Elisabeth Hobbes grew up in York, where she spent most of her teenage years wandering around the city looking for a handsome Roman or a Viking to sweep her off her feet. Elisabeth's hobbies include skiing, Arabic dance and fencing—none of which has made it into a story yet. When she isn't writing she spends her time reading, and is a pro at cooking while holding a book! Elisabeth lives in Cheshire, with her husband, two children, and three cats with ridiculous names.

UNCOVERING THE MERCHANT'S SECRET

Elisabeth Hobbes

MILLS & BOON

First Published in Great Britain 2020
by Mills & Boon, an imprint of HarperCollins*Publishers*
1 London Bridge Street, London, SE1 9GF

© 2020 Claire Lackford

ISBN: 978-0-263-27289-5

MIX
Paper from
responsible sources
FSC® C007454

This book is produced from independently certified FSC™ paper
to ensure responsible forest management.
For more information visit www.harpercollins.co.uk/green.

Printed and bound in Spain
by CPI, Barcelona

To the fabulous staff at The Day Job.
I couldn't ask for better friends and colleagues.

Chapter One

March 1346

'Are you telling me there is not one single ship that can take me to St Malo before the week is up?'

Captain John Sutton placed both hands on the table, leaned across towards the Harbourmaster seated behind it and tried to keep his temper in check. 'You assured me I would not have to wait more than two days and that was two days past!'

The Harbourmaster shrugged in an offhand manner. He rolled his eyes to the group of men huddling around the fire with mugs of wine as if to ask them to bear witness to the unreasonable demands of the English traveller. Given John's inability to establish the existence of any ship, it seemed the Harbourmaster's office was the centre for a nightly social gathering of local merchants and seafarers rather than a place to organise transport.

John gripped the edge of the table, fingernails digging into the solid oak in frustration. A captain should have command of his own ship, not have to resort to begging for passage on another man's. Much as he would like to wrap his hands round this Breton neck and squeeze some sense into the Harbourmaster, he doubted he would leave the room alive if he attempted such a thing. He was half-tempted to do it anyway and risk the consequences. Since the death of his wife, he had fought the impulse to gamble with his life until someone ended it for him. Joining Margaret was enticing when he had little to live for any longer.

'Things are difficult at the moment,' the Harbourmaster said, shrugging once more. 'The war with the English has taken its toll on our industry. Many have had to give up their business. Now with matters in Brittany being as they are…'

The Harbourmaster tailed off as John bared his teeth. Matters in Brittany were precisely why John was attempting to make the journey from Concarneau to St Malo in such haste. Although the English and French kings had declared a truce, the issue of the Breton dukedom had not been settled. Charles de Blois and John de Montfort had fought bitterly. The English success at

Cadoret followed by the siege of Quimper had caused losses on both sides, but de Montfort's death the previous autumn had left only a five-year-old heir as claimant. Now was the ideal time to be travelling safely back to England.

'That is entirely why I wish to leave with urgency. I have a report to give to my associates in Bristol regarding the state of their vineyards. Surely it is in the interest of merchants here that trade between our countries is not disrupted more than necessary.'

John gave a tight smile and spoke loudly so that all in the room could hear his words.

'I was informed that Concarneau was a thriving port and I would have no difficulty finding a ship to take me to Plymouth. Now I find I cannot even get around the coast of Brittany. Clearly, my information was incorrect and I shall be sure to make it known as widely as I can when I eventually return home so that other travellers do not find themselves caught in the same situation in this dog's piss of a town!'

There were mutters from the men by the fire who had not missed John's intended insult—hardly surprising since he had deliberately raised his voice at the end of his sentence. Disparaging comments about the reputation of their home would not be tolerated. John whipped round to look at his audience, fists bunching. He relished the thought of a brawl to rid himself of this frustration. It dulled the ever-present lump of lead in his chest where once a heart had beat.

The Harbourmaster, perhaps prompted by his audience into defending the town against such open criticism, pushed himself from his feet and came around the table. He looked up at John— a good head taller than the Harbourmaster—with an appeal in his eyes.

'It is only just March, *monsieur*. Many captains will not risk putting to sea at all until later in the year. If you were to consider taking a slower vessel through the rivers, I could direct you to three captains prepared to leave within ten days.'

The time of year could not have been worse. John's shoulders sagged as he imagined repeating this ritual daily for the next two months until conditions at sea became more favourable. By then, of course, the de Montfort faction would have rallied and hostilities would begin once more. It would be quicker at this rate to hire a horse and make the journey to St Malo by land.

'I will return tomorrow and ask again.' John set his shoulders and adjusted the clasp on his cloak. 'Perhaps you will have better news for me. Good evening.'

The Harbourmaster's eyes flickered to the

pouch at John's belt. He had already profited daily from John's generosity in the misplaced hope that it would speed matters towards a resolution. Not tonight, however. John folded his arms across his body and planted his feet solidly on the earthen floor, making it clear that his hand was going nowhere near his scrip of money. He gave a curt nod and headed from the office into the street, slamming the heavy door behind him.

He exhaled angrily and let off a string of swear words in English, causing passers-by to pause and look at the disturbance before continuing on their way. The short, explosive sounds were perfect for expressing his anger and frustration so well and he felt a little better. It was strange to him that after almost four years of living most of his time in France, his native language sounded harsh to his ears. He spoke French as fluently as any man, which made his task easier. He even dreamed in the language now, but reflecting on how far his self-imposed exile had brought him from home caused an unexpected wave of homesickness and grief to engulf him, making him reel.

A lump filled his throat. He knew from long experience it was an affliction that was best treated with a couple of jugs of wine. Not at the respectable inn where he had taken lodgings, but somewhere less reputable where a well-dressed blond Englishman would cause heads to turn, tongues to wag and, with luck, fists to fly.

He stormed away from the Harbourmaster's office towards the narrow winding alleys that led down to the port rather than up to the town, intending to find a welcoming establishment in which to drown his frustration, but had not taken more than half a dozen steps when someone fell in beside him. He glanced across and recognised the man as one who had been drinking in the Harbourmaster's office.

'What is your name and business, *monsieur*, that you should need such rapid transport?'

John bridled at being asked in such a blatant manner. His hand instinctively reached for his dagger, but he stopped and withdrew it. He ran his eyes quickly over his questioner's clothing. The man wore the thick cloak of oiled leather lined with fur and a hat familiar to anyone who had spent time around sailors. Perhaps this man could prove to be his salvation.

'My name is Jack Langdon,' John said. 'I am a simple merchant. An agent for an association of wine buyers in Bristol. They have asked me to assess the current status of production and quality. Now I need to return to England to report on my findings.'

It wasn't a lie, but nor was it the whole truth.

Captain John Sutton, aide to the King's Lieutenant in France, was no more. Now he was plain Jack Langdon, a merchant who travelled the length of western France and saw plenty to report on his travels that his *other* masters found of use.

The questioner's face brightened, radiating honesty that immediately made John suspect trickery.

'Then it is fortunate we meet, *monsieur*. I heard what that useless son of a *putain* told you back there, but he is misinformed. I'm Petrus Nevez. I am Captain of the *Sant Christophe*. I transport cargo via the coastal route back to my home in Roscoff. I am setting sail round the coast at first light. My ship is a small vessel, but if you can pay then I have room, *monsieur*.'

John considered the offer. Roscoff was not as close as he needed to be, but it was a damned sight closer than he was now. From there he could find another ship, or if necessary, travel by land to St Malo.

'You are happy to travel at this time of year?'

Nevez grinned slyly and John wondered if the sailor's cargo was legitimate or not. That might be something to investigate as he travelled. Smugglers could be useful in a war, if they had the appropriate sympathies.

'What are your terms?'

Nevez named a price that caused John to wince inwardly. He had little choice, however, so with an enthusiasm he did not entirely feel, he shook hands and memorised the location of the vessel *Sant Christophe.*

Nevez skulked away towards the port. Not wishing to follow the Captain, John changed his mind about seeking out somewhere to drink and returned to the inn that had been his lodging for what felt like eternity. He settled on to a bench as close to the fire as he could manage and called for wine and something to eat. Jeanne, the youngest daughter of the innkeeper, sashayed over bearing a tray, hips moving enticingly and shoulders pushed back so her breasts jutted forward. She greeted him with a smile that John felt was almost genuine.

'Did you find your ship, Monsieur Langdon?' she asked as she handed him a steaming bowl. John ate a couple of mouthfuls of the creamy fish stew before answering. It was excellent.

'Yes, I did, *mademoiselle.* Please tell your father I shall be leaving at first light.'

Jeanne pouted and held the wine cup out. 'That's a pity. I shall be sorry to see you leave.'

As John took hold of the cup, she quickly moved her hand so that her fingers were resting against his. She gave him a coy smile that belied the hardness in her eyes.

'Perhaps you do not wish to spend this night alone?'

John sighed inwardly and disentangled his fingers, placing the cup beside the bowl on the table. 'Thank you, but, no. My answer is the same as it has always been and always will be. I want no woman in my bed.'

Along with the other daughters of the innkeeper, Jeanne had made the same offer every night since John had arrived. When he rebuffed her every night, she accepted the rejection without rancour and did not waste much time before seeking out another potential customer. This night, she placed the wine flagon on the table and lingered beside him, regarding John with her glinting dark eyes.

'Monsieur Langdon, you look at me with longing in your eyes, but refuse, even though my price is fair. How long is it since you last had a woman in your bed?'

Too long, was the answer to that question. His grief could have sent him down two paths: spending himself in the lap of any willing woman until their faces and bodies blurred, or provoking fights to make his blood rise and leave him with tangible aches. John had chosen the latter path and it had been a year at least since he had last tumbled into bed with a too-expensive whore in La Rochelle, drunk and unable to resist the lust that consumed him. Two more before that since he had last woken in the arms of Margaret, the wife he still missed.

He examined Jeanne. She was witty and passably pretty. She might once have been beautiful before years of working on her feet and her back had caused the lines round her eyes and lips to harden. He could engage her services and relieve himself of the physical needs that tormented him. He had no doubt she would prove to be an able and entertaining companion for an hour or so, but what then? She might satisfy the needs of his loins, but would not heal the grief that filled his heart.

'I am sorry, Jeanne,' he said kindly. 'I made a vow that I would have no woman but my wife and it is one I intend to keep.'

John reached for the small cross that lay against his skin and closed his fist round it. He rubbed his thumb over the small garnets set into the front, then the engraved initials *J* and *M* side by side on the back.

'Is that your wife's?' Jeanne asked.

'Yes.'

'She waits for you in England?'

John's throat tightened. He raised his head and smiled grimly. 'She waits for me beyond the grave.'

'I apologise.' Jeanne's face was a picture of devastated embarrassment.

John shook his head. 'No need. You could not have known.'

He lifted the cross to his lips, then slipped it back beneath his clothing.

He pushed his bowl away and stood, appetite gone. 'Goodnight, *mademoiselle*.'

He took the flagon with him and went to the small bedroom in the attic. It cost him dearly, but having privacy rather than sharing with nine others in the communal bedroom was worth the expense. He lit a taper and by the dim light he packed away his belongings. He wrote a short note, detailing what he had discovered on his travels, sealed it with his signet ring and addressed it to Masters Fortin and Rudhale at their Bristol wine warehouse. This he would ask Jeanne to send via one of the inland ships that travelled the slow river in case he never reached his destination to deliver his report in person. There was another report for other eyes that he would not trust to the hands of anyone else. He possessed a pair of wooden-backed wax tablets, bound together as a book. If it became necessary, he could apply heat and erase his words. John scratched a few lines swiftly in the code known to no more than twenty men back in England. He wrapped the tablet book safely in a leather wallet and put it in a small document case. That had been a gift from his father, small enough that he could take it travelling with him without too much trouble, and watertight in case he was travelling in inclement weather.

Only after he had made all his preparations to leave did John Sutton allow himself to drain the flagon, lay his head on his arms and let his eyes fill with tears at the memory of his wife who now lay buried beneath the Devonshire soil.

The journey was rough round the end of the peninsula and as they reached the open seas, but no worse than expected for the time of year. All the same, John was glad when they started keeping the long, sweeping curve of land in view.

The cog was similar enough to John's old ship, *The King's Rose*, for him to feel at home. He spent the time drinking, laughing and gambling with the crew and found against all expectations that his spirits were high. It had been too long since he had been merry without the feelings of grief bearing down on him. He'd cut himself off from friends when he had left England in mourning, unable to bear the reminders of happier times. Maybe company was what he had needed after all, rather than isolating himself and brawling with strangers to jolt the numbness in his heart back to life.

Three days out of Concarneau, the weather grew worse. By mid-afternoon on the third day of the voyage, the clouds obscured all light and the small cog creaked ominously on waves that were increasingly violent. Now night had fallen and they were in no sight of the port Nevez had sworn they would make by dark.

John made his way from the small cabin along the planks laid down over the hull to the prow. Nevez and his first mate were gesticulating wildly at each other and the coastline, which pitched and rolled in the distance.

'What is wrong?'

'A storm. Worse than I expected,' Nevez growled.

The wind tore at John's cloak with violent fingers, trying to pull it from his body. He shivered and took a deep breath of the chilly salt air.

'We could find shelter somewhere, along the coast,' he suggested.

A wave crashed over the prow, tilting the cog and causing the three men to lurch against each other.

'Not here. There are hidden coves where a ship might hide safely,' Nevez said, adding to John's suspicions that his host was involved in smuggling, 'but this stretch of water is the home of pirates.'

'They sail under the banner of Bleiz Mor along this stretch,' the first mate added.

John narrowed his eyes. The name was unfamiliar to him.

'*Loup de Mer*, Monsieur Langdon. The Wolf of the Sea,' Nevez explained in a growl. 'His ships are both known by a black sail adorned by a white pelt. He has preyed on the French ever since they attacked Quimper, but perhaps he will not be particular at this time of year.'

If what Nevez said was true, the oddly named man was a mercenary, rather than a pirate, and one who shared the same sympathies as the English. John reminded himself to make a note in case his masters were unaware of the man's activities. A grinding sound ripped through the cog and the hull juddered, and John dismissed the thought.

'We've hit something,' he exclaimed.

'Impossible. We're nowhere near rocks.' Nevez laughed. He grabbed John's shoulder and pointed. 'See, the lights on the cliff are close. That is the harbour. We have made better speed than I had thought. We will not die tonight.'

John looked. The light that glowed brightly on the distant shore should guide them to safety. He wished he were in command, rather than a passenger, because the sound was unsettling.

Nevez shouted orders and the *Sant Christophe* pitched slightly as she turned towards shore. John scanned the blackness. Nevez's tales of pirates had slightly alarmed him, but there was no sign of any other vessel. He didn't doubt Nevez's words.

'Come below, Monsieur Langdon,' Nevez suggested. 'In my cabin I have a bottle of fine wine. Perhaps you could recommend it to your associates in England. I can give you a fair price.'

'I will shortly,' John said. 'I must complete a letter first.'

He went to his quarters in the small area at the bottom of the boat curtained off from the crew. By lantern light, he added a note to the report on his tablets he had been writing on the journey. He noted the mention of the oddly named 'Sea Wolf', but paused before committing anything to paper about Nevez. The Captain was most likely a smuggler, but to name him would be a poor way to repay the kindness. In the end, he added a single line about smugglers in general and locked the leather wallet in his document case. He put the key safely in his roll of clothing, nestled beside a thin plaited curl of Margaret's hair. He rubbed the corn-blond braid between his fingers, sadness and remorse welling up inside him. He still found it unbelievable she was not back in England as she had been each time he had returned. How carelessly he had treated her devotion, never thinking one day she would not be there patiently waiting for him.

A scraping noise made him jump in surprise, dragging him from his memories. It sounded as if something was ripping through the bottom of the boat and the floor vibrated. Cries of consternation came from the deck above and he realised that the scraping was true and the cog had collided with something. He ran up on deck and found Nevez leaning over the side, glaring.

'That is no lighthouse. This is the work of wreckers. We have been tricked.'

'What can we do?' John asked.

Nevez smacked the rail with his fist. 'Nothing! The hull is breached. There is a small rowing boat, but, other than that, our lives are in the hand of fate.'

Around them, men were throwing barrels and chests overboard and clinging to them in the hope of floating to shore safely.

'Quick, to the boat,' Nevez shouted.

'One moment,' John called. He was already running across the tilting deck to the galley. The letters to Masters Fortin and Rudhale could be rewritten, as could the report for King Edward's

Lieutenant, but the box also contained certain letters of importance to him from Margaret that he could not bear to lose. He took the steps two at a time and landed up to his ankles in water. He grabbed the document case, grateful it was small enough to stow in a satchel. He slung the satchel across his body so it hung beneath his arm and fastened his cloak over the top. There was no point being safe from drowning to freeze to death.

The boat pitched and he had to scramble on to the deck on his hands and knees. The deck was deserted. Nevez's rowing boat had moved away.

'Wait for me,' John shouted.

'Swim to us,' Nevez yelled.

John took a running jump into the sea. The waves enveloped him, pulling him down into the black, crushing coldness that left him gasping for breath. He surfaced, his lungs begging for air. As he broke through the water he discovered that, contrary to what he had thought, he cared very much about living.

He had no time to rejoice in this newfound appetite for survival or recover his breath because a large piece of wood struck his shoulder from behind. His arm went numb. He kicked his legs, propelling him towards the small boat. Something tore at his leg and he realised he was closer to the rocks than he realised. The rowing boat would risk being smashed if it came close. If he was near to the rocks, he could not be too far from the shore.

'Go without me,' he bellowed.

He could scramble over them towards safety. He aimed for the rocks when something hit him from behind, forcing him head first on to an outcrop. The impact left him reeling. He flailed and was slammed once more on to the rocks. Something warm trickled down his face, but he had no time to examine the wound.

John clambered up the rocks and crawled on his belly in the direction of the light that was burning on shore. Facing brutal wreckers would be safer than a certain death by drowning. After much slipping and sliding that left him grazed and bruised, he staggered on to a beach. He tripped over a body of one of the crewmen who had not survived the waters and gave a sob.

His head was spinning. There seemed to be two moons shining down, but even so he was finding it hard to make out anything in the moonlight. He felt his head and his fingers came away wet and sticky with blood. The sensation made him nauseous.

John staggered further up the beach, but when the hard sand changed, he slipped and lay on the damp shingle. He rolled on to his back, tangled in his cloak, and lay there. Time lost meaning and it could have been a day or a minute before he first heard the voices that called to each other across the shore. The wreckers had come.

Among the coarse sounds, John was convinced he heard soft female tones that did not belong in a place of such devastation and death. He caught a scent of something floral that was at odds with the odours of sea and blood. He decided he must be dreaming, or was at last to be reunited with his wife and a feeling of peace descended on him.

'Margaret?' he mumbled. 'I am ready for you.'

He could not keep his eyes open and had no strength left to do anything but surrender to whatever fate held in store for him.

Chapter Two

The fires had been lit in the church windows again.

Blanche Tanet slammed down her comb as soon as the faint scent of smoke reached her. Her bedchamber on the top floor of the tower room had windows at each side and she could see both shores that the castle overlooked. She leaned out, looking towards the village of Plomarc'h and, sure enough, in the window of St Petroc's Church, a light shone out to sea. The church was on the clifftop set a short distance from the village. It was visible from the sea, so sailors and fishermen would know they were being watched over, but the purpose of the beacon was far from holy.

Blanche had been preparing for bed, but could not ignore this. She muttered an oath under her breath. She tore off her chemise and began to dress in breeches and a shirt. Over the top of her padded, sleeveless gambeson she threw a heavy cloak, then tugged on her knee-length leather boots. She did not have time to braid her hair, but simply gathered it, twisting and piling it under a wide-brimmed sailor's hat, and strode down the stairs, gathering a flaming brand from the iron ring in the wall. When she reached the path that led to the beach she broke into a run, arriving on the beach slightly out of breath.

The bodies of drowned men littered the shore. When the moon slid from behind heavy, black clouds, the rocky shore looked like a battlefield. Blanche felt her stomach heave. She swallowed down the bile that rose to her throat and tightened her grip on the torch. She strode to the shore and peered out across the black rocks that glistened wet and sharp, only slightly visible above the surface. The rocks stretched out well into the sea and had been guilty of causing more deaths than Blanche could imagine over the centuries.

Barrels bobbed, surging in and out as the tide dragged at them. Wine. This had most likely been a merchant ship. All around her, the villagers hauled the debris from the sea to carry it away or load it on to the wheeled carts they had brought in preparation for such finds.

Was she the only one who felt a twinge of guilt at the way they treated the dead? A little way along the shore, a short, wide man was standing up to his knees in the water, heaving a cask back to shore. Blanche recognised him. Andrey was her cousin by her second marriage and the Captain of Blanche's ship *White Wolf.*

Blanche intercepted him as he dropped his salvage on the shingle and stood upright, stretching his arms to relieve the cricks in his neck.

'Who ordered the fires to be lit?' she demanded.

Andrey scowled and spat into the sea. 'Who do you think? Ronec did.'

Blanche's fist tightened around the flaming brand she held. Jagu Ronec was the landowner whose property neighboured Blanche's. He was also the Captain and part-financier of Blanche's second ship, *White Hawk.* He was wealthy, powerful and—as Blanche had found out only after she had allied herself with him—cruel and unprincipled. She counted to ten in her head, breathing deeply before she answered, wishing she had never thought to involve him in her crusade against the French forces. Even with this attempt at controlling the repellent emotions Ronec's name conjured, her voice was tight and full of fury.

'And you obeyed him?'

'Not I,' Andrey said. 'But the crews are growing tired of waiting for your command to sail and your insistence on only taking French ships. They look to Ronec, anticipating an alliance between you.'

Blanche flushed. There was an implicit criticism in Andrey's words and it was not without reason. Ronec had already had more of Blanche than she had wanted to give and marriage was an alliance she was determined to resist to the last. The villagers' discontent was something she would have to address soon. Ronec was not present, of course. He would not venture out to wallow in salt water in the dark when others could do it on his behalf.

'Take the bodies to the castle,' she commanded Andrey. 'They deserve a proper burial.'

Andrey nodded and began relaying the order to the men who had gathered round to watch them speaking. Andrey's loyalty to Blanche was unquestionable and she knew that the dead would be laid to rest with respect.

Blanche began to roll the barrel up the sloping beach to add it to the pile of salvage. The methods were dishonourable, but she would not let the salvage be wasted when it could be used to improve the lives of the tenants on her land.

The barrel was heavy. Blanche paused for breath beside a corpse that had been washed further up the beach than most. The man was lying on his back, one arm tangled inside a heavy cloak that must have hampered his efforts to swim and should by rights have dragged him to the bottom of the sea. Yet here he was, lying on the beach, his long limbs sprawled out carelessly. He could have been napping on a riverbank on a warm summer afternoon.

He was not a youth, nor as old as Andrey. Blanche guessed he was somewhere around his thirtieth year, only a handful of years younger than she was. Unbidden, her mind went back to her first husband who had died before his time. This man looked nothing like Mael, but the thought of stolen years upset her more than she was expecting, sorrow creeping around her heart like a winding cloth.

She knelt down next to him, barrel of wine temporarily forgotten, and held the brand close to his face. He would have been handsome when alive and it struck her as unfair that he had been snatched from life in such a brutal manner. A deep gash split his right eyebrow and ran across his temple into his sandy-brown hair. It was stark red against the paleness of his skin, though the cold and seawater had staunched the blood flow and now it was a livid, ragged-edged wound.

The laces of his shirt were untied to the middle of his chest. He must have been caught by surprise and had no time to dress properly before the cog was dashed on the rocks. By the flickering light of the brand, Blanche noticed the glint of gold among the fine, light brown hairs. She, reached beneath his collar, hooking her finger under the chain and drew out a delicate cross.

The wreckers would simply rip it from his neck, snapping the chain, but Blanche could not bear to do that with something so beautiful. She stuck the torch into the sand and cradled his head, easing it forward to slip the long chain free. Red stones glinted on the surface. Something this beautiful was too fine to leave for the wreckers to break and waste on drinking, gambling or whoring. Blanche had little care for the treasures she stole from the French beyond what good they could do to aid the cause of Brittany or her tenants, but she was gripped with the need to make sure the unknown man's treasure survived as a memorial to his life. She would not share this with anyone else so she slipped it around her own neck, tucking it deep into the bodice of her dress where it nestled between her breasts. An odd frisson made her shiver at the feel of the object that had been intimately touching him.

As she rested the man's head back, his eyes flickered open and he uttered a weak, breathy moan. He was alive! The strength of relief and joy that flooded her heart took her by surprise. He gave a heaving cough and water bubbled to his lips. Blanche pushed her hands against his ribs, pushing upwards to force any remaining water out. He bared his teeth and hissed. Mortified at having added to his pain, Blanche slid her hands gently up to his cheeks and pulled his head into what she hoped was a more comfortable position. His eyes opened once more—a little wider this time—and he peered at her. His eyes were light blue and full of confusion and pain. Though hazy, they were captivating in their intensity and Blanche could not tear her gaze away.

Blanche's hat had become dislodged when she had jerked in surprise. She pulled it off. As her thick, black locks fell freely about her, the man smiled and whispered something in a language she thought was English.

'I don't understand,' she replied in Breton, then repeated it in French.

He reached a hand out towards her hair, fumbling and clumsy. Blanche instinctively recoiled, as she did at the advances of any man, but as his fingertips brushed against her cheek with the lightest of touches, her heart fluttered.

His strength was almost spent and his arm was seized with a tremor that made it shake violently. He could not be long for this world and the awakening was only delaying the inevitable. Blood loss and shock would claim him before the night was out. Already his hand was so cold with the clammy texture of a corpse. Instinctively, Blanche wanted to pull away, but remorse and guilt flooded her once more. Her people bore the responsibility for his death, so the least she could do was bear the discomfort and act as witness to his passing. She owed him that much. She covered his hand, holding it to her cheek and feeling the quiver that raced along his arm.

He tried to pull her down towards him, tilting his head back and parting his lips as if he intended to kiss her. His fingers scrabbled deep into the hair at the nape of her neck, causing her to shiver at the intimacy of his touch. Her heart drummed a march in her breast.

'I'm so sorry,' she whispered, stroking the matted hair back from his brow.

His eyes focused again and locked on hers and he bestowed on her a smile of such overwhelming tenderness that she wanted to weep. Tenderness. So long since anyone had looked at her in such a way. Blanche closed her eyes wistfully. She bent her head and kissed his forehead with the lightest of touches. His head came up and his mouth found hers with a swiftness she would not have anticipated in one so close to death.

His lips tasted of salt and moved over hers with a fierceness she had never encountered before. He was fighting to the end; a dying man's final attempt at comfort or a sweet memory to take beyond the grave. There was desperation beneath the desire, drawing her to him and leaving her powerless to resist its pull. She kissed him back, letting her lips form the shape of his in a moment of mutual sorrow.

She felt the moment his strength gave out. Her eyes filled as she drew away and laid his head gently down.

He smiled once more.

'My angel. I am ready to come to you,' he whispered in French, then closed his eyes.

An angel?

Blanche smiled at the thought, though tears smarted in her eyes. He thought he was speaking to someone else. If only the man knew what kind of woman was peering down at him, he would not use such terms. She was Jael. Jezebel. She was the Magdalene at her worst.

His hand went limp and she placed it across his chest. She ran her fingertips along the edge of the wound on his head, probing as gently as she could so as not to cause him more discomfort, though she suspected he was rapidly slipping beyond such experiences. The wound was deep and she felt the hardness of bone. His chest heaved and he groaned, twisting on the sand. There was still strength in him. If his body was as strong as his kiss, there might be hope…

'Andrey, come help me,' she shouted. 'This one is a survivor.'

Andrey stomped over and looked down.

'Huh, better to finish him off quickly,' he said, reaching for the curved dagger at his belt.

Blanche threw herself in front of the man, arms out, and stared up at Andrey defiantly.

'No. We'll take him to the castle and give him a place to rest.'

Most likely he would not survive the night, but she could not leave him here for such a sad and lonely end.

Andrey looked appalled. 'We have no idea who these men are. He could be a spy for Charles de Blois. Do you really want to give shelter to such a man?'

Blanche stood, curling her fists. She placed them on her hips and lifted her shoulders back. Though she was only a woman, she had learned that to mimic a man's posture somehow garnered more respect and granted her authority that using her femininity did not.

'It is my home. I will not be argued with.'

Andrey still looked unhappy. Blanche softened her stance and smiled.

'I know what you say is wise, but look at him. He can be no danger to us, even if he is a spy, in this condition. Fetch a cart and help me carry him, but be discreet. I want as few people to know as possible. That will ensure word does not travel.'

Especially to Ronec's ears. Andrey met her eyes and Blanche knew he had the same thought. He nodded his head, seemingly satisfied by this precaution.

She bent down once more as Andrey stomped off, and took the man's hand. It would be sensible to at least try to find out what allegiance he might have.

'What is your name?' she asked. 'Can you speak?'

He opened his eyes and muttered a word that was no word.

'Your name,' she repeated, leaning close so that her ear was close to his lips. 'Who are you?'

He muttered something that may have been *Jacques*, then his eyes closed and his mouth went slack.

Andrey brought the cart and began to re-arrange the contents to make space. Blanche pushed the man's cloak back and saw he was wearing a satchel. Blanche eased it free. It contained a small, shallow casket made of dark wood.

'At least we'll have some spoils,' Andrey said with a grin.

Blanche held it to the light. It was plain and looked well used. Probably a document case, but maybe a jewel casket.

'It may contain the key to learning who he is,' Blanche mused.

'Key! Not one I've found.' Andrey laughed. 'Best break it open.'

Blanche put the bag and casket on to the cart.

'There'll be plenty of time for that later. Keep it safe for now.'

If the man lived, she would ask him herself. If he didn't, then she would permit Andrey to open it and put an end to their curiosity. She helped Andrey lift the man, slipping her arms in the crook behind his knees, and made sure he was laid carefully on to the cart. His long legs were crooked, reminding her of a discarded marionette, and she straightened them before putting the box beside him. She followed the cart up the beach and along the rutted track that led to the sea gate of the castle. In the courtyard she paused, as the first seeds of doubt began to grow.

'We won't put him in a bedroom,' she decided. 'There's a small storeroom in the cellars of the outbuilding. Take him there.'

She saw that the man was taken where she

instructed and a pallet with a mattress was provided. She dismissed Andrey and his suggestions that she call a servant to tend the injured man.

'The fewer people who know, the safer it will be for all of us.'

In truth, she felt responsible and wanted to tend the man herself. The moonlight shone through the small, barred window, falling across his face, which even in the dim light she could see had a deathly pallor. She loosened his wet shirt and eased it off his body, thinking how long it had been since she had undressed a man and how welcome it was knowing this one was in no position to paw at her or expect a candle's worth of rutting. She pressed her palm over his heart. The beat was barely perceptible beneath the mound of his chest. He began to shiver, tremors passing through what Blanche recognised was a powerful frame. She drew a sheet high up to his chin and covered him with a pair of wolf pelts. She spooned weak ale laced with something to ease his pain between his lips.

If he survived the night that would be miraculous, but she left him and went to her own bed satisfied that she had done what she could.

Chapter Three

Long fingers of light fluttered across the wall. They played over his legs and moved slowly, languidly up his body until they reached his face and began to climb stealthily upwards. Because of this, he knew time was passing, but his limbs felt heavy and he had no desire to move. He was lying on a mattress, though the lumpy sack filled with stale-smelling straw hardly dignified the description. Everything was unfamiliar. This was not his home.

His head ached as if he had been beaten around it repeatedly and his muscles felt torn, but he didn't know why. He reached a hand up to touch the main source of the dull throbbing on his temple and discovered his arm was weak and the effort brought a sweat to his brow. He succeeded in feeling his head. It was bandaged, which meant he had suffered an injury of some sort, but he had no idea what or how he had come about it. Nor did he have any idea how he came to be in this place.

The last thing he remembered was—

And there he was forced to stop, because although he had the vague sense of scents and tastes, and the sound of screaming and splitting wood in his ears, he had no recollection of what had happened. He knew for certain he did not know this place, but how he knew that, he was unable to explain. The smell was musty and old with a hint of yeastiness to the air. If he didn't know better, he would say he was in a bakery or storeroom.

He rolled his head to look at the source of light and realised the narrow slit of window was barred. Panic constricted his chest as he realised he must be a prisoner. The fact he had no idea who his captors were, or why he had been imprisoned, increased the terror tenfold. The agitation heated his limbs and he felt his blood spring to life as it surged around his body. He took a deep breath and decided he would hammer on the door until someone came, but when he embarked on this plan his legs buckled before he had crossed half the small space, and he crumpled to the ground. He lay in a heap on the cold stone floor, noticing now that he was naked from the waist up. So, he was in a barred room with a stone floor and a small door. That probably meant the ground floor or cellars. Which meant a big building. The effort of coming to this conclusion made his head reel and did not, in fact, help him in any real way, but a small part of him cheered in satisfaction that he had noticed the surface he was lying on. He had not lost all his wits.

He cried out in English, but when no one answered, something in the back of his mind told him this was not the only language he could use. He repeated his words in French, gratified that the words came as easily. Still no one came, so when he felt slightly stronger he crawled his way back on to the pallet and pulled up the sheet and furs. He lay there shivering, his mind in turmoil, knowing that he had no choice but to wait until his captors deemed it fit to visit him. He slept again.

When he woke it was daylight now. The sun was a warm orange and there was a faint scent of sea in the air, accompanied by a hint of sweet blossom. He inhaled deeply, taking pleasure from the only thing of beauty in his life that he could clutch on to.

A metallic scraping sound caught his attention and he realised it was coming from the other side of the door. It was the sound of a bolt being drawn back. He looked to the door slightly too sharply and the movement caused his head to spin. Lights burst behind his eyes and he blinked furiously to clear them, so that when the door opened he was lying with watery eyes and staring at the ceiling so he did not immediately notice who had entered.

Someone walked to the corner of the room and he heard a pot of some sort set down on a table he had not noticed earlier. He waited patiently to see what would happen. An instinct was telling him to try overpowering whoever it was and try to escape, but he knew he didn't have the strength to do anything of the sort. He opened his eyes and craned his head weakly. A short girl in a plain gown was placing a jug on a small table.

'Where am I?' he asked in English. 'Help me!'

His voice was rasping from the dryness of his throat. The girl shrieked and jumped back and the jug toppled over. Before he could speak again she had fled from the room, banging the door behind her. He heard the bolt scrape, confirming he was a prisoner. He groaned weakly and licked his lips, thirsty beyond endurance and with a belly that ached from emptiness. He didn't think he would be able to sleep, but his head began to spin and he lapsed into a fitful sleep.

* * *

He was awakened once again by the bolt drawing back and someone entering the room. The person began to hum softly in a voice that was soft and female. This time he had the sense to remain silent and lie with eyes half-open. It was a different woman this time, taller and dressed in a deep brown, flowing surcoat. She was standing by the small table doing something Jack could not see. She came to the bed and he realised that she had a cloth and a bowl of water. Another servant of whoever was holding him, he suspected.

He closed his eyes so she would not realise he was awake. She unwound the bandage from around his head and bathed the wound, then moved from working on his head to tending the grazes on his body. She slid her cool hand slowly up the length of his bare belly with the softness of a lover beginning a caress. He drew a sharp breath as an overwhelming sense of pleasure combined with the sting of the cuts. Realising he could no longer feign sleep, he opened his eyes.

'Ah, you are awake again,' she said in what he recognised as the Breton dialect.

That mended another rip in the cloth that was his mind. Now he knew which part of the world he was in. She did not sound particularly happy at the discovery.

'You frightened Marie,' the woman said. She was looking at him severely so his first impression was of forbidding black eyes. 'She ran to me crying tales of nonsense words growled at her.'

He swallowed and opened his mouth to try explaining what had happened.

'Don't try to speak,' she instructed. 'Wait there.'

She moved to the table and came back bearing a wide-rimmed earthenware cup. She slipped a hand beneath his neck and raised him slightly to cradle his head, then held the cup to his lips. It turned out to be cider and he drank greedily until the cup was empty.

Her cool fingers trailed across the back of his neck as she withdrew her hand and laid his head back. He shivered once more with unexpected desire and gave a soft moan. She must have interpreted this as pain because she peered down at him and concern banished the severity of her expression. Something woke inside him as her face filled his gaze: a deep sense of familiarity and the certainty that he had seen this face before. The memory fluttered from him like moths circling a lamp and evading fingers trying to seize them, leaving only vague shapes and the sensation of intimacy. Like the moths, he felt pulled towards her flame. His lips twitched.

'Can you speak now?' she asked.

'I did not mean to frighten her,' he croaked.

'I'm glad to hear it. I would not like to think I am giving shelter to one who would terrorise girls.'

They were strangers, then. So why did he feel such a connection to her? He furrowed his brow.

She gave a brief smile. 'Think nothing of it. Marie is silly and jumps if the kitchen cats mew behind her.'

With an effort of will he was able to focus on her with a little more clarity now, though his eyes kept blurring. From the high singing voice, he had thought she was not much older than a child, but now he saw she was past her youth. A few faint lines had begun to appear at the corner of her eyes and mouth and a short frown line ran between her brows to the top of a straight, sharp nose. The severe expression must be habitual.

He reassessed his opinion that she was a mere servant. Her surcoat was plain brown with wide sleeves, but the close-fitting green kirtle beneath had a wide band of embroidery around the straight neck and wrists that spoke of quality. Beneath the linen band across her brow, there was a glint of gold combs that swept her black hair up into rolls at each side of her head. They looked expensive, indicating wealth, and she wore rings on three of her fingers.

More than that, the way she held herself and the expression on her face suggested she was used to any command she issued being obeyed. She was clearly waiting for him to respond. He tested his tongue and found it looser.

'My head aches,' he said in a croaky voice. 'I do not know this place. What happened to me?'

She frowned, deepening the small line between her straight black brows.

'Do you remember anything of how you came to be here?'

He knew better now than to try to shake his head and simply murmured, 'Nothing, *madame*. I remember nothing. What can you tell me?'

She did not answer and her eyes narrowed. He rose up as best he could and clutched at her hand and felt her fingers straighten. Her eyes widened and without knowing why he put a hand to her cheek. Immediately, the gentleness with which she had nursed him was gone, replaced by ice.

'Take your hands off me,' she snapped, her face becoming thunderous. She leaned closer to him and with a twist of her wrist she had slipped from his grip.

'Pardon me,' he said. He fell back on the pillow, panting slightly from the effort it had cost him. 'But, please, if you can tell me anything, I beseech you to do so.'

'I will tell you what I can. Be warned, *monsieur*, no man touches me without my consent, even an invalid.'

'I understand.'

She gave a brief, tight smile of approval and settled back on to her knees, arranging her skirts with practised elegance, then rested her hands neatly in her lap.

'You were on a ship.'

She paused and looked away. Her face closed down. She looked wary and, despite her sharp, striking features, this uncertainty gave her an air of fragility. He waited, examining her in the bright sunlight as her eyes darted quickly around. He wanted to stroke her arm and encourage her to continue, but her warning rang in his ears.

'What do you know?' he prompted.

'There was a shipwreck. We found you on the beach among the debris and the dead.' She leaned closer and her eyes raked over him, scrutinising him so intimately he imagined he was being undressed. 'Do you really remember nothing? What is your name?'

And this was when he truly began to panic. With rising terror, he realised he did not know the answer.

'I can't remember!'

He heard alarm in his voice, but the woman looked suspicious. Her expression became stone.

'Are you sure?' She leaned closer. 'Are you a spy? How do I know you are telling the truth?'

He reached out to clutch her sleeve to emphasise his integrity, but remembered her warning in time to stay his hand in mid-air. They both regarded it. He clenched his fist, holding it to his side, then lowered it to the fur. Their eyes found each other's and the woman nodded. A brief moment of understanding passed between them. In any other circumstances he would find the situation extremely erotic, but the fascination he had for her had to compete with the disorientation, weakness and confusion he felt.

'I have no proof, but believe me, please. I am telling the truth. I cannot remember who I am.'

He ground his fingers into the thick white pelt that covered him and gazed at her, willing her to believe him. She eyed him steadily, her dark eyes moving slowly over his face, up to the wound on his head and down again, further over his body. It made him feel uneasy to be examined so frankly by a stranger. More than that was the fact of her sex. The fascination he felt for her was being pushed deep inside him by a stronger, more painful emotion that cautioned him to resist and retreat. The presence of a woman felt even more unfamiliar than the unknown surroundings, but it came to him that it was not just her. He would not feel easy with any woman at his bedside, but did not know why. It was slightly reassuring because the warning voice meant that deep down inside him, some knowledge of himself still existed and could hopefully be unearthed.

'Shall I suggest some names and see if anything seems right?' the woman asked.

He nodded slightly.

She spoke names, pausing after each to give him time to respond and looking questioningly at him. 'Philippe... Michel... Charles... James... Jacques...'

A dart pierced his stomach.

Jack.

That had a familiarity where the others did not. She stopped and her head tilted to one side.

'You are Jacques? Or Jack, as you are English, I suspect. You muttered something on the shore when we found you which could have been that.'

'You were there?' He raised himself to his elbows, more astonished by this revelation than a possible nationality and name.

'I was.' She pushed herself to her feet and walked away, gracefully crossing the room to the table. She stood with her back to him, wrung out the cloth and returned. She pressed it to his forehead and used the motion to lay him back down again.

'It was I who found you. You were the only survivor that we found.'

Her full lips twisted down with sadness and Jack—as he decided must suffice for now—was filled with warmth for her compassion. Who had time to grieve for strangers? He could remember nothing of the men who had perished, though he must have known them, and remorse chilled him.

'I thought you were dead, but then you opened your eyes,' the woman said in a matter-of-fact voice, as if she was recounting a day at market. 'I was unsure if you would survive, but we brought you back here anyway and hoped.'

We? Did she have a husband? A woman of her age usually did, unless she was widowed.

'Whose house am I in?' he asked. 'Where is its master?'

Her lips twitched and once again she paused before answering, filling Jack with the suspicion that there was an undercurrent he was not aware of.

'You wish to meet the master of this house? You have no idea whose house you are in, but you assume naturally that there must be one.'

Jack said nothing, wondering if his assumption was wrong. This woman was fascinating.

Perhaps she was the mistress and sole chatelaine of wherever he was.

'Shall I call you Jack?' she asked.

He nodded. The shape of it felt well enough in his mouth and he would be content to live under that name for the time being. If he discovered another, then he would relinquish it. If he never recovered his memory—and the thought of that made him want to scream with horror—a plain name would suit an unknown man.

'You should sleep again,' the woman said. 'I'll have food sent to you as well as water to bathe in and clean clothing.' Her gaze raked him once more. 'We didn't want to touch you too much for fear of injuring you further, but I can imagine some fresh attire would be welcome.'

She wrinkled her nose slightly and Jack realised with a sense of shame that his body and hair felt filthy. There was an odour clinging to him that had the taint of seawater and stale sweat. Bathing was suddenly the most enticing thing he could think of.

'Last night,' he said. 'On the shore…'

The woman raised her eyebrows.

'Monsieur Jack, you have been unconscious for five days.'

Five days! His head swam and he shook his head, causing waves of dizziness to envelop him. 'How?'

'A fever took hold of you. I thought you would die. It was only last night that it broke and you were able to rest.'

She looked thoughtful, then placed her hand on his chest, over his heart. His skin flamed beneath her touch. Even with the deep sense of unease that had cautioned him to keep his distance, he did not want to discourage her from touching him in the slightest. Quite the opposite. He watched her face to see if she was equally affected. She slid her eyes to his and smiled like a cat watching a mouse and his heart gave a violent thud.

'Your heart is strong, *monsieur,* even though you are weak. I think you are strong when you are well, yes?'

Jack flexed the muscles in his arms and felt them tighten easily. He felt weak and ill, but there was strength in his body that would return in time. His heart was racing, but that was from the sensation of her hand on his flesh.

'Perhaps,' he agreed.

She nodded in the manner of a queen receiving homage from a subject, then left. Jack listened for the sound of the bolt being drawn across, but heard nothing. He had been a prisoner before, but apparently was no longer. Or perhaps the woman rightly suspected that even if he had the inclination to roam about, he didn't possess the strength yet.

It was only as he finished the cider and lay back to try to sleep again that it occurred to him he had not asked her name, nor had the bewitching creature given it.

Chapter Four

Blanche walked to the end of the passageway. She took three breaths to regain her composure before she smiled down at Andrey who was sitting on a stool.

'That was interesting,' she said. An understatement, indeed.

Andrey grunted and sheathed the sword that he was conspicuously wearing.

'What did you find out?'

'Very little.' Blanche frowned. 'He claims to have no memory of who he is or where he is from.'

'Do you believe him or do you think he is lying?'

Blanche considered the conversation that had taken place. The man's—Jack's—air of confusion and the look of horror that had crossed his face when he had been unable to supply a name had appeared genuine. The film of perspiration that had arisen across his brow and chest could not have been feigned. Her hand twitched as she recalled the shape of his chest muscles beneath her palm, firm and smooth. A younger body than she had touched for so long. It had taken control not to explore further down to his belly and beyond and see if everything was as well toned. She shook her head to rid herself of the image.

'I believe him. More's the pity,' she said. She looked back at the door to the storeroom. A twinge of guilt took her by surprise as she considered what an inhospitable room it was for a man in his circumstances to find himself. A bare room, little more than a cell. She had not bolted the door, but she wondered if he was aware of that, or if he even suspected he had been confined at all. There were other, better rooms and other beds. She blinked, surprised at the direction her thoughts were taking. It was that kiss which had done it. She should never have yielded to the temptation on the beach.

'We'll have to keep him here a little longer.'

'Why?' Andrey's eyebrows shot up in surprise.

'He has no money, no possessions.' Her conscience gave a twinge; there had been a box somewhere and she had the cross in her room.

'He has no name.'

'Assuming he is telling the truth,' Andrey said.

'Assuming that.' Blanche sighed, wishing she

had never brought him to the castle. 'However, we cannot send him out to wander the countryside like a vagrant. Who knows whom he might encounter? Here he is safe from harm.'

'And causing harm,' Andrey pointed out. 'Marie didn't like him.'

'He made her jump, nothing more,' Blanche said. Andrey was protective of his wife to the point of inanity and Marie's reaction to being surprised would not have helped Jack endear himself.

They walked back up the stairs and out into the courtyard. The window that was high in Jack's room was at ground level in the wall of the storerooms so a breeze could keep grain fresh. If Blanche knelt down beside it, she would be able to look over his bed. Was he sleeping now or lying awake, wondering who and where he was? The fever that had almost claimed his life had been fierce, and his skin had burned even as he shivered. His muscles did not lie—he must be strong indeed to have fought that off.

She decided against looking in case he was awake and saw her.

'Put a guard on his door,' she told Andrey. 'Someone loyal to you.'

She straightened her sleeves and thought back to the way Jack had seized her by the wrist. He had moved so quickly, but there had been no panic in her. The abhorrence she usually felt at being touched without permission had been mild and she had snapped at him as a matter of course. When the impulse had clearly filled him to try to touch her for a second time he had stayed his hand and that had endeared him to her even more.

'A pity he has no memory,' she mused to Andrey. 'I would like to know who he is and what he is doing.'

She crossed the courtyard from the building where Jack was being housed and climbed the outside stairs to the main tower of the fort. She paused as she always did and pressed her palm against the door. Compared to the grand home that she had shared with her second husband, Yann, it was small, but it belonged to her and no one else. Jack had believed the house belonged to a man, naturally, and the knowledge rankled. But why would he not?

She lifted her head, proud to have done something so few women would dare to try or succeed in doing. There had been times after Yann's death when her courage to continue down the path she had chosen had wavered. But she had continued, and Bleiz Mor lived and fought, her name a tribute to the wolf pelts that had decorated their walls.

'Brittany will triumph,' she whispered to Yann's ghost. 'You did not die in vain.'

She climbed the stairs to her private room on the top floor of the tower and sat in the high-backed chair at the window, shivering a little in the breeze that crept round the threadbare screens. Winter had not fully loosened its grasp, but each time she considered spending some of her plunder on her own comfort she thought of the widowed women who struggled in bare cottages to feed fatherless children, or the men toiling to grow crops in fields turned to battlefields. She did not need it as much as they did.

She turned her attention to the cross that lay on the table. Keeping this was an indulgence. She had examined it over and over in the days before Jack regained consciousness and could picture it with her eyes closed. It was engraved on the back with the initials *J* and *M* on either side. She had been right to suspect his name might begin with that letter. She wondered who *M* was and a little jealous flame flickered in her breast. She hoped it was his family name and not that of a wife or lover. Perhaps he would remember if she showed him the cross. She would wait until he was well rather than risk agitating him now.

She held the cross tightly and pursed her lips. That was not the only reason for delaying. If his memory returned and he was proved to be a supporter of Charles de Blois, there were matters she would have to face. Taking a man's life in combat or on the seas was one thing, but callously executing him in her own home after giving him care and shelter was entirely another. She worried she was allowing her sense of sympathy for his injuries and pity for his circumstances to cloud her judgement. Perhaps he thought a woman would be more easily tricked or cajoled into believing his lies, or that her opinions were of no consequence. He would not be the first man who had tried to dismiss her in such a way.

She walked behind the tapestry screen and into the shallow alcove of the window and glanced out over the sea, deep in thought. She occupied the whole of the top floor of the tower as her bedchamber and private solar. From her window, and hers alone, high on the highest floor of the tower, it was possible to see that the coast with its shallow inlets and jutting rocks dipped in more deeply and curved round behind the cliff in a loop.

It was in this concealed cove, safe from the tides and from passing eyes, where her two ships rested at anchor. She inhaled deeply, tasting the salt air in the back of her mouth and feeling the wind enfolding her. She had not sailed since the night before Jack's shipwreck.

Although she was still furious at the way the villagers had defied her and lit the church lights, she knew they were growing restless with the continued assaults on houses loyal to the de Montfort cause. She had sworn vengeance on the French, yet had kept her ships at harbour since the night of the shipwreck, the thought of more death turning her stomach in a way that was new and unpleasant. News had come to her earlier in the day through the network of men in her pay of a French ship making its way along the coast. It would not be allowed to pass further up the coast.

She summoned Marie—the only person Blanche permitted inside her private sanctuary—and sent orders down to Andrey to ready her two ships, *White Wolf* and *White Hawk,* by dusk.

She descended to the large room on the ground floor where her household ate and joined them, passing around the tables to speak with each man and woman. Like her, everyone here had lost someone dear to the French after the siege of Quimper or in other battles. Like her, they had sworn to wreak revenge on those who had taken arms against the rightful claimant to the dukedom of Brittany, but only Blanche had the determination and courage to do what she had done and rebuild her life stronger than she had been before. They loved her for it and were fiercely loyal. She had no fears that her identity would be revealed by anyone within the walls of the castle.

She could not help but feel proud of what she had accomplished as she looked round the room. Lamps burned brightly on every table, richly coloured tapestries hung along each wall and they drank from ornate goblets. Anyone who visited would be awestruck by the riches on display and understand that Blanche Tanet's spirit had not died when her husband Yann had been executed.

She stood on the raised dais before the fire, knowing that her silhouette before the flames was dramatic, and waited for silence.

'Luring the ship on to the rocks was cowardly and short-sighted. We could harm our allies as much as our enemies. That must not happen again.' She waited while the inevitable muttering subsided. Jagu Ronec was sitting beside Andrey, his face thunderous. Blanche smiled at him warmly, despite the stirrings of anxiety inside her, and addressed her next words of flattery to him.

'You are all brave men, strong and determined, and have no need of such tricks. Tonight, my friends, we attack the French ship that is sailing down the coast from Concarneau. I wish you success. We will win and Brittany will triumph.'

She held her goblet aloft, fingers closing round

the jewelled stem, and led the toast. The wine they had salvaged from the wreck was excellent quality. She stepped down and spoke to Ronec.

'I'll sail with you tonight. *White Hawk* leads the advance.'

Ronec's eyes gleamed. Blanche hid her revulsion as his lips brushed the back of her hand. If she had been more far-sighted, she would never have thrown her lot in with him, but it had seemed a good idea given that he was her closest neighbour and a friend of her first husband. He was fiercely passionate about the cause, but lacked the acumen to come up with such a bold venture himself. A week of nights in his bed had been a price she had reluctantly accepted in return for the money she had needed and the provision of a crew, but he clearly expected the transaction to continue even after he had paid her what she needed for *White Hawk*. That she had staved him off for over a year was a source of amazement to everyone, most of all to Blanche, and it was a constant worry that she could not hope to do so for ever.

The assault was a success. *White Hawk* lay in wait for the French cog while *White Wolf* came from behind. When the sail was hoisted it caught the wind, the square billowing out, proudly displaying the symbol of the wolf pelt. She saw *White Hawk* do the same. Blanche's mood lifted, as it never failed to once she felt the waves lifting and breaking. The symbol of Yann's favourite quarry now struck fear into the hearts of the foe who had taken him.

The crew were suppressed with ease and little bloodshed. Blanche strode back and forth before the bound crew who knelt on the deck at sword point. Dressed in Bleiz Mor's disguise, the sense of power never failed to thrill her. Even in the height of summer, she wore a thickly padded gambeson beneath a heavy leather jerkin. As well as protecting her, it gave her a masculine shape. The impression was of a stocky man. To complete the disguise, she wore a low-brimmed hat and grotesque *jongleur*'s leather mask in the form of a wolf's upper face. It added an air of menace and ensured that any opponent would not realise he was facing a woman. She suspected she could forgo the padding and still go undetected because how many women ever faced and defeated men as she did?

'Thank you for your donation to our cause,' she smirked. 'John de Montfort will be grateful for your weapons and the people of Brittany will eat well with your wages.'

The Captain stared at her with hatred in his

eyes, but his defiance subsided as she stood over him. She tore the hat from his head and grasped him by the hair, ready to slit his throat, but stayed her hand on seeing the shock of unkempt blond hair and the crisscross of scars on his brow. He reminded her too much of the man lying in her storeroom.

'Let them live so they can pass our message to their commanders,' she said. She waited until the crew had been thrust into the rowboat and tossed the flaming brand on to the deck of *Charles Roi* herself.

Both of Blanche's ships returned home wealthier than when they had left. Cheered by the thought of gold, Ronec had barely objected when Blanche took the opportunity to tell him of the survivor's presence. It had been fortuitous.

It was almost dawn when Blanche returned to the castle, the scent of woodsmoke in her nostrils and cries for mercy in her ears. As soon as Ronec left to return to his own home, Andrey spoke to Blanche in an undertone.

'The guard I left on the stranger's room came to speak to me. Your survivor has been creating quite a disturbance. He has been demanding to speak to you.'

'Demanding?' If he was capable of such, then

he must have made a swift recovery since Blanche had spoken with him.

'Requesting, then. But forcefully and frequently. He has eaten and bathed so he no longer stinks.' Andrey frowned. 'I am not happy with him being here. We should slit his throat, or at the very least surrender him to someone who has more proficiency in discovering the truth. It would gain you some credit.'

Blanche recoiled. 'You mean torture? No.'

Andrey grinned. 'Are you showing mercy again tonight, Cousin? Since when have you shown compassion to your enemies? You have cut down men in their dozens without a second thought.'

Blanche closed her eyes. She smelled the iron odour of blood, felt the cold steel in her hand. Each man she had cut down in the assault on *Charles Roi* had been one strike against Charles de Blois and his army in revenge for the loyal Bretons who had died. Why did the existence of one stranger attack her conscience so powerfully? Her strange compassion to the surviving crew was his fault.

'We are in a war. I will kill when I know the men are my enemies,' she said brusquely. 'I don't know that this man is. He may be an ally or, if he does follow de Blois's cause, he may be a use-ful hostage. We can hand him over at any time.'

She glanced towards the building where Jack was being housed. She had few servants, but even at dawn the building was buzzing like a beehive, alive with the sounds of daily life. A visitor lis-tening to the chatter of maids washing could be-lieve he was in just another household, not the stronghold of a feared pirate.

'He might respond better to a man asking questions. Not all men think women worth speak-ing the truth to.'

Maybe it was time for Jack to receive a visit from the Sea Wolf. This would test him and allow Blanche to see whether she received the same declarations twice.

'I will speak to him once more.'

Andrey looked her up and down. 'Like this? What if he recognises you?'

Blanche gave him a tight smile. 'It isn't likely. He'll see what he expects to see—a man in a mask. Why would he assume I'm a woman be-neath the disguise when I do something so un-womanly? He's only seen me briefly in any case.'

She made her way instead to the storeroom. Andrey's guard was sitting at the end of the cor-ridor, dozing. He jumped at her sharp whistle.

'Has he been any trouble tonight?' Blanche asked.

The guard shook his head.

'Wait here for my word,' Blanche instructed, taking the lantern from the table. She pulled her mask on, tipped the brim of her hat lower over her face and swung the door open.

Jack was lying on the bed, stretched out on top of the furs. His hands were behind his head and one long leg was bent at the knee, crooked over the other. He appeared to be asleep and looked much as he had on the beach the first time Blanche had seen him. She was half-tempted to try to wake him and see if he repeated his kiss and in turn regained some memories, but as she stepped over the threshold his head jerked up.

'*Madame*, is that you?'

His tone was eager. Blanche paused, wondering what in her step had made him recognise her? She lowered her voice more, making it into a husky snarl.

'No.'

Blanche hung the lantern on a hook beside the door and stood, arms folded and legs planted apart. She stuck her hips forward and lifted her head. The mask would disguise her face and as always she spoke in a deep growl to hide the feminine tones.

'My men tell me you have been calling for her. Why? Is there something you need?'

Blanche swept a hand around the room, taking in the mattress with fine furs. She looked pointedly at the table where an uncorked wine bottle stood beside an empty wooden plate. She knew he had been sent water to bathe earlier in the day.

Jack set his jaw. 'I have no cause to complain of my care. I have everything I need except my freedom.' Jack's expression became bullish. He lowered his hands and sat upright, swaying slightly. 'Are you the master of this house?'

'No. You have met its mistress, Madame Tanet.'

She watched as he digested this information. When he looked back at her, his eyes were sharp.

'She is your wife?'

Blanche laughed. 'Madame Tanet is a widow. She belongs to no man.'

Jack cocked his head, his eyes flickering with interest. Blanche's palms grew sweaty inside her leather gloves. Most women did belong to someone and Blanche woke every day knowing how fragile and unusual her independence was.

'Then how come you are here?' Jack asked.

'The lady and I have come to an arrangement that works well for both of us.' She thickened her accent as an extra precaution until she sounded more like the common fishermen in the village.

Jack's eyes widened, then narrowed slightly. Interesting. He was obviously speculating what sort of arrangement it was and no doubt coming to the conclusion Blanche expected. Knowing he had no suspicion of whom he was talking to gave her a rush of pleasure and power. She drew her sword, but held it at her side. Jack's eyes followed the movement and his powerful shoulders tensed.

'Madame Tanet tells me you claim to have no memory of who you are.'

He gave her an angry glare. 'I do more than "claim".'

He was dressed now, wearing one of the servants' loose tunics and breeches. The tunic was tied by two points, leaving the top two open. Blanche tried not to look too obviously at his chest. He swung his legs over the bed and indicated the table.

'May I have some paper and the means to write?' he asked.

'You can write?' Blanche raised an eyebrow. 'You know this, yet you do not know your name?'

He looked perplexed. 'I know some things, though I don't know why or how. I can speak. I can dress myself, as you can see. I hoped if I had the means to write or draw, some memories might come to me.'

He probed carefully at the edge of the bandage. His hands were long, with slender fingers and well-kept nails. She knew from nursing him there were old calluses on the ridge at the base of each finger that had started to soften. If he was a sailor they would be hardened. He was a mystery. Solving it teased her intriguingly.

'Who are you?' she breathed.

He looked surprised and Blanche realised with alarm that she had almost let her guise down for a moment and revealed her true self.

'Tell me the truth,' she said, more sternly. 'I have no time for men who speak falsehoods to me.'

'I don't know,' he said, his voice rising in frustration. He bunched his fists, pressing them to the side of his temples, then pounded them on the wall in frustration. His expression darkened and he looked unexpectedly dangerous. He stood and faced Blanche, arms crossed and head high. His sleeves were rolled up and his arms were toned, but did not have the deep tan of men who were used to working outside all day. Good arms. Strong arms, Blanche thought, then despised herself a little for noticing such a detail.

'I have told you what I told Madame Tanet. Present me with another visitor and I shall swear the same to him. Where am I? I have told you everything I am able, yet no one will tell me where I am or who is keeping me here.'

He stepped towards her and she raised the sword. 'Do not move.'

'Who are you?' Jack growled. 'You come in here, threatening me with a sword. I demand to know why I am being kept here.'

'I'm not threatening you,' Blanche snarled. 'This is for my protection.'

'Against what?'

Jack curled his lip. He spread his arms wide and turned in a slow circle, giving Blanche a perfect view of his tall, strong body. He would conquer her easily if he decided to attack. She gripped her sword tighter. When he faced her there was no fear in his eyes, only anger held in check. If she held a sword to his throat, he would not quake like the Captain of *Charles Roi* had.

'I have no way of attacking you or defending myself. Until this morning I could not even raise myself from the bed. You are treating me poorly, *monsieur*, and I would like some answers. If I were myself again and in possession of a weapon of my own, I would take them from your lips at sword point.'

'If you were yourself, you would not need to fight me for the answers,' Blanche pointed out. She lowered the sword, her hand trembling a little as the thought of what he had already done to her lips sent a shiver through her belly. 'But you obviously think you are capable, which tells us both something about you, does it not?'

He glared at her, then spun away and walked to the window, his frustration clear. Being a storeroom, the window was high set and narrow. He raised himself on to the balls of his feet, craning his head to look out, and grabbed hold of the bars as if he intended to pull his entire body off the ground. His arms were muscular and Blanche considered that he would have no problem doing that.

'What do you see?' Blanche asked, curious to discover what would command his attention. 'Tell me what it tells you.'

He looked over his shoulder at her. Light drenched his hair, picking out the blond among the sand and casting shadows over sculpted cheekbones. 'Is this a test? Will I earn my freedom if I pass?'

She cocked her head to one side and gestured. Their eyes locked and for a moment she was fixed by the certainty Jack recognised her, despite the mask, but he looked away. He was silent as his head moved from side to side. Blanche held her breath.

'There is a rounded tower on the building opposite with a window set high into the top. I know I am below ground here because I can see doorways and steps.'

He sniffed. 'From the smell of grain I think this is a storeroom, not a cell.'

He breathed again, more deeply and slower. His shoulders lifted and his torso expanded. He had a powerful body, Blanche thought. She caught herself wondering what it would be like to run her hands over the solid muscles of his back that moved beneath the tunic, imagining them to be as solid and sculpted as those in his chest. She took a step closer.

'I can smell the sea,' Jack murmured. 'And when it is quiet in the night I think I can hear the waves.'

He let go of the bars and dropped on to his feet with a lightness that took Blanche by surprise, and stood upright.

'I already know I am by the coast because Madame Tanet told me they had only brought me a short way. Where is she?' he asked.

Blanche was struck by the eagerness in his voice. He obviously found her attractive from the way his eyes filled with life. She wondered how deeply the memory of their kiss was buried and what it would take to make it resurface.

'You'd like to see her again?' she asked. 'A pretty woman, isn't she, for all that she is older than you, I think? Don't men your age hanker after young virginal girls?'

'I don't hanker after anyone,' Jack snapped. He raised his head and his eyes were hard, though pain whispered at the edge of his voice. 'I would like to see her again because she was kind to me when I woke and I believe it is down to her I owe my life. I would like to thank her.'

Blanche sheathed her sword and adjusted her cloak and gloves.

'Perhaps you will see her again. However, I will pass any messages on to her that you wish. I will leave you now. I have matters to attend to.'

'Am I a prisoner?' Jack asked, anger in his voice. 'Is the door to be bolted once more?'

Blanche jerked her head up in surprise. She had not drawn the bolt when she had left, which meant that if he knew of its existence he had either opened the door or had heard it before. Which in turn meant he had been feigning sleep when she entered to bathe him. Her sense of fairness told her he had perhaps half woken and was lapsing in and out of sleep and had not intended to deceive her. The contemptuous part of her that knew what she did of men was unsure.

Jack flexed his arms. 'I have been still and sleeping for too long and ache to stretch my legs.'

Blanche looked at the limbs in question that he now planted apart. They were long and lean with—she couldn't help but notice—a sizeable bunching of cloth between them. She had thought her desire for men had been ground out of her by the degrading exploits she had put herself through since Yann's death, but to her consternation, heat rose to her face. Images of lovemaking began to bud in her mind like wild blooms after the winter frost.

'You stay here for now. For your safety as much as anything else. Madame Tanet had to fight to bring you here and her men will not trust a stranger as readily as she will. These are difficult times.'

She hammered on the door with a fist. Jack tensed, looking as though he was about to spring forward, but when she held out a hand he stood back. He clearly didn't like the answer. She didn't blame him.

When the door opened, Blanche dropped into a low bow, sweeping the hat from her head with a flourish, and swept out. She bolted the door, taking care to make as much noise as possible so Jack knew what she had done.

She leaned against the door and pulled the mask from her face, then fanned her neck with her hat and faced Andrey who was waiting at the end of the passageway.

'I think he's telling the truth.'

'Did you mention what we found in the barrels?' Andrey asked.

Blanche shook her head. What they had discovered had been surprising, but it had not seemed an appropriate time to throw it in his face. It had been interesting to see how Jack's manner had been when he believed he was speaking to a man. He had been polite, yet this time she had sensed an undercurrent of belligerence he had not shown to Blanche. She'd half expected him to attack her even without a sword in his hand.

She believed his memory loss was true, however, though how to help him regain it was going to be a challenge. And she did want him to. He fascinated her beyond explanation. She would have to think about it, but now she craved her bed.

'I want one more interview with him later on,' Blanche insisted.

She pressed her ear to the door and could hear Jack muttering to himself but could not make out his words. She wondered what he would be like in a fight. She wondered what he would be like in bed. She wasn't sure which excited her more.

Chapter Five

Jack was torn from sleep by the sound of the door slamming back and wood hitting stone. He had been awake until dawn rose, considering his conversation with the mysterious man before giving into his body's demand for sleep.

His body jerked and he gazed blearily at the two figures who had entered. They had not visited him before and were dressed in well-cut coats of wool, but their belts were adorned with various weapons that looked well used.

'Get up,' the younger of the two—a handsome dark-haired man who Jack thought looked about forty—barked. 'You're wanted.'

Jack frowned. He pushed himself on to his elbows, cursing the fact that he still felt slightly dizzy when he moved too suddenly. 'Who by?'

'You'll find out when you get there,' the man

replied curtly. 'If you don't come willingly, we'll take you.'

He pulled the edge of his cloak back to reveal a pair of iron cuffs linked by a heavy chain. Jack pushed himself from the bed, his temper flaring and his fists bunching. He reined it back in. Though the man's tone caused his temper to rise, he was not prepared to suffer the indignity of being shackled. Besides, this was his first opportunity to leave his room and he would be unwise to pass it up.

He pulled on a loose-fitting jerkin over his tunic and hose. At the end of the bed was a pair of boots. They were well-worn brown leather, scuffed at the heels and toes, and reached to mid-calf. When he pulled them on they fitted him perfectly, fitting to the shape of his soles and toes, so were most likely his own. He inspected them curiously for a moment, waiting for some sign of recognition, but beyond the sense of striding he got nothing.

The men stood by, the one who had spoken drumming his fingers on his crossed arms with an impatient look on his face. A spark of mutiny reared up in Jack and he took time to run his fingers through the side of his hair that wasn't muffled in the bandage, to adjust his borrowed clothes to his liking and to rub a finger round his teeth to freshen them. He caught a flash of a smirk on the face of the short, wide man.

'I'm ready,' he said, addressing the short man. 'Where are we going?'

'You'll find out when we get there,' Dark Hair growled.

They led him along a passageway. Jack gazed round curiously at the rooms he passed. He was, as he had suspected, in a storeroom. The other rooms he passed were being used to store food, including a particularly pungent cheese that made Jack's mouth water.

They climbed the stairs and emerged in the small courtyard that Jack had seen from his window. He looked back at the building and identified what he thought was his room at the furthest end. He tried not to think of it as a cell because the idea of his imprisonment made his body grow cold with perspiration. He began walking across the courtyard towards the round tower that was the only other building within the walls.

'Not that way,' said the short man. 'Follow us.'

They walked at either side of him and led him through the gateway round the back of the tower. Wind buffeted him, catching his hair and the loose sleeves of his tunic. He inhaled deeply, relishing the fresh air after the stifling yeastiness of the storeroom. A rutted track led down and away from the castle. Jack looked back, ignoring the urging of the two men. The round tower was a squat, wide building with windows set at intervals that revealed three storeys. It clung to the edge of a cliff, with a sheer drop to the rocks below. Jack felt dizzy even looking at it.

'Come on,' said the short man, while Dark Hair gave him a rough shove between the shoulder blades.

Eventually, they emerged on a long, curved beach. By the time they arrived, Jack's back and armpits were clammy with perspiration and the tunic was sticking to him. He hadn't realised how weak he still was. He walked unaided, though his speed had slightly irritated his captors. He was determined he would not show any weakness to them.

When his feet crunched on the sand, he had to resist the urge to sink down to his knees. Instead he stood and gazed around, moving his head slowly from one end of the beach to the other.

Smooth black rocks rose out of the sea at each end of the cove, providing a natural end, with others scattered along the length, half-buried beneath grey shingle. The tide surged in and out, revealing other rocks concealed beneath the sea. The wind was fierce and cold, and the tide crashed on to the beach in violent rolls that sent spray upwards. White rolls churned further out, indicating there were more rocks. Gulls circled lazily across the pale grey sky, their cries the only voices punctuating the crashing waves.

A lone figure stood on the flat, black rocks just above where the tide reached. He was facing out to sea. He wore his hat pulled down low and a heavy cloak of black trimmed with white fur that billowed in the wind. It was a dramatic pose, clearly contrived for maximum effect. This was the same man who had visited Jack's room earlier on.

'We've brought him,' the short man said.

The man on the rock turned slowly, sure-footed on the treacherous rocks. He was wearing the unsettling animal mask. He tilted his head back.

'Thank you, Andrey. Bring him closer.'

Andrey was the friendlier of the two men. He made to take Jack's arm, though without much effort, and Jack shrugged him off easily. Andrey seemed to hold no grudge, but followed close behind as Jack walked across the shingle. Jack stopped short of clambering on to the rocks to join the man. The surface was black and they glistened with weed. Jack felt an overpowering sense of nausea and dizziness as he imagined himself flailing, losing footing and crashing into the sea.

The man gestured around him.

'Well, Master Jack?'

'Well?' Jack echoed. He folded his arms and stared at the man on the rock.

He was slightly shorter than the other two, though held himself tall with poise. Beneath the cloak that reached to his knees he wore a bulky leather surcoat, loosely belted at the waist. His chest looked thickset and Jack imagined that the neck and chin beneath the tightly wound scarf would be equally corpulent. If only he would reveal his face. Being able to see only the black eyes was unsettling.

Clearly, the man expected Jack to be cowed and a sense of rebellion swelled in him. He folded his arms across his chest and planted his feet wide.

'You have me at a disadvantage. I do not yet know your name.'

The man looked at Andrey and the other man. Were they servants or companions? He folded his arms.

'I am Bleiz Mor.'

Jack started forward, mouth open, then stopped and drew back as fog rolled across his mind once more.

'You have heard of me?' The suspicion in the man's voice was the first hint of emotion Jack had seen.

'No. Yes.' Doubt filled Jack's mind, but there had been a flicker of something.

'All sailors and Frenchmen have heard of the Sea Wolf,' the dark-haired man growled. 'They know to fear him.'

'Thank you, Ronec,' Bleiz Mor said. He tilted his head on one side. 'Is Ronec correct?'

'I don't know.' Jack heaved a sigh, feeling frustrated. 'Your name seems familiar, but I don't know where I have heard it. You seem familiar, but I don't know if we have met. I wish I could remember.'

'It would be to your benefit if you could,' Bleiz Mor prompted, somewhat unnecessarily to Jack's mind.

Jack walked closer to the rocks. Bleiz Mor did not move.

'Some memories are locked inside my head,' Jack said. 'I have tastes and smells, sometimes voices or faces, but they jumble together and I don't know where they are from.'

He closed his eyes and held his hand out as if he could snatch the memories back that way. The man cocked his head to one side. Again, Jack was filled with a tormenting sense of familiarity he couldn't explain.

'Is Bleiz Mor a name or a title?'

'A perceptive question. If you know my name,

then you should know I am to be feared. I do not know if you can be trusted. You may be an ally of the French or a spy for Charles de Blois. I do not know if I can trust you not to betray me.'

'Then perhaps you should not have told me it,' Jack pointed out.

'That's what I said,' Ronec growled.

Ronec had clearly spoken out of turn because Bleiz Mor's head came up sharply and he spat words at Ronec that were too quick for Jack to catch. The intent was clear, though, and, from the resentment in Ronec's eyes as he bowed his head, Jack realised there was some animosity between the two men.

'Have you brought me here to be judged?' he asked. 'What is my crime?'

'Crime?' The head tipped to the side. An inflexion of surprise.

'I presume I must have committed one to be held in such circumstances and threatened with being chained to be brought to you.'

'No crime has been committed as far as I am aware,' Bleiz Mor answered.

'Not by me at least,' Jack said. 'But you have the appearance of having no love of the law, otherwise you would not disguise yourself.'

He kicked the sand, sending a spray of small pebbles cascading into the sea, causing a musical ripple, and looked again at the man on the rock.

'The vessel I was on was wrecked,' Jack said grimly. 'But I am unsure whether it was an accident or intentional. Are you responsible for my situation?'

White-hot fury surged inside him. He was weary to the bone and wanted to be lying down, not standing on a windswept beach with someone who would not even show his face.

'Am I to be kept in captivity for the simple fortune of not dying along with everyone else?'

He spun towards the man, exhilarated at the thought of plunging into a fight with his fists and feet. Bleiz Mor showed the first sign of agitation Jack had seen, but it didn't seem to be the threat of attack that had hit the mark.

'I swear to you now that I had nothing to do with that,' he spat, his voice rising. 'And I have not brought you here to be judged or sentenced.' He lowered his voice. 'You assume everyone else died.'

Jack considered before answering, 'I think so. My identity is in question and you clearly wish to know as much as I do. If there was someone who could reveal the truth, I don't believe you would keep that from me. What would be the point?'

Bleiz Mor nodded. 'You are a clever man. We have no other survivors. Perhaps some lived and were washed ashore further along the coast, but we have seen no one. You were lucky.' His voice softened unexpectedly. 'I am sorry for your loss.'

Jack hung his head. Heaviness and a sudden sense of grief enveloped him like a thick mist, chilling him and filling his stomach with blackness. Loss felt as familiar and well fitting as his boots. But who he grieved for, he could not name.

Bleiz Mor swept round to Jack once again.

'Does this place seem familiar to you?'

Jack walked to the edge of the sea and knelt back on his heels, staring out across the rocks. There was nothing familiar. The sea stretched out and jagged rocks rose above the surface in the distance, but nothing significant struck Jack.

'Is this where you found me?'

'It is.'

There appeared to be a flat surface stretching out beneath the tide, turning the sea a black, oily colour. At low tide, it might be possible to walk out.

'How far does this stretch?' he asked.

Bleiz Mor shrugged. 'Far enough that if a ship heads in at the wrong place it will run aground.'

'Like mine did.'

'Like yours did.'

'How did I survive?'

'My best guess is that you clung to the rocks and were somehow washed ashore. It would explain the gash on your head and the grazes on your body.'

Jack's hand went instinctively to the bandage. The pain was no longer a blinding throb, but a dull ache he could ignore most of the time. The lacerations on his chest and belly were at the stage where they itched rather than stung. He touched his chest and his mind filled with the memory of Madame Tanet's hand gently soothing him. His skin grew prickly as he realised he craved her touch again and he lowered his hand, bunching it into a fist at his side.

He lifted his head and found Bleiz Mor had been watching closely. The mask and hat made his features impossible to see, but his stance and the tilt of his head radiated arrogance and authority.

'You tell me nothing that helps me,' Jack said. 'And, as you know, I can tell you nothing that helps you.'

'It might have been safer to let you die,' Bleiz Mor said with a cruel laugh.

Jack raised his eyes, his body growing rigid with anger.

'Perhaps so,' he snarled. 'What is the point of me living if I am to stay here in this half life not able to remember anything? If I dash my head against the rocks once more will that restore my memory or snatch what I still know away from me?'

'I cannot answer that. But I will offer some consolation—once you remember more, I can decide what is to become of you and if I am to let you go.'

'And what if I never do? Am I to remain here for ever?' Jack asked. He was filled with a reckless urge to put an end to the torture of his existence.

'I have done with your insinuations and constant questioning. Kill me now rather than that.'

He strode to where Bleiz Mor stood and dropped to his knees on the shingle, bearing his throat and gesturing to the sword Bleiz Mor wore at his side. He willed the bastard to strike, meaning his words more sincerely than anything he could remember.

Bleiz Mor drew the sword slowly and stepped back, holding it at arm's length so the tip was a finger's width from Jack's heart. The organ in question hammered in Jack's chest, loud enough that it must be an easy target. Jack waited for the blow that would end his life, staring up with a challenge, and determined to meet his fate with open eyes. Part of his brain told him this was what he had been craving for a long time.

'You do not fear death?' Bleiz Mor murmured.

Jack gritted his teeth. The sudden longing for death had felt like the greeting of an old friend. What had his life been like if that was true?

'It appears not.'

The sword wavered, then Bleiz Mor sheathed it with a smooth gesture.

'You are fearless as well as clever. If you do not regain your memory, I could make use of a man like you.'

'As a pirate?' Jack sneered.

'As someone defending Brittany against those who would lay claim to her,' Bleiz Mor answered. 'We fight to regain our land for the true Duke. There are worse lives than mine.'

'And better,' Jack spat. 'Honest men do not hide their faces and threaten people.'

Bleiz Mor jerked his head and Jack steeled himself for a blow, but instead the masked man leaned close and spoke in an angry whisper.

'You talk to me of honesty. Do you know what was in the barrels we salvaged? Sunk to the bottom of cheap wine? Weapons. Swords and knives. Your ship was a smuggling vessel. Don't assume you are any better than I, *monsieur*. Can you honestly say you haven't killed or stolen?'

Jack dropped his head. He had no answer and the remembrance of the rage and craving for a fight indicated he might indeed be that sort of man.

Bleiz Mor gave a short laugh. He did not press Jack for an answer, but addressed Ronec. 'I'm satisfied he knows nothing. Are you?'

'So shall I slit his throat?' Ronec growled, fingering the blade of his knife.

Bleiz Mor appeared to consider the offer. Jack lifted his chin, baring his throat.

Ronec laughed and said something in a dialect Jack didn't know. Bleiz Mor retorted angrily and the two men squared up to each other, both shouting furiously and rapidly. Ronec was taller and wider, but the squat man showed no signs of backing down and, against his will, Jack found himself impressed by his captor's tenacity. He laughed and both men turned to face him. It seemed to break the tension between them as they shook hands.

'We'll have no murder in cold blood here,' Bleiz Mor insisted.

Ronec sheathed his knife and gave Jack an unpleasant grin.

'Wait a short while, then take him back to the

castle,' Bleiz Mor said. He swept away up the path Jack had been brought down, leaving the other three men standing on the beach. Jack stared at the short figure, striding away. A sense of loathing welled inside him. It might not be his doing that Jack was in this predicament—the outrage had seemed genuine—but he had made no attempt to make it easy for Jack. His manner rankled.

'I'd kill the son of a *putain* now,' Jack muttered beneath his breath.

Where was he going? Did he live in the tower alongside Madame Tanet? Jack stepped forward to follow him, but Ronec and Andrey were alongside him instantly and took an arm each. Jack attempted to throw them off, but they held tight. Jack flexed his muscles and twisted in their grasp. He was strong, despite the fever that had sapped his strength, but so were they. Under normal circumstances he might have stood a chance of freeing himself, but not now. He would grow stronger and bide his time.

He watched as Bleiz Mor walked away up the path and disappeared round the bend. Jack vowed to himself he would have vengeance on the man for speaking to him in such a manner. He'd tear the arrogant tongue from his mouth and choke the life from him. But within him, a bud of anxiety was beginning to shoot. Knives and weapons concealed in wine barrels?

Was he involved in foul play like the pirate and would he ever discover the truth?

Chapter Six

What to do now?

Blanche removed her disguise. She folded the cloak and gloves and placed them in her wardrobe. She dropped the mask in the hat and put them beneath the table towards the back. She bathed in cold water and brushed her hair loose, then dressed in a gown. It was always a relief to put away her disguise, especially the uncomfortable mask, but the restrictiveness of her tight bodice made her long to wear breeches and a tunic all the time.

She sat by the window, rubbing beeswax into her nails. It would not do for her hands to show signs of labour or exposure to the elements. From there she could see the path that she had walked up. She watched as Jack was brought back to the castle. He was walking slowly, head bowed and shoulders hunched. She was pleased to see

Ronec's manacles had not been necessary, but frowned none the less.

He cut a lonely figure, his large frame folded up on itself as he walked ahead of Ronec and Andrey. He was still weak and looked haggard. She had half expected him to drop dead on the beach—in fact, when he dropped to his knees she had believed his life was giving out.

Blanche drummed her nails on the stone sill and remembered the feeling that had come upon her as Jack had knelt on the sand, his chest smooth and toned, bared and waiting for her to strike. The bruises and grazes were healing and fading. Even if she had intended to end his life, the idea of marring the perfection further had been repellent. She had been consumed with the urge to remove her gloves and run her fingers over his body in a caress, to feel the hardness of his muscles and the softness of the palm-sized area of light hair that reached between his nipples.

She'd expected to see fear or resignation when she drew her weapon, but the blue orbs had been brimming with challenge. When he had begged for death it had not been entirely a surprise. She frowned. Not begged. Demanded. What was his past that he should seek out an end so boldly? Jack was a brave man, whoever he was, and he was not afraid of death. The offer of employment had been sincere, though he had taken it as a taunt and rejected it. If he continued to have no memory, perhaps he could be persuaded.

What to do…?

If you have someone or something, you would produce it.

He had sounded so desperate and agitated that she had almost feared for his mind. She walked to the other window and opened her jewel casket to take out Jack's cross. This could be the key to release Jack's memory, or one of them at least. She bit her lip, reminding herself that she did not know where the box was. She had told Andrey they could open it, but then hadn't done and since coming back to the fort had lost track of it among all the other salvage. It would not be fair to Jack now he was conscious. She ran her fingers over the garnets on the front and let the chain slip through her fingers. She would return it to Jack in a day or two, when he had fully recovered.

She left her room and ordered the servants to prepare a room for Jack. Even though she was now the chatelaine of a lonely tower, she had not forgotten the rules of hospitality that she had been brought up with since childhood. She had sorely breached them and now she had decided Jack would have to stay, she could not house him in a storeroom for ever.

* * *

When she received word that his room was prepared she made her way down to the storerooms. Marie was loitering at the end of the passage, holding a bowl and looking nervous.

'He won't bite you,' Blanche chided gently. She took the bowl of white cheese and honeycomb from Marie and sent her off to find Andrey.

Blanche knocked at the door before she entered. There was a short delay before Jack's low voice answered.

'Who is it?'

'Madame Tanet,' she answered. She pressed her hands against the door.

There was a pause before he bade her to come in. He was standing, leaning against the wall facing the window, arms raised around his head, as if he had been pulling himself up to look out again. He turned and gave her a warm smile that made her toes curl with pleasure.

'Good day, *madame*. I saw you leaving the tower and hoped you might be coming to visit me.'

Blanche's throat tightened at the thought he had been watching while she was unawares. She wondered what else he had seen.

'You were spying on me?'

'That's a severe verdict!' He glanced over his

shoulder at the high window. 'I have little else to occupy me. Do you blame me for wanting to see what is happening?'

She dipped her head in part acknowledgement and part apology, then held out the bowl.

'I've brought you some food.'

Jack took it from her and began to eat, picking morsels of the cheese delicately between his thumb and forefinger. He ran his finger round the bowl to catch the final crumbs and trace of honey and licked them clean. He almost certainly didn't intend the action to be seductive, but Blanche's neck prickled at the sight of his tongue running meticulously around the tips. She licked her lips as if they were covered in honey, too. He noticed her watching and frowned.

'Excuse my lack of manners. I haven't been allowed a knife.' The rebuke was gentle.

'You have an appetite and are out of bed at least,' she said. 'This is good.'

'Yes. The pallet is not the comfiest place for a man who is not insensible and close to death.'

He rolled his shoulders back and stretched his head from side to side, illustrating the cricks and aches he must have developed and giving Blanche a good look at the firm tendons in his neck and broad shoulders in the process. Jack still looked tired. The shadows beneath his eyes had diminished slightly and his face was a little less lined, but he was clearly still weary. Blanche recalled how he had looked while she had nursed him through his fever, flushed cheeks in an otherwise grey complexion, with a sheen of sweat covering his supple chest.

'Perhaps the news I bring will be welcome in that case,' Blanche said. 'Will you come with me, please?'

He narrowed his eyes and glanced behind her at the passageway, presumably checking if Ronec and Andrey were there to escort him.

'Of course.'

He pulled on his boots and followed her out. He walked slowly and carefully, his eyes watchful and body held in readiness in case he needed to move into action. Whether or not he remembered it, this was a man who was used to assessing his surroundings. They walked across the courtyard, but when Jack began heading towards the beach path Blanche took hold of his arm. His forearm tensed at her touch and he jerked his head towards her, eyes vividly bright. She removed her hand quickly, recalling how she had cautioned him not to touch her. She should at least give him the same consideration.

'We're going in here this time,' she said, gesturing to the tower.

Jack raised an eyebrow. 'So you know that I was taken to the beach.'

'I do.'

Jack's face became guarded, but his eyes grew watchful.

'I know where you went and who you met,' Blanche said. This was the test; whether he now admitted he had recognised her or if her disguise had held.

'Considering your recent illness, confronting Bleiz Mor was foolhardy. Most men would not live if they tried that. Many have died for less.'

Jack's face contorted with rage that made Blanche quake.

'Ruthless or not, he toyed with me, taunted me and made accusations that I could not confirm or deny.'

'But he needed to be sure you were not an agent of the de Blois faction,' Blanche pointed out. 'Your memory loss could have been a trick, or you could be unwittingly putting us into danger by your presence.'

'Nevertheless, I took exception to his manner,' Jack snapped. He seemed to recall he was talking to a woman and lowered his voice. 'The next time I encounter him, I hope to have a sword in my hand.'

An air of power emanated from him. Blanche

curled her fingers, anxiously tightening them into fists buried deep in her skirts. He spoke with such hatred in his voice and with fair reason. She swore to herself that she must never make the connection between them.

'*Madame*, I must ask, are you in danger here?'

Her instinct was to laugh scornfully and tell him she was perfectly capable of keeping herself safe, the same answer she had given to Andrey when she first started on her venture. However, Jack was looking at her with such genuine concern on his face that the words died on her lips and she just stood there, open-mouthed. Jack jerked his head towards the beach path.

'From that vicious cur. You seem agitated and you have turned pale.'

Blanche lifted a hand slowly to her cheek. It felt hot, the fires stoked by this unexpected show of concern and the intense look that blazed in Jack's eyes.

'I'm not in danger from Bleiz Mor,' she said, her voice barely more than a whisper. It was all she could manage.

Doubt filled Jack's blue eyes. He must have taken her wavering voice as an admission that she was frightened because he moved even closer, arms outstretched, as if intending to protect her from unseen assailants who might even now be attacking. Or preparing to enfold her within an embrace.

Blanche felt the long-forgotten need to be in someone's arms and took an uncertain step towards him. Jack reached a hand to her face, but hesitated before his fingers brushed her cheek, his hand wavering in mid-air. The suspense twisted Blanche's innards and she could swear she felt his touch from the way her nerves shouted. He took another step closer, but still did not touch her. Blanche realised she was holding her breath. Slowly, Jack lowered his hand again.

'If you are sure. But if I can be of any aid to you, however small or slight, please, know I am here.'

A lump filled her throat that Jack—a stranger who had no reason to care for her well-being— was offering himself as protector when he had such unbearable troubles of his own. For so long she had relied on no one but herself, and the very idea that someone else might be her champion was strange and disconcerting.

'Thank you,' she murmured. She held an arm out. 'Please, come with me. The wind is getting chilly.'

He fell in beside her and took it. She led him inside the tower, highly conscious of his body close to hers. The sound of lively music and low murmurs of servants' voices came from the Hall where the tables were being laid for the evening meal.

'Up here…' She gestured, indicating the stone staircase. She dropped his arm and led the way up the stairs. She paused on the first turn to confirm Jack was following her and caught his eyes flickering away. A flash of guilt crossed his face, but he threw it off. Blanche hid a smile. He had been gazing at her body as he walked behind her and was interested in what he had seen. She could not censure him for that. She found it hard to keep her eyes from roving over him in turn. His broad shoulders and great height were so charming.

She led him to the first floor and opened the door, gesturing for Jack to enter, then followed.

'This room is for you.'

Jack stood in the centre and gazed around. The room was one that Blanche used for visitors and as such was well decorated. A small but comfortable bed, with a luxuriant coverlet of green wool embroidered with blue silks, stood against one wall. A similar coloured tapestry decorated the wall opposite, above a small fireplace. A table and chair stood before the window.

Jack looked suspicious. 'My new cell?'

'Not a cell,' Blanche said. 'I'm sorry you believed your previous room was one.'

'The door was often bolted,' he countered.

'But, as you see, this room has no bolt, except for one to give you privacy,' she said gently, walking to the door and running her fingers over the iron. 'Jack, you are welcome to stay as a guest in this house. With luck something might emerge which could help heal your broken memory.'

Jack walked to the window. Unlike Blanche's chamber, which covered the whole of the top floor, this room only had one window, slightly offset beneath Blanche's, but which faced the same direction over the courtyard. Jack would not be able to see all the way to the beach.

'Do you trust me now?' he asked, glancing round at her.

'Possibly,' Blanche answered. 'At least, enough to believe that you will not intentionally cause me danger. Besides, it was inhospitable to keep you where you were.'

Jack smiled. 'Then I thank you.' He walked to the bed and rested his open palm on it, pressing it up and down to test the firmness. 'This is certainly an improvement.'

His eyes clouded and he frowned as if the sight of the bed had sapped his strength and reminded him how weary he must still be feeling. He sat on the edge, then reclined back, stretching himself out fully. He stared up at Blanche and she could not ignore the inviting expression in his eyes. Her heart had leapt to her throat at the sight of the reclining man, stretched out with his long limbs sprawled invitingly—then his posture reminded her of a time when she had had no choice in whether to join a man in his bed and she recoiled.

'What are you doing? Do you think I intend to share this bed with you?'

Jack shot upwards, surprise suffusing his face. 'No, Madame Tanet. I would never presume such a thing. I was only appreciating how comfortable this bed is compared to my previous one. Not that I am ungrateful for what you gave me before.'

He stood and moved away from the bed as if the mattress was filled with thorns and thistles, not barley straw.

'Please, pardon my clumsiness.'

They smiled at each other awkwardly.

'No pardon is necessary,' Blanche said. The conclusion was one she alone had reached, imagining a demand that had not been issued. She walked to the window and looked out, conscious of Jack's eyes following her movement. She felt the heat between her breasts and in her loins intensify.

'You must understand, I am a widow and live here modestly. It is I who should beg your forgiveness for implying you would assume such liberties could be taken.'

She felt her cheeks colour at her words. Jack didn't know that since Yann's death she had allowed a number of men to take whatever liberties they had wanted when necessity or expediency had prompted her to. If he had done, he would have been perfectly right to assume she might tumble into bed at a moment's notice. He joined her at the window and placed his hands on the stone lintel. He looked down at the courtyard and craned his head to look beyond the walls at the distant fields and edge of the shore.

'Am I confined to this room?'

Blanche looked around. The room was a good size and considerably more luxurious than the grain store. She remembered the way he had strode along the beach in his fury at Bleiz Mor. His vitality was returning after his illness, his strength growing almost before her eyes. This was a man who needed to move, not be enclosed. His presence filled the room, even as he stood motionless at her side. An attack on the French-held town across the bay was planned for two nights hence, however, and she could not risk him discovering it.

'It is best if you do not leave this room without me to accompany you.'

Jack's eyes narrowed, already heavy with weariness from his exertion, then slid towards the door.

Blanche sighed. 'You are not a prisoner as I keep telling you. I will order my servants to treat you as a guest. You may join my household for our evening meal after a night or two. It is a modest affair and I am little used to company so you must forgive me if I appear ill at ease.'

He breathed deeply, then tilted his head to one side and gave Blanche a measured stare.

'Tonight I could perhaps dine with you here,' she suggested.

It was difficult to know which of them was more surprised by Blanche's offer. The impulse had seized her suddenly. She was drawn to him and the idea of spending time learning about him appealed.

Jack's smile reached his eyes and his weariness seemed to lessen.

'I would like that,' he said.

They held each other's gaze for a moment longer than was appropriate and something passed between them that made Blanche's skin quiver. He was staggeringly attractive. In Blanche's head, a warning bell sounded. She looked away quickly, breaking whatever connection had bound them.

'I should leave you to get used to your room.

Is there anything you wish to be brought from your other room?'

Jack shook his head. 'I have nothing. The paper is just scrawls. I was trying to see if anything came to my mind, but alas, nothing did. Thank you, *madame*—I am in your debt, as I continually seem to be. I shall look forward to seeing you again soon.'

She walked to the foot of the stairs leading upwards.

'What is up there?' Jack asked.

'Those are my private quarters.' Blanche held his gaze firmly. 'That is the one place you may not roam—no one goes there except for me.'

Jack bowed and as he stood he closed his eyes and swayed a little. His colour drained. Blanche reached her hands out to steady him, one on his chest and the other on his arm.

'I'm fine.' Jack reached a fumbling hand for the door frame. 'You don't have to help me.'

He had turned pale and seemed far from fine, however much he might protest otherwise. His determination was admirable, but Blanche put her hands around him. Blanche was strong, but not enough to bear his full weight if he should fall, so she eased him back against the wall for support. His body was warm and the muscles were every bit as firm as she remembered when she had bathed him. She spread her fingers wider over the slight inward curve between his ribs over his heart. The beat was strong but rapid, gradually slowing. Their bodies were close together. She could feel the hardness of his chest and legs pressing against her. She felt the muscles in his arm tense and flex beneath her touch and a rush of desire spilled from deep inside her, flooding her limbs and veins and making her feel almost as weak as Jack was.

He opened his eyes and looked down at her, his gaze warm and settling on her like a feather bolster. She slid her hand up his chest and on to the skin over his collarbone, noting how smooth and delicate it felt, despite the sudden perspiration that had appeared like dew. He made a small noise in the back of his throat that caused her stomach to tighten and an answering hum to begin rising deep inside her.

'Do you feel faint still?' she asked.

She was close to that herself, enveloped by a mist of lust she had not experienced for so long. She could not let him know how such a small sound was capable of causing her such sensations.

Jack gave a wry smile, as if admitting such a thing pained him. 'Today has been hard. I am not as strong as I should be.'

'You should sit,' Blanche murmured. The lon-

ger she stood close to him, the harder it would be
to resist kissing him.

'Thank you, but I think I would prefer to lie.
If you permit it?'

He took an unsteady step forward.

'You don't need my permission in your own
room. Will you…allow me to help you?'

He gave her a sidelong look and she wondered
if he was too proud to be helped by a woman, but
he merely smiled.

'With your assistance, then.'

Blanche took his arm again. He leaned on her
outstretched arm, but Blanche noticed he was
careful not to put too much weight on her. She
walked with him to the bed and helped him lie
down, sitting on the edge of the bed at his side
while she plumped the pillow behind his head
and settled him back.

She looked down at him and felt a thrill at how
close she was, their earlier misunderstanding still
fresh in her mind. She'd been this close while he
had been in a fever, but now he was conscious,
and despite being weak, he was watching her
closely. It had been too long since she had taken
a man into her bed that she had actually wanted to
be there and, seeing this powerful figure lying so
still, with an air of vulnerability, was unsettling.
She drew the fur across his lower half.

'Thank you,' he murmured. His fingers reached down and he buried them in the thick, grey fur. Something flashed in his eyes. 'You like wolves, *madame*?'

A fist squeezed Blanche's guts. Did he suspect her? Was this a test?

'Yes. They are fierce and loyal to their pack. Nothing surpasses their fur for warmth. My husband was a skilled hunter and brought down many of them. He always said an animal that could take down the hunter was the only prize worth winning.'

She kept her face neutral and pulled the fur a little higher. Yann had not won against the French and his death had not been that of a hunter. Just one more for the French to slaughter. When she had sworn to avenge his death, Blanche had chosen her alias in tribute to Yann's favourite target and to remind her why she pursued her course.

Jack stifled a yawn, the tendons in his neck rippling. 'Madame Tanet, I think I shall decline your offer of company tonight, if it will not cause offence.'

'Not in the slightest,' Blanche said, relieved that she would not have to spend time with him or explain his presence for the time being.

'Is something troubling you?' Jack asked softly,

his brow furrowing even as his eyes grew heavy with sleep.

'Nothing that I need share.' Blanche shook her head, touched by his consideration. She rested her hand close to Jack's on the bed, noticing how his long, elegant fingers flexed, indicating he was aware of how close they were to touching. She stood and straightened her skirts.

'I think for now the best thing you can do is sleep. I'll have food and wine sent up. I have few servants, but they will all be happy to attend you. For now, sleep and heal.'

'You are my hostess. I shall do as I am bid.'

He closed his eyes. Blanche made her way to the door. She watched until his breathing grew shallow and he appeared to be asleep before leaving.

Andrey was waiting by the fire in the Great Hall, warming his hands. The wind rushed in from the sea and, even though the windows were shuttered with strips of horn, soaked and flattened to lie together, it was impossible to rid the castle of every draught.

'He's resting,' Blanche told her cousin. 'He'll stay in his room until I call for him to join me.'

'Do you think he will?' Andrey looked sceptical.

'I think so. He's still weak. Put a man on the

door, just in case. A trusted servant. I should be hospitable, but I am no fool.'

'Some might say that keeping him alive or moving him from his cell proves you are,' Andrey said. They both knew whom he was referring to. Ronec and Andrey had both argued vociferously against moving Jack from his previous room but, as always, Blanche had prevailed in her own house. How long this state of affairs would continue was something that gnawed at her mind.

She would have to be very careful when Ronec met Jack again. She could not imagine he would take kindly to sitting at the same table as the man who had threatened to chain him and Ronec would be equally unhappy.

'I draw the line at murder in cold blood. The sooner he recovers, the quicker he will regain his memory and can be gone. Then we can continue in peace doing what we have to.'

'Killing in cold blood?' Andrey asked, smirking.

'Avenging the deaths of good men and fighting for our country, as well you know.'

They clasped hands. She swept from the room without looking back. Instead of calling a servant to collect Jack's papers, she went back herself. She folded the furs from the bed, holding them close to her face to breathe in the scent and wondering how much of the warm muskiness was the fur and how much was a trace of Jack's own scent. She inspected the papers, which had been neatly stacked. As Jack had said, they were mainly scrawls, with the occasional attempt at capturing the shape of the rocks in the bay. The main part consisted of Jack's name, written over and over in columns. The writing grew more confident as it moved down the sheet, finishing with a final flourish of a signature.

She took them back to her room and put them next to the cross on the table. She sat at the table and, chin in her hands, stared at this small collection of Jack's possessions. Every moment she kept the cross's existence from him, she was doing Jack a grave disservice, but she remembered the hatred in his eyes when he had faced her in her disguise.

She would return them when he joined her to dine in a day or two. For now, she looked forward to his company with a pleasure she had not anticipated for a long time.

Chapter Seven

For two days, Jack obeyed Madame Tanet's orders to remain cloistered away. He was happy to do so, finding that the time of enforced rest gave him time to recuperate. His head gradually healed and his body felt stronger.

He slept a little less each day and was not so weary by nightfall. It was probably this reason that caused him to wake late in the night when the sound of voices pierced his dreams. It was dark outside and the air was cold and damp, and at first he was confused and thought he must be dreaming vividly of covert happenings. Something crashed and the voices grew louder. An irate female one caused his eyes to flick open.

He was not dreaming and the sounds were coming from the courtyard. Madame Tanet was among them. He looked from the window in time to see a huddle of black shadows slipping around the edge of the courtyard.

Bleiz Mor. It had to be him. Jack pulled on his tunic and heaved the door open. He took two steps before colliding with a man sitting on a low stool in the small space outside his doorway at the turn of the stairs. The door might not be locked, but he was being guarded.

'What's happening outside?' he demanded.

The guard stood up and Jack realised he was quite an old man.

'Let me pass.'

He tried to dodge round the guard, but the man was quick to spread his arms. 'You must stay here. *Madame* told me to watch over you.'

'Where is Madame Tanet?' Jack demanded. 'I want to speak with her.'

He hoped she was safe where Bleiz Mor could not reach her. He turned to go up the stairs that led to her rooms, but the man tugged him back with one hand and drew his sword with the other.

'No one goes up there. Return to your room and I shall tell her you wish to see her.'

Reluctantly, Jack agreed. He left the door open, but the guard closed it with a meaningful look. Jack listened carefully. The footsteps went down, not up. He had not been imagining Madame Tanet was outside.

* * *

After a while she arrived, carrying a lantern and dressed in a flowing mantle that covered her from neck to feet.

'Are you safe?' Jack asked.

'Why would I not be?' she asked.

Her eyes grew watchful and he felt a rush of protectiveness. He wanted to hold her close and swear that everything would be all right. That whatever danger had caused her to cry out was over and he would protect her. His whole being urged him to keep her safe. If she gave any indication that she wanted him to hold her, he would not hesitate, but she just smoothed her hair down and pulled her collar tighter.

'I heard shouting,' he explained. 'It woke me.'

'Nothing is wrong,' Madame Tanet said. 'Some of the village men drank more than they should have done and decided to venture out to sea to fish at night.'

Her hair was loose and her face and neck were flushed. She glowed with vitality. If she had come from her bedroom, Jack would have assumed the brightness of her eyes and the tangle of her hair had been the result of lovemaking. Was the Sea Wolf her bedfellow? A stab of envy caught him unawares, forcing him to acknowledge how much he desired her himself.

'Why were they inside the grounds?'

Madame Tanet stepped closer to him. She placed a hand on his arm and his blood began to race.

'Jack, thank you for your consideration, but really there is no need.' She looked up at him with an expression of clear-eyed innocence. 'Everything has been dealt with. Go back to bed. You aren't yet fully recovered. You need to rest.'

She yawned and rolled her head around, extending her elegant neck to reveal a creamy curve where the pink flush had started to fade.

'I would like to go to bed, too.'

Jack suppressed a yawn. He *was* tired. He could no longer say how many of the voices and crashes he had dreamed and what was real. If Madame Tanet was not standing in front of him in what he assumed covered her nightclothes, he would have doubted he had heard her voice. He wondered if she was naked beneath her mantle, then wished he hadn't speculated on that because the ferocious stirring between his legs caught him unawares. He didn't know when last he had been aroused—certainly not since waking in the storeroom—but the thought of Madame Tanet naked made him hard immediately.

She ran her fingers through the tangled waves of hair, making an attempt to smooth it and caus-

ing the blackness to glint with scarlet in the glow
of the lantern. Jack grew harder, his chest tightening and stopping his breath. His fingers itched
to touch it, but a voice that had been hitherto buried deep urged him to hold back. A brief image
of pale gold locks flashed through his mind.
It caused him to stay his hand and killed his
arousal. Was there a wife elsewhere waiting for
him whose face was buried in his mind? Guilt
consumed him. However much he desired Madame Tanet, he must not act on it until he knew
the truth.

'Sleep well,' he said, stepping away from her.

Madame Tanet dipped her head. She went up
the stairs to her own room, footsteps echoing in
the silent stairwell. Jack followed her until she
disappeared around the corner. Her long mantle
trailed behind her and as she lifted it slightly he
caught a glimpse of heel. Jack returned to his bed
and was half-asleep as the thought came to him
to wonder why she had taken the time to put on
riding boots as well as her mantle.

Madame Tanet visited Jack the following
morning, bringing a bowl of warm water and
cloths. Jack let her place it on the table as he sat
in the chair by the window, but when she dipped
the cloth in the water he took it from her hand.

'You are my hostess and the lady of the house,' he said. 'This is a job for a servant.'

She looked amused. 'Don't be foolish. Marie is still a little scared of your presence and there is no one else, unless you would prefer Andrey to nurse you. Besides, I've done much worse in my time.'

'How so?'

'I have two children. Once you have dealt with some of the messes they produce, a little blood is no great matter.'

She spoke jokingly, but her eyes flickered and her smile solidified like cooling wax. Jack had seen no evidence in the castle nor heard any childish voices. He felt a pang in his chest and wondered if he was a husband and father.

'Tell me about your children,' he said to distract himself from those thoughts.

'Why do you want to know?' She looked suspicious and he recalled she did not necessarily trust him. Did she believe he might be trying to trick her? It made him more eager to know.

'I am just making conversation,' he said, shrugging. 'I don't mean to intrude. Do you have boys or girls?'

He gave her what he hoped was a disarming yet sincere smile. She hesitated then spoke.

'I have one of each. Maelle is my daughter. She is fifteen years now.' Madame Tanet's face closed with grief. 'Her father did not live to meet her. Mael and I married when I was fifteen, but he died when I was eighteen and pregnant.'

Jack's heart fluttered in sympathy. How sad to be left with a fatherless child so young. He tried to imagine an eighteen-year-old version of the woman before him but found it impossible. He wondered what she would have been like in the first flush of youth. Her features were sharp and the fine lines at the corners of her eyes and lips suited her. He wondered whether she would have been beautiful, or if it was only now her eyes regarded the world with wisdom and she was surrounded by an air of stateliness that her character shone through.

'And your son?' he asked.

'Fransez is eleven now.'

It did not take much skill with numbers to realise what she said did not make sense. She watched him work it out and a small smile edged on to her face, softening her features.

'You've had more than one husband?'

'That's right. Yann, my second husband, was his father.'

Jack wondered how soon she had remarried after being widowed and how long since she had been widowed again.

'I haven't heard any children here.'

'They aren't here. Maelle is in a convent to the south of Brest. She chose that path in life. I can't say I understand and such seclusion would be a torture for me, but her faith is sincere and she is happy.'

Madame Tanet shook her head wonderingly, as if contemplating the eccentricity of youth.

'Fransez is… A young boy needs men around him to show him how to behave. I was fortunate enough to secure him a place in a great establishment far away from danger and war.'

Her eyes shone with pride as she spoke.

'Don't you miss them?' Jack asked. 'How could you bear to let them go?'

She pressed her lips together briefly until they went white.

'Of course I miss them, but a mother knows her children are not hers to keep for ever. I want the best for them.'

She folded her arms and gave Jack a stern look. 'You would not ask a man if he could bear to part from his children, would you, and yet men do so every day. Did you part from yours easily, if you have them?'

'I don't know that I do have any,' Jack snapped.

An awkward silence hung in the air. Jack dropped his head down. His hair fell clumsily over his brow. Madame Tanet reached out and pushed the locks back behind his ears with gentle fingers. It was excitingly intimate and caused the breath to catch in Jack's throat and his pulse to speed up.

'You can clean the wound yourself if you prefer, but don't refuse my help on some odd sense of propriety,' Madame Tanet said gruffly.

Clearly, the conversation was over. She was talking sense, so Jack opened his hand and she took the cloth from his open palm. She unwound the bandage. It was less bloodstained than the previous ones had been. The gash was healing and the wound did not burn as angrily when the cold air touched it.

Jack probed with his fingers, feeling how it ran deep and long.

'I think you'll have a scar,' Madame Tanet said regretfully.

Jack shrugged. 'That doesn't matter. It is the least of my concerns.'

He sat as still as he could while Madame Tanet began wiping away the crusted blood from around the wound. He found this harder than expected as she leaned forward to examine her work, bringing her face close to Jack's. She caught his eye and momentarily held his gaze. She was remarkably beautiful, but in the way a hawk was, with an angular chin beneath the slash of a red mouth, high cheekbones and very dark brown eyes that were currently piercing him with her gaze.

Her sharp, dark eyes were beguilingly framed with thick lashes that curled upwards almost to her straight, black brows. The faint lines at the side of her eyes suited her and Jack wanted to trace his fingertips over them. The lines beside her mouth called out to be kissed. So did the lips themselves.

'How does your head feel now?' she asked briskly.

He reached his hand up to feel the bandage, grateful she had changed the subject. 'Better than it was.'

Madame Tanet smiled. 'I'll bring fresh bandages tomorrow or send a servant if I cannot come myself. Promise you won't frighten Marie next time—I've told her you aren't to be feared.'

He frowned up at her balefully. 'I did not intentionally before,' he said, indignation tingeing his voice.

'I know. The fault is hers, not yours. She's always been a mouse.'

Madame Tanet took away the cloth. She stroked the good skin at the edge of Jack's brow with her thumb, before running it down the side of his face. He couldn't suppress the sigh that her touch induced and she drew her hand away hastily, looking down at the cloth in her hands.

'Were you really scared for me last night?' she asked.

'I heard your voice and you sounded angry,' Jack admitted. 'I was worried for you. What had happened?'

'The fishermen decided that it was too rough to sail. They came visiting in case my servants would give them sustenance.'

'Drink, you mean,' Jack said.

'Exactly.' Madame Tanet raised an eyebrow and her lips twisted into a grin. Jack smiled back and for a moment they were allies, sharing amusement. It gave him the first sense of belonging he'd felt in a long time.

'You heard me because I was ordering the men to leave.'

'Was the Sea Wolf here?' he asked.

'Why do you ask that?' Madame Tanet looked startled.

Jack shook his head. It had been the first thought that sprang to mind. 'I imagine that if there was trouble he would be involved. As long as you swear you were under no threat, I believe you.'

'If I had been in any danger I have loyal servants who will not let me come to harm. But thank you. To hear you say that means a lot to me.'

She briefly placed her hand over his, but looked away. Jack turned his hand over so their palms were together. Where the mounds at the base of her fingers and thumb touched his, his skin felt intoxicatingly sensitive. She gave him a shy smile, then gently tugged her hand free, stood and dropped the cloth into the bowl.

'I think you should leave the bandage off now, Jack. At least while you are awake. When you are sleeping it might be better to cover it in case you roll on to your front and cause the scab to split.'

'I don't think that's likely. I always sleep on my back,' Jack said.

Her eyes flickered, the long lashes batting down and up rapidly. He felt his neck grow a little warm as he told her how he lay, especially as he couldn't forget the misunderstanding where she thought he was inviting her to share the bed with him.

'You should be fine in that case,' Madame Tanet said. 'However, if you discover otherwise, please try not to bleed on my coverlet.'

She crinkled her eyes to show she was at least partly joking and Jack laughed softly. He could see the bed now from the corner of his eye. He wondered what she looked like when sleep claimed her, whether she sprawled on her back with her hair loose about her or curled tight in a shape that a man could readily wind himself about. The thought of carrying her to the bed and discovering what lay beneath her gown was a tantalising notion, but he strongly doubted she would react favourably. Besides, the same warning had risen in his breast as it had the night before. Something inside him was urging him to suppress all emotions and lusts and he didn't know why.

He looked out of the window at the courtyard. It was busy, with more people than he had seen previously. Male servants were hefting boxes around and carrying scythes and long knives.

'Where are they going?' Jack asked.

Blanche peered out. She shrugged and gave Jack an airy smile.

'There is nothing untoward happening. They are simply preparing to harvest buckwheat grown over winter to clear the ground for spring crops. It keeps the soil rich, I believe.'

'Where I come from, most crops aren't ready until much later,' he remarked.

Madame Tanet gave him a look of surprise. 'You can remember where you are from?'

Jack was silent as he delved into his mind. He had spoken without thinking and returned from his memory with an image of gentle hills. He described it to her.

'I only wish I knew where this was.'

His throat tightened and he dropped his head. Madame Tanet put a hand on his shoulder.

'You will, I'm sure of it. It is a good sign that you can even remember that.'

Jack raised his eyes to hers and found them full of compassion. They flickered and something in her expression hardened subtly.

'When you are healed and can travel to England, more memories will surely return,' she said.

'I hope so,' Jack agreed. He was only tolerated here, he reminded himself. He had no idea where to start looking or how he would make his way back to England.

Madame Tanet picked up the bowl. At the door, she turned back.

'Would you feel well enough to join me downstairs tonight?' she asked. 'I have some other company—my cousin and the master of a neighbouring manor will be attending, along with some of the villagers. Your presence won't be questioned.'

She looked anxious, as if worried he might refuse. Nothing could be further from his mind. He thanked her and accepted, then lay on his bed, arms behind his head. An evening in the intriguing Madame Tanet's company would be just what he needed to lift his spirits.

To Jack's frustration, he was seated nowhere near Madame Tanet. She had said they would not be alone, but he was not expecting as many people to be present in the hall. Two long tables were end on to a smaller one on a slightly raised platform in front of a stone fireplace. There was a hierarchy as the guests dressed in more elaborately cut and trimmed clothing sat closest to the fire, while those dressed in plainer garb such as Jack wore were further away. Jack was motioned towards a seat halfway down. He sat silently, listening to the other guests talk of their lives, but not able to join in. No one spoke to him. He might as well have been invisible and wished he had not come. He used his time watching for clues to the identity of Bleiz Mor in case the pirate was among them, though the man could be anyone, given that Jack had only seen eyes between the mask and hat. Did even Madame Tanet and the two men in her company know his true identity? Jack reasoned they must. He could not speak for the men, but his hostess seemed far from being a fool.

Madame Tanet sat at the table facing the room. Ronec and Andrey, who had taken him to the beach, sat at either side of her. Despite this, she smiled at him and gave every impression of being attentive to his words.

Jack gave his attention to the fish and vegetable stew with a hint of cider in the liquor. It was exceedingly good and he finished his serving quickly, wiping his bread around the bowl to scoop up the last traces. He sat back and looked up again and found Madame Tanet's eyes were on him. As Jack met her gaze the corner of her mouth tilted upwards. He smiled back, pleased that she had noticed him. She gestured towards her bowl and raised an eyebrow. Jack grinned, tilting his bowl to show it was empty. Madame Tanet called a serving boy across, whispered in his ear and Jack's bowl was refilled before he realised. He gave a flourish of his hand in thanks and her eyes grew merry.

Presently, Madame Tanet stood and began to walk around the room, making conversation with her household. Ronec followed close behind her. He leaned in and whispered something in her ear from behind. It was clear that Madame Tanet did not welcome Ronec's attentions from the way she leaned away from him and her shoulders tensed. He would not have been able to see her brief expression of distaste but Jack, watching closely, did not miss it.

She moved with grace about the room. She was not as young as the maids they whistled after—and Jack thought that it would be a brave man who catcalled at Madame Tanet—but she moved with poise and a knowing look in her eye that meant each man's gaze lingered after she had passed beyond his presence, even when they had a wife or woman sitting beside them. Most of the guests obviously desired her and Jack added himself to their number. She passed Jack just as he was lifting his cup to his lips. She didn't stop to speak to him but, as he stared at her over the rim of his cup, her eyes slid sideways to settle briefly on him. She slowed her pace and her eyelashes beat rapidly before she carried on.

She returned to her table and stood before it, then began speaking. Silence descended. Servants began handing out small cups of something that, from the meagre measures, was probably deadly strong. Jack sniffed it and caught apples. Madame Tanet thanked the villagers for attending, praised their work on her land and reminded them that this was the way to prosper, not the dishonourable act of wrecking. She ended with a toast to the rightful Duke of Brittany, which was taken up with loud enthusiasm. She held her cup aloft, then tipped the contents down her throat in one, tilting her head back to reveal the creamy throat and angular jaw. Jack couldn't picture anything more erotic than the lines of her bared neck leading down to the dip at the base of her throat. He wondered what she would look like beneath her gown, when her breasts were released from the captivity of the bodice that currently pushed them into round mounds, and the curves of her thighs and belly were revealed rather than hinted at by the folds and sway of her skirts. Jack tossed back his own cup and coughed as the drink burned his throat and wound a hot path down into his belly.

Madame Tanet slipped from the hall while the musicians struck up a lively tune and guests rushed to form a circle, performing a dance that they had clearly done many times before. Jack watched until the shrill pipes began to make his head feel like a hive of bees had taken up residence, then left. A walk in the courtyard would clear his head before he went to bed.

As he reached the door, he heard Madame Tanet's voice coming from the floor above. She sounded angry, then footsteps started to descend rapidly. A low mutter of a male voice answered and the tone was definitely threatening. Jack's scalp prickled and he paused, recognising the voice. He should return to the hall or leave the building, but leaving Madame Tanet to face an angry-sounding Ronec was not in his nature. Quickly he slipped into the shadows and waited.

Chapter Eight

Madame Tanet rounded the spiral staircase, closely followed by Ronec. Even if Jack had not overheard the angry exchange, the look of ferocity on her face would have been enough indication that she was extremely angry. Ronec seized her by the arm, halting her descent.

'Hear me out,' he growled.

'Take your hands off me,' Madame Tanet exclaimed. 'In my house, with my servants around, you dare do this!'

She was furious, but Jack sensed fear beneath the anger and had no doubt Ronec noticed it, too, as he appeared to have no intention of obeying her. Jack's hackles rose. He'd already taken a dislike to Ronec and this confirmed his hatred was well founded. He stepped forward.

'I believe Madame Tanet asked you to release her.'

Both Madame Tanet and Ronec turned. Jack

kept his body purposefully relaxed, though temper was surging inside him, keen to be freed.

'Do as she says,' Jack said softly. He bunched his fists. If Ronec decided to fight, Jack knew he would lose, but he would give it his best. He hoped Ronec would not realise how weak he still felt.

Ronec slowly released his hand from Madame Tanet's arm, glaring at Jack all the while. He dusted his hands down his front as if wiping away grime from a journey and stared into Madame Tanet's eyes.

'Think on what I said.'

Madame Tanet drew herself up straight and glared at Ronec.

'I warn you, Jagu, touch me again without my permission and I will tear your member off and feed it to my cats!'

Ronec cast her a look of contempt, which he then turned on Jack and stalked away, leaving the building. Madame Tanet watched until he was gone, then rounded on Jack.

'There was no need for that,' she said. She could have been rebuking a child for throwing stones at apples. 'I would have got rid of him by myself before long.'

'There is always a need to assist.' Jack frowned and decided not to mention that he had seen relief flash in her expressive eyes when she had seen he was there. Jack's presence and intervention had clearly helped restore her poise and he was glad he had intervened. He stepped closer and folded his arms across his chest to indicate he was not intending to touch her.

'Why reject assistance if it is available?'

'Because it rarely is,' Madame Tanet said crisply. 'It is not wise to grow to rely on other people. I must remember to start wearing my dagger when I am in his company.'

'That sounds like a way to ensure you are hurt,' Jack snapped. He furrowed his brow, wondering why he was speaking with such rudeness to his hostess and why the thought of her in peril alarmed him so much.

'I can defend myself,' she snapped back. 'You know nothing of me.'

She clamped her mouth shut, as if regretting her words, and lowered her head. 'I was rude to rebuff you, though. I apologise. And thank you.'

Jack's eyes followed in Ronec's direction. 'What did he want?'

'What all men will try to take, if they see an opportunity.' Madame Tanet rolled her eyes. 'He drank too much and forgot himself. He won't try it again.'

'Not if he wants to keep his manhood from becoming cat food,' Jack said, giving her a grin.

'It would be a meagre meal,' Madame Tanet sneered. She smiled at Jack. 'I don't actually have a cat.'

'You should. They're pleasant companions,' Jack said.

'Do you like them?'

'I suppose I must.' He raised his eyebrows in surprise and gave a delighted laugh. 'That's something new I have learned about myself. Thank you, Madame Tanet.'

She held a hand out. 'Please, call me Blanche as you are my guest. It does not seem right that you have no other name but Jack and I speak to you informally.'

It was the last thing he had expected and he paused. She looked uncertain and began to lower her hand. Not wanting her to think he was rejecting her overture, he reached for it as she drew it away, holding it a little too tightly at first, loosening it as she extended it again. They both went through the awkward play of making noises, nonwords that signified apology, forgiveness, acknowledgement that the other meant no offence. Finally, Jack held her slender hand in his and raised it to his lips. Her skin fluttered, he was sure of it, and it caused the fine hairs on the back of his hand to stand to attention. He wanted to turn it over and examine the long, tapered fingers or run his thumb over the lines on her palm and see if the gesture made her shiver with delight.

Blanche. It meant white. A good name for a woman with skin so pale amid the mass of black locks.

'I'm glad you felt well enough to join us tonight. I trust your room is comfortable?' she asked.

'Much better than my previous,' he said. 'I was right that the bed would be better.'

He looked away, recalling his idle thoughts of tempting her there and not wanting her to see that he very much desired her.

'Were you going there when you overheard us?' she asked.

'I was going outside to take some air.' He held out an arm. 'Would you care to join me, Blanche?'

'That would be pleasant. Wait here a moment.'

She went upstairs and returned wearing a cloak of deep orange brocade, fastened across her chest with slits at the side for her arms. Jack offered her an arm, but she shook her head and walked on. Maybe after her encounter with Ronec she was wary of being too close to another man. They completed a slow turn of the courtyard, walking slowly and silently side by side.

A dozen ways of opening the conversation rose to Jack's tongue, but he ignored them, content to enjoy the peace of Blanche's company. The court-yard was quiet and the sound of waves drifted on the wind. The scent of the tide filled his nostrils and a wild fancy thrust itself into his mind.

'I want to go to the beach.'

'Now?' Blanche wrinkled her brow. 'It's late and will be dark.'

'I know. That's why. When I was there before, I didn't recognise anything. Now the circum-stances will be the same. I might recall some-thing.'

She looked doubtful.

'I'm afraid there is no one now who could escort you there. All my servants are busy and Ronec has gone. I won't ask him to come back and I don't think he would be the best person to ask to take you in any case.'

'No one needs to take me,' Jack said. 'I can go alone.'

Blanche's eyes filled with suspicion. 'I can't let you do that while your identity and motive are still under question.'

It was a fair point and he did his best to swal-low down his frustration.

'I can't do nothing and simply hope my mem-ory returns. Will you come with me?'

Her dark eyes flooded with wariness and her jaw tightened. No doubt she thought he might be trying to lure her to an isolated spot for the same purpose Ronec had.

'Madame, I don't intend to harm you. I can assure you I want to go there for one purpose alone. You are perfectly safe in my company.'

Her gaze raked over him, giving Jack the impression she was seeing beyond his clothes to his soul. A feeling of familiarity spread over him as he stared back into the black depths. It was torture that he could not remember why he felt so drawn to her.

'I have no doubt, given your current state of health—however, I appreciate your words. Few men would be so considerate.' Blanche glanced at the castle, then towards the gate. 'Very well. I'll come. I'm curious to see if it works. Wait here a moment, please.'

She walked swiftly back inside and returned a short while later. To the girdle at her hips she had attached a scabbard with a short, wide-bladed knife. Jack grimaced.

'A weapon? It would be easy enough to take it from you and I could do more harm to you than you could to me.'

'You sound very certain,' she said. 'Are you confident in what you are capable of?'

She met his eyes with a challenge that sent a thrill through him. Was she daring him to try?

Jack looked her up and down. Tall but slight. He could have her in his arms and the knife from her belt before she realised.

'I don't think I'd need to be that capable.'

'But you don't know what I am capable of,' she said, lifting her chin. Her fingers slid to the knife, stroking the hilt delicately. 'I'll keep the knife or we don't go.'

'As you wish,' Jack replied, grudgingly impressed that she would argue so boldly. A woman living alone in charge of a household must live with these sorts of trials daily.

They walked through the small sea gate and down the path. Where it turned steeply Jack paused and looked back towards the castle. The moonlight silhouetted the tower, turning it into a dark outline against the sky.

'Your home is beautiful,' he said.

Blanche snorted. It was not ladylike but was all the more appealing for that. 'No, it isn't. It's squat and ugly, but it serves the purpose it was built for.' She gestured at the rock face that fell away into the sea. 'It is called Fort Carouel. It was built for defence over sixty years ago and does that admirably.'

'Is this where you lived with your husband?' he asked, then winced. He had no idea why he had asked something so intrusive. It was nothing to do with him what Blanche's husband had done.

She did not seem offended by the question. 'We never lived here, but we visited. My first husband and I, that is.'

Blanche moved away from his side and walked a little further without speaking. Despite his curiosity, Jack didn't push her for more details, conscious that he could not answer any questions about himself. Loneliness descended on his shoulders like a cloak of lead. He stayed a few paces behind, walking silently. At the next bend she stopped and pulled her cloak round herself a little closer.

'The fort passed to Mael's older brother on the death of their father. He inherited the family castle, too, and was gracious enough to sell the fort to me when I needed somewhere to live.'

'You bought it outright?'

Her chin came up and her eyes filled with determination.

'I prefer that than being beholden to a landlord. I shall pass it to Maelle in turn, though doubtless she will gift it to the convent.'

'Did your second husband leave you no home?' he asked.

Her face closed down once more. 'Yann left me nothing. He would have if...'

Her straight, black brows came together, giving her an air of melancholy that looked similar to the one Jack had been feeling. He wondered if her second marriage had been for love or convenience, but it was not his business to ask that question. 'It was not Yann's fault. He had no choice.'

'What happened to him?' Jack asked.

Blanche's eyes narrowed. 'Do you remember anything of what is happening in Brittany, Jack?'

'Little. I understand there is conflict over the succession. Was your husband caught in that?'

Blanche bit her bottom lip, drawing it between her teeth in a manner Jack found more than a little distracting. He almost lost all interest in her husband with the desire to kiss her. Ronec had clearly been trying to do it and Jack knew better than to try the same thing, but it was incredibly tempting.

'Another time, perhaps,' she said.

She walked on. Jack followed, intrigued. The path was growing soft underfoot where the stones were turning to sand. It was still quite a strenuous walk and he was growing fatigued. He set his shoulders and strode out, determined not to reveal his weariness to Blanche.

'Is something wrong?' she asked.

He looked at her in surprise, not expecting her to be so perceptive.

'I'm just thinking that the last time I came here I was threatened with shackles. It's good to have some freedom.'

She rolled her eyes and put her hands on her hip. 'You are not a prisoner. How many times must I tell you that for you to believe me? You are free to go whenever you choose. If you wanted to, you could walk away now and no one would try to bring you back or stop you.'

No one, Jack thought darkly. The loneliness was overwhelming, coming closer to unmanning him than any physical injury had done. Knowing that he had no attachments here crushed him. Not knowing whether he had any elsewhere was worse. At least a jailor might care about his whereabouts.

'What should I do if I left? Wander France in the hope of seeing a familiar face? I may have a life, but I don't know where it is.' He clenched his fists and groaned in exasperation. 'I don't even know if I can trust myself. That *putain* Bleiz Mor told me what was in the barrels. Weapons hidden in wine. Am I a pirate like him, or a smuggler? How do I even know which side I would choose in this matter of the succession?'

'I think you must have been a passenger on the ship.'

'What makes you say that?' He grasped her

words like a drowning man might clutch at a piece of driftwood.

'You aren't French, you're English.'

'I believe so. But why only a passenger? It could have been an English ship.'

'No. Parts washed up and what we…they… managed to salvage had French marks on the boxes. You were well dressed. You might be a merchant of some sort.'

'What you managed to salvage? What the wreckers claimed, you mean.'

Fury flashed across her face. 'I do.'

He looked at her sharply. What hold did Bleiz Mor have over her that she would allow him access to her home when the wrecking clearly angered her? Was she as innocent as she claimed, or was she as mired in the pirate's activities as Ronec and Andrey?

'Why were you on the beach the night of the wreck, Blanche? Were you part of it?'

'No!' She rounded on him with fire in her eyes and voice. 'Believe me when I say I would never be involved in something so dishonourable.'

Her voice reeked with contempt that sounded so real it was hard to believe she could feign it so convincingly.

'It was the villagers. I smelled the smoke and heard the cries. I went to see what was happening. I am as disgusted as you that they would do something so cowardly. I told them so at dinner that I would have no more of it, you heard me.'

Jack looked along the beach, trying to picture men heaving bodies and cargo from the sea, picturing himself among them. If Blanche had not found him, would he have perished at their hands or died from the wound on his head? He put a hand to his neck, rubbing his finger and thumb around his collarbone and feeling that something felt wrong, but unable to place it. He dismissed it.

'Was Ronec involved in the wrecking?' Jack asked.

Blanche didn't answer.

'I don't like him,' Jack growled.

'He isn't easy to like.'

'He seems to like you,' Jack commented.

Blanche's eyebrows knotted. 'Ronec doesn't like me, you fool.'

Jack was startled at the vehemence in her voice.

She turned away abruptly and walked to the edge of the sea. She hugged herself as if suddenly cold. Jack watched, feeling the bite of the wind that lifted her hair and played around her skirts, creating interesting silhouettes and shadows.

Jack followed her. The waves were calm now, lapping across the rocks and gently whispering, as if imparting secrets if only he could understand their language.

'I said the wrong thing, didn't I? That was foolish. I saw how he was when he thought you were alone.'

She nodded slowly.

'He hates me, but he desires me. He wants to possess me and everything I own. We are neighbours. It would suit him for us to marry.'

'But it would not suit you?'

Jack's eyes bored into her. It was more than a dislike for Ronec that gave his blood such heat—it was a liking for her. He was jealous.

'No,' she said, firmly, lifting her chin and facing Jack. 'But then again, marriage to anyone would not suit me.'

'A widow has more independence than a wife, I expect,' Jack said.

She smiled at his understanding. Their eyes met and Jack felt something akin to friendship forming. It had only happened a few times, but he wanted more of it. Blanche was the first to look away, casting her hand out towards the sea.

'Now we're here, what do you want to do?'

Jack walked barefoot down the beach and into the sea. The water was cold and his muscles tensed. He ground his toes into the shingle, sharpness pricking the soles of his feet until he became

accustomed to the temperature. The tide was far-
ther out than when he had stood there before two
days ago with Bleiz Mor, and the rocks that had
been beneath the surface were now visible. He
took a few steps out along the ridge, slipping as he
walked gingerly for a dozen paces, arms slightly
outstretched to balance.

He looked down. If he stepped off the rocks, he
would be waist deep. He leaned forward, wondering if he could see the seabed in the moonlight.
The waves lapped around his ankles, occasion-
ally stronger and calf high. The tide was turning. He could feel a pull as it attempted to catch
him and carry him further out. He was tempted
to let it and put an end to his uncertain existence.

'Be careful!'

Jack looked around. Blanche was close to the
sea, skirts held up in one hand out of the way
of the tide. She sounded alarmed and her whole
body looked tense, her free hand bunched into a
fist at her side.

'What are you doing?' Her voice was unnatu-
rally calm, as if she was talking to a child.

'I'm wondering what it felt like to be out there
and what it would feel like again. I think I could
probably get a long way.'

Something inside him whispered this was what
he wanted. What he had craved for a long time.

He only had to step backwards from the rock and the pain in his heart would end. His grief would be over, though he would die without ever discovering the reason for it.

'I didn't save you from death and nurse you for you to throw your life away,' she shouted.

'Why do you think I would do that?' he asked, unnerved that she had read his thoughts.

'Because I know you asked to die the other day.'

She looked poised to run into the sea and grab him if he decided to hurl himself off. He wondered if she actually would. As he stood in the moonlight he felt he was faced with a choice. He could hurl himself into the sea and hope for the death that seemed quite appealing and which he had challenged Bleiz Mor to grant him. Death would be quick. Blanche would never reach him in time before he was swept away. Or he could walk back to shore and make the best of his situation.

He faced away from the sea and looked past Blanche at the castle, which he could make out at the end of the path. Blanche was standing very still, her eyes fixed on him. He could not make out her features in the moonlight, but he could picture them clearly. A memory surfaced of her bright eyes scrutinising him in the darkness of night, looking down on him from above.

He was certain it was the first memory from before he had woken in the storeroom. She had not done that since he had regained consciousness. He laughed with elation and began picking his way carefully back to shore. Blanche's relief was palpable.

'I remember!' he said. 'I remembered your face. At least, I saw it in my mind.'

He took her hands and kissed them, laughing in glee. She did not respond.

'That was so dangerous,' she said, her voice tight with fury.

'Did you really think I was about to drown myself?' Jack asked, surprised once more at her perceptiveness.

'I…I don't know.' She clutched his hands tighter, then dropped them. 'I know you have a wish for death. Don't deny it.'

'I don't know why I have that urge. It feels like a habit ingrained in me, like a pattern burned into old wood.' Jack rubbed his eyes. 'I wonder what happened before to make me long for such a thing as that. One more secret I'm hiding from myself.'

'Wouldn't it be a relief if you never found the answer?' Blanche asked gently. 'What if what you left behind is better forgotten?'

He saw the earnest expression in her eyes. In

the moonlight, her cheekbones were sharp and her eyes were like twin pools of blackness that were almost as enticing to drown in as the sea. Her mouth was set in a firm, decisive line. Jack longed to take her in his arms and kiss them until her lips softened and yielded to him. Such strength of desire took him by surprise. He ran his fingers over the wound at his temple and took his time before answering.

'Whatever my past is, I want to face it. To do otherwise would be cowardly and I do not like to think of myself as a coward.'

'I don't think you are,' Blanche said warmly. 'You intervened when you didn't have to and you faced the Sea Wolf with courage.'

Tiredness washed over Jack. He shook his head sadly. 'If only there was something that could help me regain my memory. Let's return to the castle.'

As they walked side by side to the castle, Jack was acutely aware of her presence. They weren't touching, but from the corner of his eye he could see the way her skirts swayed as she walked and could imagine the hips moving gracefully that caused the effect. His blood seemed to effervesce as it rushed through his veins, causing his heart to leap, reminding him he was alive.

For the moment, that was a great thing and

being close to Blanche and sensing the way she moved at his side was enough to sustain him. His yearning to touch her, to be close to her—to anyone—grew stronger, so once again he offered her an arm. She hesitated, then rested her hand on his wrist. Her touch was light, but to Jack it felt like the weight of a thousand coals lighting fires beneath his skin. There was a warmer look in Blanche's eye though she held his arm stiffly as if not quite at ease, but they walked together as far as the gate to the castle, where Blanche slipped her hand from beneath Jack's arm.

'Is my face all you remember from our first encounter?'

'Yes, but it is a start. If I remember you finding me, I might remember other things, too.'

'Yes, you might.'

She regarded him with the eyes that seared his soul and Jack burned with the desire to kiss her, stronger than ever before. His conscience pricked. He might have a wife already which was why the warning voice in his head told him not to act on his feelings. To be contemplating trying to kiss Blanche was dishonourable and his conscience could not deny the possibility he was being unfaithful. He stifled a sigh. His attraction to Blanche Tanet would have to be strongly resisted if he was not to pile further troubles on to his conscience. It was so hard when she stood before him with rare warmth radiating from her.

He bowed and stepped back, watching her closely for any sign that she might be disappointed, but she only smiled.

'Goodnight, Jack. Thank you again for your company. And for your aid earlier.'

Once she had disappeared from sight, he made his way wearily to bed and slept sounder and more peacefully than any night since his arrival.

Chapter Nine

Blanche lay awake long into the night. She had truly believed Jack would hurl himself into the sea when he was standing so precariously on the rocks and had been more relieved than expected when he did not. His wretchedness spoke to her own sense of loneliness and she wanted to help him.

His memories were starting to return, but slowly and in no particular order. He remembered her, but not kissing her. She put her fingers to her lips as the memory of the kiss made them pulse and sighed with longing. She was half-tempted to try to kiss him and see if that brought memories back. At least, that was the excuse she told herself even as she knew it was for her own ends.

He needed something to help him, but she was loath to give him the cross. Explaining how she had come by it would be difficult and the all-too-brief flicker of what could become friendship was too fragile to risk quenching if he realised her deceit. There was something else, though, which would be more likely to hold a clue to his identity, if only she knew where it had gone. She rolled on to her front, trying not to picture Jack in bed lying on his back almost directly beneath her.

She rose early the next morning. She found Andrey sitting with a piece of driftwood and a short-bladed knife, whittling it into the shape of a woman.

'When we found Jack on the beach, do you remember there was a satchel with a case in it?'

'Yes. You wouldn't let me break it open.' He scowled and his voice was accusatory. Given the circumstances they now found themselves in with a man with no past, it was fair enough.

'What happened to it?' Blanche asked.

Andrey shrugged and made another few strokes with his knife, scraping the splinters into smooth lines. 'It didn't seem valuable.'

'How could you tell?'

He grinned. 'The box was plain. It didn't rattle when I shook it. I don't think it was full of gold or treasures. It probably ended up in one of the cellars, or perhaps Ronec took it.'

Blanche's stomach tightened, but if Ronec had opened it and had found some clue to Jack's identity inside, then he would have lost no time in telling her and disposing of Jack if he were a danger.

'Why not ask again if your lost soul will join our crew? Tell him who he was really speaking to on the beach and he might not be so quick to refuse next time.'

It was tempting. Jack was strong and fearless. He was not scared of throwing himself into a fight given how he had approached Ronec, first on the beach and then again in Blanche's defence. But the hatred in his eyes and voice when he spoke of his encounter with the masked man chilled her. What if Andrey was wrong and he rejected her?

'He believes me to be a virtuous widow living quietly,' she answered. 'I'm quite happy to play that role while he remains here.'

'How can you be sure his memory loss is even real?'

'Because I have asked him over and over, nicely and as a threat. Every time, the answer is the same.'

She didn't add that the pain in his eyes, the frustration in his voice and the way his whole body tensed with the effort of trying to remember were more convincing than any words that might trip from his tongue. Once again, sympathy for his predicament was a stone in her heart.

'Do you want to know what I think?' Andrey asked. 'I think you want him to be trustworthy.'

'I'd like all men to be trustworthy,' Blanche said with a bitter laugh. 'Sadly, that rarely proves to be the case.'

She thought of the English King's officer, who had agreed to provide ships and men, then only given half what he had promised, his excuse being that agreeing to take Fransez to England and train him would be costly. Of Ronec, who had seemed a sensible ally until he had demanded more nights in her bed in return for keeping her identity secret. How would Jack disappoint her if she let herself grow too close? Doubtless there would be something.

Andrey gave her a long look of scrutiny that made her blush. She left him and changed into her oldest gown and tied her hair under a veil. The cellars beneath the castle were cold and smelled of decay. Blanche hated them. She spent a fruitless morning searching through the boxes and piles of detritus that had been salvaged from wrecks over years and had been considered too worthless or useless to take. Anything of value had been taken and shared and the cellar was a memorial to lives lost at the wreckers' hands. It sickened her to see the evidence of the villagers' grisly efforts.

She retained her composure up until the point when she discovered a child's doll. It was missing a leg and had been tossed among piles of mismatched shoes and rags and left to fester. It reminded her of Maelle's favourite doll and for a horrible moment Blanche had an image of her daughter sinking to the bottom of the sea. Her throat filled with bitter acid and she sat cross-legged on the floor, clutching the doll and weeping silently, reminding herself that Maelle was safe in the care of the sisters at the convent.

Had there been children on Jack's vessel? Did he once have a family now lost to the wreckers? He was older than both Mael and Yann had been when they became fathers. The thought caused her such pain. She had a terrible understanding of what torture Jack must be enduring. Would it be better never to discover the truth than to unearth such horrors?

She swore, sitting in the shadows and candlelight, that there would be no more beacons lit in the church at Plomarc'h, however much she angered the villagers and Ronec. It had used to happen rarely in peacetime when the land provided what people needed, but they had done it three times in the past two years.

When the lamp began to splutter and dim, she stirred. It was time to give up her search. If the satchel had been here, she would have found it. With a heavy heart she admitted she would have to go speak to Ronec.

She made her way out, blinking in the bleak sunlight. She made her way round to the door, intending to go to her room until her emotions were more stable, but heard her name. Jack was hailing her from the other side of the courtyard. He had been chopping logs into firewood, but laid down his axe and strode towards her.

'Good morning, Blanche.'

He had been working hard and a sheen of perspiration covered his brow and cheeks, but rather than the sickly pallor of his fever, this gave him a ruddy glow.

His tunic was loose at the neck, but clinging where his broad chest was sweat damp. Her stomach coiled with longing and her fingers tingled with the urge to feel the slickness of his firm muscles. He looked more at ease than Blanche had seen him before. He ran his fingers through his ruffled hair in an attempt to smooth the disorder. His eyes took in her appearance and he raised his brows.

'You look as dishevelled as me! What on earth have you been doing?'

'I was in the cellars, searching for…for…' She shook her head and her mouth wobbled.

Jack's smile dropped, replaced with concern. 'Something's wrong!'

After the dark thoughts that had assailed her in the cellar, he was the last person she could face without guilt searing her soul.

'How do you bear it?' she whispered. Her eyes blurred. She blinked and felt her cheeks grow damp. 'Not knowing who you are. What you've forgotten.'

'Are you crying for me?'

He sounded incredulous. He moved towards her, taking her face in his palm. He ran his thumb over the curve of her cheek to wipe the tear away. There was a gentleness emanating from him and such tenderness was unnerving. It had been so many years since anyone had cared to comfort Blanche and she found it infinitely more appealing than any attempt at seduction or show of strength he might have tried.

His eyes were soft and brimming with grief. The steely determination and despair with which he had begged for death had vanished and she realised that a trace of moisture was glinting above the thick lashes of his lower lids. Such visible pain made her want to weep for him. She covered his hand with hers and laced her fingers between his.

'You shouldn't be comforting me when you have lost so much,' she murmured.

'Why can't we comfort each other?' Jack asked.

Their eyes met and *something* bloomed in the air between them. A sense that this was right. That this was inevitable. An attraction so vibrant that it almost took on a life of its own, demanding to be acknowledged and obeyed.

'Hold me,' she whispered.

They moved at the same time, meeting with arms ready to embrace. Blanche wound her arms around Jack's waist and felt him do the same back, drawing her tightly into an embrace. She rested her cheek against his chest. He smelled as sweet and earthy as she had imagined, his body warm and enticing, pressing against hers. She knew every contour of his chest from nursing him, but to feel it pushing against her, his chest rising and falling against hers as he breathed, sent warmth rushing through her, coiling hot into her belly and loins. She could feel her breasts swelling and hardening beneath her clothes. She burned to press herself closer, crush herself against him.

Shame brought heat rushing to her neck.

Jack was comforting her and she should be doing the same to him, not daydreaming about tearing the clothes from his back. If only he knew what she was considering, he would be disgusted.

'Why are you not insane with the uncertainty?' she asked.

'I believe I might have lost my mind if it hadn't been for your care,' he murmured. 'I owe you more than I can ever repay.'

'I haven't been a good hostess,' she said. 'I was short-tempered and irritable. I saw you as an inconvenience. Will you pardon my rudeness?'

Jack stroked her hair. 'Blanche, you have nursed me, given me shelter and food. That I am not dressed in rags or naked is thanks to your generosity. There is nothing to pardon.'

Blanche bit her lip hard, partly in guilt for the warmth with which he addressed her and partly because the thought of being naked with Jack, with nothing between his body and hers to prevent her savouring every inch of him, was overpowering.

When she raised her head, Jack's eyes were fierce and brimming with raw, undisguised hunger. This craving was mutual. Blanche moved her leg to balance her weight and brushed against his thigh, which had somehow insinuated its way between her legs. If she shifted her hip slightly upwards, she would brush against that area men apparently had no control over and could discover for herself whether he was nearing her own state of arousal. Jack's hands tightened in the small of her back, fingers skimming down to rest on the rounded swell of her buttocks.

Blanche parted her lips, tilting her head to the side as Jack leaned closer. She realised she was holding her breath, anticipating what was about to happen. Jack put his lips to hers with a gentle pressure, then jerked his head away, leaving only the memory of warmth. He pulled his hands away abruptly, stepping back.

'*Madame*, I'm sorry! I don't know what I was thinking to do such a thing!'

'Don't you?'

Blanche gave him a wry smile and took a step back before she threw herself at him and kissed him as thoroughly as she wanted to. 'I think you know very well. I think we both do. You felt what I felt, didn't you?'

'I felt something I shouldn't have,' Jack muttered. He looked genuinely contrite and Blanche felt another twinge of guilt that she had thrown the decorum required of a hostess to the floor and ground it beneath her heel.

'Shall we both accept that we were indiscreet?' she suggested, a little shakily. 'It has been a long time since anyone has held me in such a way and I forgot myself.'

'Since your husband died,' he said. 'I didn't think. It must seem strange to you.'

Blanche said nothing. He didn't know of the men she had been with since then, but he was partly correct. It had been so long since a man had held her without negotiating terms, whether in coins or assistance promised. Jack had expected nothing in return. That had been a part of the attraction that had caught her unawares. He wanted nothing from her and she wanted nothing from him beyond what their bodies urged them to do. A man like that was dangerous to be around.

'I think…it felt strange to me, too,' Jack said.

'Does that mean you have no wife waiting for you?' Blanche asked.

He closed his eyes, shaking his head. 'I do not know. I may be guilty of breaking my marriage vows or I may have no ties.'

Blanche laughed softly. 'In some ways I almost envy your loss of memory. You have a rare opportunity to start your life afresh. Like a newborn babe, you have a life ahead of you with no attachments and nothing on your conscience.'

He gave a wry grin. 'What you envy is what plagues me most. The attachments I do not remember.'

His sadness was still there, beneath the surface, but he was concealing it well. He was stronger than Blanche had given him credit for. She held her hand out to Jack, sideways as a man would shake it rather than palm down to be lifted and kissed. He took it and they shook firmly, but Blanche couldn't prevent the frisson that shot up her arm and plunged, white hot, between her breasts.

'I have to leave the castle for a short while,' Blanche said. 'I have business with a neighbour, but I will return by sunset.'

She gestured to the abandoned wood and axe.

'Jack, you are my guest. You do not have to chop wood.'

'I wish to work for my keep. And truthfully, I found it enjoyable to be moving and using my body after so long feeling weak and inactive.'

Jack gestured around the courtyard, then rolled his shoulders back and flexed his arms, causing the muscles in his forearms to shift and tense.

'Then I will not stop you if you wish it,' Blanche said with a smile. 'There is always work to be done. You could take Bleiz Mor's offer of employment,' she suggested.

Jack set his jaw. 'Honest work, *madame*. I believe I am an honest man. And if I wasn't before, I intend to be now. Is there anything else I can do for you besides chopping wood?'

Blanche remembered how she had paid for her own bread on occasions since Yann died when she had needed to. There were so many things Jack could do for her and none of them involved working in the castle grounds. A reckless part of her wondered what he would say if she made the suggestion that had been made to her so many times. She felt a stab of lust low in her belly again and an aching swell of heat between her legs at the thought of Jack inside her, bringing her to the point of complete surrender. How many nights in her bed, making love to her, would he consider adequate payment for his bed and board? Her legs almost buckled at the thought.

She would like to stay and watch him and admire how his muscles moved as he hefted his axe, but left him before her cheeks flamed visibly scarlet and betrayed her scandalous thoughts.

Jack finished the logs and stacked them neatly. He put the chopper down and stood back admiring his work. The day was almost over, but the weather was far too pleasant to return to his room. He drew a long breath, filling his lungs with balmy salt air. He tried to keep himself busy. Andrey was mending fishing nets, his deft fingers moving back and forth with a bone needle Jack's eyes could barely keep up with.

He begged the older man for a lesson and, to his surprise and pleasure, Andrey agreed. They moved from the shade to catch the end of the sun and settled side by side on the bench. Jack soon discovered he had no natural ability, but persisted, determined to get the net finished before giving up.

'Whatever you did before, it wasn't that,' Andrey said pleasantly. 'The fingers don't forget.'

Jack agreed. His animosity towards Andrey was beginning to diminish since their first meeting. He learned that Andrey was a cousin by marriage to Blanche and when she had been left widowed he had taken it upon himself to guard her. Despite being ten or more years older than Blanche, he was still a well-looking man whose body was hardened and whose face was tanned from a life at sea. If he hadn't been devoted to the frightened mouse of a serving girl, Marie, Jack might have suspected he would be a possible husband for Blanche.

Servants and workers from Blanche's village started to appear in preparation for the evening meal. They stopped to spend a few moments with Andrey, and Jack found himself gradually included in gossip and anecdotes.

Being included in a household, even slightly, made him feel warm inside. Happy, even. He started to realise his mind was healing a little, as his body already had.

The net was finished, though Jack suspected Andrey would be redoing half of Jack's portion later.

'I want to work to earn my keep here,' he told Andrey. 'I don't know what I can do. Not net mending, I know. What does Blanche need that I could provide?'

'That's something you'd have to ask her,' Andrey said, a strange look crossing his face. 'You were offered employment and you turned it down. You didn't want to work for Bleiz Mor.'

Jack curled his lip.

'Blanche said that, too. I told her I want lawful work. Where is the Sea Wolf now?' Jack asked. 'I haven't seen him since that day.'

Another odd look crossed Andrey's face.

'He's gone for now,' was all Andrey said. He gathered the nets and cocked his head at the sea path. 'You might want to bathe before you dine tonight.'

Jack sniffed. It had been days since he had properly washed and the hard work had made him sweat. What must Blanche have thought of him when she ended up so unexpectedly in his embrace? He'd offered to comfort her, but that had been the last thing on his mind when he had opened his arms to her, hoping only to receive a moment's consolation. He shivered and grew hot, reliving the sensation of her clinging to him and the lightning bolt that had speared him when their lips touched. A cold swim would be welcome.

He followed Andrey and a handful of the men to the shore and joined them in stripping bare. A momentary sense of dread filled him at the thought of stepping into the sea that had almost claimed him, but the emotion was welcome. He knew now that he wanted to live.

Andrey was watching him.

'Do you think you could get on a boat again?' he asked as they waded in.

Jack looked further out to sea. The thought of it made his stomach heave a little. 'I don't know. It depends on the size. If I want to return to England I'll have to.'

'The village depends on fishing,' Andrey explained. 'If you want to make yourself useful, you could go out on the boats.'

Jack realised with a sinking feeling that the men who took boats out to fish were most likely the same ones who caused ships to be wrecked or crewed for the Sea Wolf. He swallowed the bile that filled his throat and waded back to shore.

On his way back up the path he paused and looked towards Blanche's window. She must know, or at least suspect, what went on around her and he didn't like the thought that she was unable to prevent such violent behaviour. He was glad now that he had no current means to leave because the feeling of protectiveness that had begun to grow inside him was increasing each time he thought of Blanche. While he remained in her home, he would devote himself to keeping her safe.

Best to concentrate on the protectiveness, because the other emotions that stirred inside him were nowhere near as honourable or pure.

Chapter Ten

Ronec's home was past St Petroc's Church and the village of Plomarc'h, along the headland and set back from the sea. The distance was easily covered on horseback and Blanche arrived all too soon at his gates. His home was newer and grander than Blanche's. It reeked of wealth and ambition and was as unwelcoming as its owner. Each time she felt qualms over her piracy, she reminded herself of the difference in their lives. She was better than Ronec was, who thought only of increasing his status among the wealthy and powerful families in the neighbourhood. What she did, only attacking ships of war, was not the same as wrecking.

It sounded increasingly hollow to her ears. She hoped the conflict would be ended soon and the French vanquished so she could leave it behind her.

Ronec was practising archery with some of his companions when Blanche was admitted to the courtyard. Ronec had never come close to assaulting her, but the night before he had been unexpectedly forceful in his suggestion that she spend the night with him. She wished she were dressed as Bleiz Mor with a sword at her waist. He was cowardly beneath the bravado and would never dream of such an assault then.

Once again she was glad Jack had intervened and strengthened her resolve to get him what he needed.

'This is a welcome surprise, Blanche,' Ronec said. 'Have you come to try your hand with a bow? Would you like to hold mine?'

A couple of the other men laughed, but she silenced them with a glare. Ronec loosed his arrow, which landed slightly off the centre of the target to Blanche's private gratification. Blanche curtsied to the men, recognising the *Prévôt* of Benestin, the local town. She smiled nervously. Erwan de Larrion knew of her other identity and only turned a blind eye because he was fiercely anti-Blois in sympathies. A handful of the other men had crewed *White Hawk* under Ronec and at least one of the men from Benestin received a share of any spoils from wrecking in order to buy his silence. Even so, Jack's presence was not public knowledge and she intended to keep it that way.

'I think this conversation is best conducted discreetly,' she said to Ronec. 'May we speak in private?'

'Where would you like to go?' He drew her to one side. 'My bedchamber, perhaps,' he whispered. 'You've seen it before, after all.'

She curled her lip and ignored the taunt.

'Perhaps here will do as well for what I wish to say,' she said, meeting Ronec's eye with a challenge, then flicking her attention to the *Prévôt*'s face. Erwan de Larrion might ignore the Sea Wolf, but he would take a dim view of wrecking. As she suspected, Ronec did not want that. He bowed to his guests.

'*Messieurs*, I must bid you farewell for the time being. I hope I shall not be too long with Madame Tanet.'

He gave her a lecherous grin and held his hand out. Blanche felt distaste and her skin crawled as she took his proffered arm. She would endure his company for Jack's sake.

'What do you want?' Ronec asked. 'You've only come here of your own accord once before. Dare I hope it is for the same reason?'

'You know my feelings about that,' Blanche growled.

'Perhaps they had better change,' Ronec muttered darkly. 'You have been widowed for long enough and can't remain unmarried for ever.'

'I will not speak to you about this now,' she said firmly. 'I've come about a different matter. There was a box brought back with the survivor on the night of the wreck. Do you have it?'

She described it. Ronec raised his eyes to the sky and pretended to think. 'A memory stirs. Come with me and I'll see what I can recall as we take some wine.'

He escorted her inside to a small room furnished with chairs and a small table. He bade her sit down and bellowed for a servant. She waited with growing impatience as he ordered wine and settled into the chair opposite her. He was clearly enjoying the delay, fussing with wine cups, pouring slowly and taking his time to answer.

'A box, you say. Why do you want it? Was your share not enough for you?'

'I took no share,' Blanche reminded him.

'Of course. Your principles wouldn't allow you to benefit from such a cowardly venture, I remember.' His voice dripped with contempt. 'Why do you want part of my share?'

'You do have it?' Blanche said, sitting forward.

He gave a supercilious smile. 'If I did, what

would be the benefit of giving it to you? Tell me why you need it.'

There was no point in prevaricating or trying to concoct a lie. The quicker she had her answer, the sooner she could leave Ronec and return home.

'It was found beside Jack. I think it belongs to him. Whatever it contains might help restore his memory.'

Ronec's expression grew dark.

'You desire that man,' Ronec muttered. 'Would you take him as a lover? Are you hoping to gain favour with him?'

'That is none of your business.'

It was the wrong answer, but outright denial hadn't even occurred to her. Ronec seized her arm, pulled her roughly forward in her chair to face him.

'It becomes my business when you are in debt to me and have been delaying payment. I have a notion to call in the debt now.'

'You wouldn't dare!' she exclaimed. 'When your guests are within earshot of my cry.'

'Would they stop me?' Ronec laughed. 'Half of them look to me for leadership anyway.'

Blanche pulled her arm, but he held tighter, digging his fingers in. She ground her teeth, refusing to give him the satisfaction of seeing her discomfort, though fear surged through her blood at the idea he would openly assault her. She flexed her hand, preparing to rake her sharp nails down his neck and leave him with something to regret.

'You know I want no lovers,' Blanche said.

'So you keep telling me,' Ronec said. 'I don't know if I believe you.'

He leaned in close and put his lips to Blanche's ear, speaking in a low voice that only she could hear.

'You're growing weak, Blanche. Forbidding the beacon lighting hasn't done you any favours. There are some in the village who would gladly turn you over to the authorities. Erwan de Larrion ignores what you do, but if he sees the chance to gain favour with his superiors he would not hesitate to hand you over.'

'You'd be caught at the same time,' Blanche growled. 'You can't increase your wealth from inside a cell or on the gallows.'

She regarded him scornfully. He was greedy, but cared more about his name and reputation at the end of the day.

'You agreed to work with me, Jagu, and to let me lead as Bleiz Mor. You trusted me to plan carefully and I have never failed us. Listen to me now—de Larrion might turn his face from our ships, but he has no time for wreckers. My hands are free of that blood, but the consequences for you would be dire.'

Ronec released her arm and sat back, waving an arm carelessly.

'Perhaps. Perhaps not. A man finds it easier to keep his friends when trouble appears, never forget that. A husbandless woman has no one to speak for her.'

'Do you have the box?' Blanche asked through gritted teeth.

'Yes, I do. How much do you want it?'

'Stop playing games,' Blanche said. She stood and smoothed her sleeve. 'If Jack's memory comes back, he will have no reason to stay. I don't want him here any more than you do. Every moment we spend trying to keep things from him increases the risk of him discovering what we do. It will be spring soon and the campaigns will begin again. I want to be ready.'

'If you just killed him it would end the problem, memory or not,' Ronec pointed out.

'I honour the laws of hospitality even if you don't,' Blanche said scornfully.

Ronec sat back in his chair. 'I hate a woman who thinks she can talk sense.'

Blanche hid her triumph at this admission that

she was talking sense and he agreed. He wasn't going to make it easy, though.

'You still owe me two nights in my bed. You can have the box in exchange for a third.'

'It isn't worth that,' Blanche said. 'Goodbye.'

She walked to the door without looking back. At least she had not mentioned the purpose of her visit to Jack. To have the prospect of his box within his grasp only to have it snatched away was too cruel. Jack would not expect that sacrifice of her, though. No one would.

'A kiss,' Ronec called after her.

She paused and looked round.

'Bring the box.'

He motioned her to wait, but she followed him out of the room and waited in the entrance hall. She did not entirely trust him to stop at a kiss and had no intention of getting trapped with no escape. He laughed when he saw her and held the leather satchel out, then withdrew it.

'Payment first.'

She sneered. 'Do you think I'm a child on my first trip to market? I'll see what I'm buying, thank you.'

Ronec opened the satchel and drew out the box that Jack had been guarding so carefully that, even through all he had suffered, he had not loosened his grip. It was plain and unassuming, something that could easily be overlooked. The wood had long gouges in it and the lock had been forced.

'You opened it?'

She reached out, but Ronec stepped back.

'It might have contained gold or jewels, but there were just papers,' Ronec said. 'I put them back, don't worry.'

Blanche concealed a smile. Ronec was a poor reader. For all his wealth and cunning he struggled to write more than his own name. He would have been unable to read the contents. It was one of the reasons he agreed to help Blanche. Her intelligence balanced his brute strength. They complemented each other. If only he was content to be partners in name only, the arrangement would have been perfect.

He stuffed the box back in the satchel. 'If you want it, I'll take my payment now.'

Blanche nodded. Papers were more useful to Jack than treasure. Her mind flitted to the cross and chain that she had kept from him and her conscience jerked. Ronec squared up to her, looming close. He didn't touch her, but he was closer than he had ever been. She recoiled in distaste, remembering his hands roving across her naked body and wishing in that moment that she had never gone to him for help.

He took her face between both hands and held her still while he brought his mouth over hers and wriggled his tongue between her lips and inside her mouth. She kissed him back, feigning enthusiasm, knowing he would not be satisfied with passivity. She tried to pretend he was someone else. Someone she liked. That had worked in the past, when she had been able to invoke the image of Mael and make the grim deeds endurable. Now she tried to bring Jack to mind, but as soon as she managed to fix his image in her mind she dismissed it. The tenderness he had exhibited as he held her should not be sullied by something this base and lacking affection.

Ronec released her and held out the satchel. She took it from his hand. Ronec seized her, fingers tight around her upper arm. He pulled her round to face him.

'It would breach no laws of hospitality if *I* kill your friend. Remember that.'

He released her and she ran with his laughter ringing in her ears. She didn't stop running until she reached the stables and mounted her mare. She rode at a gallop, satchel slung across her back, until she reached the road that led home. Then she slowed to a walk and led the mare along the cliff edge to avoid the village. She rode past the turning. Until she had bathed and rid herself of the taste of Ronec, she didn't want to see anyone, and she knew where best to restore her equilibrium.

At the end of the headland beyond the fort were a dozen large boulders known as the Maiden Stones that had been dragged into a rough circle some time so long ago no one living knew how they had come to be there. Blanche secured the bridle to the shortest and made her way on foot to the turning that led down to the small inlet where her ships were moored. The path was almost concealed behind the thick gorse bushes that grew wild. Everyone in the village who needed to knew of its existence, but to a stranger it would not be obvious.

The tide was in and the ships at anchor bobbed up and down, rigging creaking gently. The sight soothed Blanche's heart. She had a sudden longing to be on board *White Wolf*, following the tide and the wind, not to attack or harry any other ship but for the simple pleasure of feeling the surge of the sea beneath her.

The ships were cogs, low and flat bottomed with single masts where the sails emblazoned with the Sea Wolf's colours were currently furled. *White Wolf* was her favourite, even though the two ships were almost identical. They had been cargo vessels before being repurposed and a faint scent of spices still imbued *White Wolf*'s hold which made Blanche think of winter nights and hearty dishes.

She put a hand on *White Hawk*'s prow. She needed a different captain to Ronec, but where to look, and how to rid herself of him, was too much to think about now. She tucked her skirts up and climbed the ladder on to the deck of *White Wolf.* There she sat on the raised platform in front of the aft tower with Jack's box beside her.

The urge to open it and read what the papers said was almost irresistible. She wanted to know who he was almost as much as he did. She lifted the lid. There was a leather wallet, tightly wrapped around something that looked like a book. With a careful fingertip she lifted that. Beneath it was a similar packet and beneath that were loose letters. She left the packages untouched, her conscience already biting for prying this much. At least Ronec had not destroyed the contents.

Blanche sniffed. The thought of him brought back the memory of his tongue between her lips and his hands on her face. She could even smell him from here. With the grime from the cellars and the taint of Ronec on her, she felt truly filthy. She had privacy in this cove as no one came without her permission so she climbed on to the harbour and peeled off her clothes. Naked, she plunged off the end of the dock and swam out. She gulped a mouthful of seawater, swilling it round her mouth and spitting out the taste of Ronec. The sea was bracing and goosebumps rose all over her flesh. She swam back to the jetty and heaved herself out, invigorated and feeling cleaner, but planning a hot soak in a tub when she returned home to warm her through. Now, at least, she felt able to face the world with a show of strength. She rubbed herself down with her shift and dressed quickly before the cold made her teeth chatter and her legs shake, thinking how nice it had been to ease into the warmth of Jack's arms for a moment of comfort and how different he was from Ronec and almost every man she had known.

Mael had been her first love and she had mourned his passing deeper than the more recently deceased Yann. She had been fond of her second husband, but marrying him had been the choice of her head, not her heart. Mael had been a youth himself, with the reckless exuberance of a young man with no imminent responsibilities and their time together had been full of laughter, whereas Jack was older than Mael had ever lived to be and possessed an air of maturity. He was a few years younger than Blanche, but she had not felt a gap between them. She gazed at the box, knowing that once she gave it to him he would have no reason to stay. She was torn between hoping for his sake that his memory returned and selfishly wishing it never did. She shook herself from the reverie, wondering where this uncharacteristic sentimentality had come from. She wanted rid of him. He was an inconvenience and the sooner he was gone, the sooner she could concentrate on wreaking havoc on the French as she had said to Ronec.

She made her way up the steep path cut into the cliff side and arrived at the top hot and sticky, with burning legs and lungs, and was glad to let her mare take the strain of the return journey. She arrived home in a better mood than she had begun that particular journey. She left her horse to be stabled and walked into the courtyard. Jack was nowhere to be seen, but a neatly stacked pile of logs told her he had been hard at work. She was thankful he wasn't there because she didn't want to present him with the box without a prelude. She would find a quiet moment that evening. She summoned Marie and ordered the bath to be filled, then sent the maid with instructions requesting Jack to join her for dinner that night.

Blanche lay back in the warm water and closed her eyes. After chopping logs Jack would be as much in need of a bath as she was. She contemplated inviting him to join her in the deep wooden tub and taking turns sponging away the dirt and doing what would naturally follow once they were both clean and crushed together in the tub. She moved her hands languidly over her body, imagining they were Jack's and wondering when she had passed from detesting the idea of a man's hands on her to craving the touch of one in particular, until a fresh picture arose of Jack simply holding her while she embraced him in turn. She hugged herself as a wave of loneliness killed her pleasure.

The sooner he was gone, the better it would be, and she would be spared such distracting, dangerous thoughts.

Jack ate at the same table he had the night before. The household was smaller now Blanche did not have company. This time, rather than sitting silently, Jack found himself included in the laughter and joking by the men of the house he had bathed with that afternoon. He caught Blanche's eye as Andrey was comically miming Jack's efforts with the net and she gave him a grin. When the meal was ended and people started to leave, he found her at his side.

'I am staying here for a drink. Will you come join me, please?'

Jack followed as she led him to the end of the hall, past the table and behind the screen. Two carved chairs with low arms and high backs were in front of the fireplace. They had thick, padded cushions on the seat and additional cushions to rest on and looked inviting. A low table stood between them with a carafe and two wine cups decorated with an intricate pattern of leaves.

Blanche held her hand out. 'Please sit.'

Jack moved to her chair and drew it back, motioning for her to sit first. She smiled round at him and dropped gracefully on to the seat.

She reached past him to take the brass jug. As she leaned in, a sweet floral scent washed over Jack. The hairs on his arms stood to attention. He hadn't noticed her wearing this before, yet for some reason it was as if the scent had gone straight through his nose and into his brain, picking at his memory and stroking his senses as it did. She noticed him watching and drew her arm back.

'What's wrong?'

A small line appeared between her brows and it pained him to think she was troubled by anything he did. He leaned in close.

'That scent,' he murmured. 'It is familiar. What is it?'

Blanche hesitated, then held her arm out again.

Jack leaned in close to her wrist, his hand hovering beside hers.

'May I?'

She nodded. Jack rested her wrist in the palm of his hand and lifted it. After resisting touching her, this slight contact was enough to send the blood racing through him. Her skin was so pale as to be almost translucent and the fine network of veins wove a pattern. Jack's pulse sped and he had to fight to resist the urge to press his lips against the delicate skin and see if Blanche's heartbeat matched his own.

She held still and allowed him to inhale deeply across the velvety skin, though quite what she must have thought of his action was anyone's guess. He knew she was still a little suspicious that he was lying and must have thought his actions those of a madman. When he raised his head, he found her eyes full of curiosity.

'I know the scent,' he said. He ran his thumb across the mound beneath her thumb and looked at her. 'What is it?'

'Narcissus from Glénan. A local plant, crushed in oil to release the perfume,' she said. 'It is not flowering yet.'

'Why are you so familiar to me?' he asked. 'Were you wearing it the night you found me on the beach?'

Her eyes became guarded. She tugged on her arm and Jack opened his fingers to release her. She pulled her sleeve down to cover her wrist. The haughty look appeared in her eyes again, but this time Jack understood that it was not stand-offish but cautious. She was keeping her own secrets.

'I believe I might have been,' she admitted.

'Then when you found me I must have smelled it.'

'Perhaps.' She sat forward on her chair. 'You are starting to remember more things.'

'I don't remember exactly,' he said.

The scent of the flowers, mingled with Blanche's skin, reached to the part of his brain that controlled his desire, the result of which was pure, unbridled lust. He flexed and stiffened his fingers and looked around. No one else was at their end of the room. They were completely private, concealed behind the screen that kept the draughts away from the fire.

'What happened on the beach?' he asked.

Blanch poured a little wine into her cup and filled Jack's. 'I told you.'

She held the cup to him, but Jack shook his head and folded his arms, refusing to take it.

'Everywhere I turn I feel secrets. I think you are hiding something from me.'

Blanche replaced the cup and sat back, folding her arms to mirror Jack's pose. 'I thought you were dead. I leaned over you. You moved.'

Her cheeks coloured and her eyes filled with a determined glow. She licked her lips swiftly. The pink tip of her tongue darting in and out across her scarlet lips sent Jack wild with the urge to kiss her.

'And then what?' he prompted.

She looked him in the eye. 'Then you kissed me.'

Chapter Eleven

Jack wasn't prepared for that answer and the shock burst through him like lightning spearing a dry tree. Blanche pressed her lips firmly together, waiting for his reaction. He steepled his fingers and put them to his lips, pressing firmly in an attempt to stop the desperate urge to press his mouth to hers and once again taste the sweet lips that tormented him.

'You must forgive me,' he said. 'I have no recollection of that in the slightest.'

'I assumed as much.'

Jack took his cup and gripped the stem tightly to stop his hands from trembling. He was aware of turmoil stirring his belly. He had kissed her. This beautiful woman whose lips had commanded his attention at every opportunity. Who drove him wild and who he fought daily to resist. How could he have lost the memory of something he had been burning to do almost since they had met? The slight brush of their lips in the courtyard could hardly be called a kiss. He gave a soft laugh tinged with bitterness.

'It is amusing?' Blanche asked. She raised her head, her eyes cold. Jack wanted more than anything to see them soften.

'Not in the slightest,' he said. 'Alas, it is one more reason to curse this loss of memory. That is one memory I would very much like to regain.'

Blanche blinked and he feared he had crossed the line between hospitality and rudeness.

'My apologies, that was too frank.'

She reached forward and rested her hand on top of his, causing his pulse to drum.

'No pardon is necessary. You were almost insensible. I thought you were about to die. Perhaps that is why I permitted it.' She looked into his eyes and the faint lines at the corner of hers deepened.

'And why I kissed you back.'

'You kissed me?' The revelation was astonishing. Devastating that he could not recall it. 'You told me you want no man.'

She shook her head. 'I told you I shall be submissive to no man and that is true. I did not say I want no man. If, and when, I choose to take one, I do it on my terms.'

There was a challenge in her eye. Jack felt his determination to ignore his growing feelings melting like ice in the sun.

'When you kissed me this morning, did it waken anything?'

Jack said nothing, acutely aware of what sensation it had caused to spring to life within him. Had it done the same for her? He searched Blanche's face for signs of admission of the fact and found them in the crinkling of the skin at the side of her eyes.

'Any memories, I mean?' Blanche added. Her eyes sparkled with amusement and he knew she was thinking the same thing.

'No memories, I'm afraid,' he said with a sigh. He lifted his eyes to hers. 'Though I'd barely describe that as a kiss if I'm perfectly honest.'

'Barely,' she agreed. He heard the clear longing in her voice and his belly fluttered.

Blanche had brought him to this private spot for a reason, and after their embrace his mind filled with possibilities. He could kiss her now and no one beyond the screen would be any the wiser. Maybe she was hoping he would. She had warned him when they first met not to touch her without permission, but he had done so on a number of occasions without consequence.

'I find I do not object to your touch,' Blanche murmured.

Jack realised she was giving her assent to the question he hadn't asked aloud. He leaned forward and cupped the back of her head, drawing her close and finding her mouth with his.

She tasted of the wine they had shared. This time he didn't pull away instantly but let his mouth linger, tasting the sharpness of the fruit on her yielding lips. Blanche's lips parted in response to his touch and all Jack's intention to remain chaste until he knew who he was crumbled. It troubled him momentarily, but when her fingertips rested on the flesh beneath his ear, tickling enticingly, his mind emptied.

He'd once stroked a cat on a thundery day and a sharp crackle from its fur had stung his fingers. The sensation that jolted his heart as their tongues brushed felt almost the same. The kiss was brief, but all the sweeter for it, tantalising him with a glimpse of what he was denying himself. Blanche slid her hand from behind his head and brought it to his chest, pushing him gently away. Reluctantly, he obeyed, but the loss of her touch was like a burst of winter after the warmth of summer. Blanche's cheeks were suffused with a soft pink that made Jack think of early roses.

'Do you remember now?' she asked. No, not

asked. *Purred.* Her voice was creamy and sending vibrations through his limbs.

Jack shook his head. He forced himself not to put his hands to his lips or the spot on his neck where Blanche's fingers had rested. He didn't think mentioning that his only stirring recollection had been of the cat would be complimentary to her.

'I wish more than anything I could say yes,' he sighed. 'It is no reflection on you.'

She gave a gentle laugh. 'I have had worse failures.'

They smiled, sharing the jest. It seemed the safest thing to do, in Jack's mind, because he sensed that attempting to repeat the kiss as he wanted to would not end in the same way. He would find it harder to stop at a kiss and he suspected Blanche's tolerance of his touch would only stretch so far before snapping back.

'What happened after we kissed?' he asked.

Blanche smoothed her hair down, then placed her hands in her lap. She looked past him, eyes distant. 'You called me an angel. Then you closed your eyes and I thought you were dying.'

'I remember none of that. Nothing until I awoke with you in my room,' Jack admitted. He wanted to weep. There was nothing in his mind. He looked at Blanche, thinking of all the ways she had been good to him, despite her clear wish to be left in solitude in her house.

'I don't think it was me you were thinking of,' Blanche whispered.

Her words crushed him. Whom had he been thinking of? Kissing Blanche had been a betrayal of the unknown woman, but now even trying to bring a face to mind felt like disloyalty to Blanche. As he tried, nothing came to him beyond a lingering despondency, tinged with the habitual frustration that he could not remember.

'I'm sorry,' he said. 'I wish I could remember.'

'You will, in time.'

He nodded, but without enthusiasm, because he was aware that once he did, he would have no further need to remain a guest in Blanche's home. He stared towards the window, picturing the sea beyond, and beyond that, England. Somewhere he knew was his home, or had been once, but to where he felt no ties. When he knew who he was, he would have to leave. He would want to, surely, but the thought of tearing himself from Blanche who, after only a few days, he wanted to know better was an impossible thought.

'What are you thinking?'

He realised he had been staring silently for a long time.

'Whether people are waiting for me. Maybe missing me.'

Was there a mother or wife weeping for him? A father who thought him dead? Hoped he was alive?

'If you have friends and family, they will surely be missing you,' Blanche said gently.

'Why?'

'Because I think you are a good man.'

The simplicity of her answer and the certainty of her tone almost undid him. He buried his head in his hands so she would not see the emotion her words caused him.

'I just wish I knew.'

Blanche drained her wine and put the cup down with a firm bang.

'Jack, will you go to your room and wait for me there?'

Jack's scalp prickled. Was she intending to offer herself to him? Blood coursed through him. He felt the awakening between his legs and shifted awkwardly. She obviously saw what he was thinking and smiled.

'Not for that reason. There is something I must show you, but this is too public. It must be in private. I will come to you shortly.'

He did as she instructed. A few moments after he had entered, he heard her foot on the stair as she passed without stopping. He stuck his head round the door.

'Where are you going?'

She half turned, looking over her shoulder. Her slender silhouette twisted and Jack longed to run his hands over the full mounds of her breasts and down to the curve of her belly. 'To my room. What I need to fetch is there.'

He put his hands on the door. 'Wouldn't it be easier if I came up there with you, to save you coming down again?'

'No. My room is my sanctuary and no one enters.'

Jack sat at the desk. Stood immediately, pacing around in anticipation of what Blanche was about to reveal. Sat down again. He counted, picturing her turning the stairs, up and down. He was beginning to think she was not returning when a soft knock came at the door and she entered.

Jack leapt to his feet. Blanche halted, taken by surprise, and he saw apprehension flit over her face before her expression settled.

'I have something for you,' she said. 'I think it is yours.'

In her hands was a small box of dark wood, bound with leather and hinged in brass. She offered it to Jack.

He took it between his hands. It was instantly

familiar, like an old friend. The weight and shape fitted into his hand. He lifted it and caught the smell of oil and wood and knew without question it was his. He closed his eyes and ran his fingers over the lid, probing the knots and scratches in the wood. A candlelit room. The strong bitterness of ink and sealing wax. Scents and sounds danced around his head.

'I know this,' he murmured. 'Where did you find it? Why did you think it was mine?'

Blanche looked nervous again. 'It was on the beach. Caught in your cloak.'

Jack's temper flared like a brand dipped in oil. There was a lock, but it had been forced and crude scratches had dug into the wood.

'You took it from me?' he said angrily. He held the box close to him, as if she might snatch it away once more.

'I did.' Blanche held her head high, though there was anxiety in her eyes and she took a step back from him. 'I didn't want it to be destroyed. Then I lost sight of it. When you said you hoped there might be something that could help you, I remembered and went in search of it.'

He thought back to earlier in the day. She had been agitated when he had met her coming from the cellars. Even now he could recall in exquisite detail the way her body had cleaved to his as they held each other. Her dress had been dusty and Jack had smelled mustiness on her hair when they had embraced. She must have been looking, but without success. Then he recalled what she had told him she was going to do and it must have been late when she returned because he had missed seeing her.

'Was this your errand?'

She nodded.

The pulse in Jack's temple throbbed. 'Who had it? Was it that bastard Bleiz Mor?'

'It was Ronec.'

The distaste in her voice was clear and Jack's throat tightened. She'd brought him what he needed and he had responded with anger and accusations. 'Was that the neighbour you were visiting?'

She nodded and something in the way her lip curled sent Jack's senses ringing with warning.

'What did it cost you to get the box?' he asked.

Blanche walked abruptly to the window and looked out. 'That doesn't concern you. All that matters is that you have it now.'

Jack put the box on the table. The contents called to him, but discovering them could wait. He reached for her shoulder and pulled her round to face him.

'That isn't all that matters. You should have

told me where you were going. I would have come with you.'

She tipped her head on one side. 'As my protector? I told you I don't need one.'

'Your manner now suggests otherwise,' he retorted. 'You should have given me the choice.'

'What if I had told you and then he didn't have the box? I didn't want to do that to you.' She turned her sharp eyes on him, filled with challenge and not a trace of remorse. 'And would you have given me the choice to refuse your company if you had known who I was visiting?'

He shook his head. No power in the universe could have kept him from accompanying her into Ronec's presence.

'What did he ask of you?' He fixed Blanche with a stern gaze, folding his arms across his chest, partly to show her he was serious and partly to resist his all-consuming urge to take her in his arms and belatedly protect her from whatever had occurred. 'If he hurt you…'

'He didn't.' Blanche put her hands on Jack's cheeks, turning his face to hers. The shock of being touched so intimately sent him reeling. 'He didn't hurt me. He only demanded a kiss.'

Demanded.

'And you gave him what he wanted?' The thought of Ronec holding Blanche, kissing her, of her kissing him back, sickened Jack. Had Ronec found her lips as willing as Jack had, or had he sensed her distaste and ignored her reluctance? Jealousy wound sharp fingers around his throat, constricting his breath. Relief prised them free that she had not been forced to submit to anything more intimate.

'Don't scorn me for what I did!' Blanche's eyes flashed with anger. She had misunderstood his meaning. Jack held a hand out to her and gave a gentle smile.

'I don't scorn you. I'm not angry at you for doing it. It is the thought of him exacting such a price that boils my blood. Why did you agree?'

'It was the only way I could see of getting what I needed.'

Blanche drew in on herself, an uncharacteristic air of vulnerability shrouding her. Jack shivered even as his limbs grew hot and his blood raced. He wanted more than anything to wrap his arms around her and hold her to him. Would she reject him or cleave to him as she had done in the courtyard? Either outcome would unsettle him in different ways, but the thought of her turning from him was not worth the risk. He settled for touching her gently at the elbow, hoping that the comfort he wanted to pour over her could somehow find its way through that insignificant gesture.

'The price was too high,' he said firmly.

She gave him a faint smile and touched his hand with her fingertips.

'No, it wasn't. You needed the box and it was my fault you didn't have it. As I have gone to the trouble of retrieving it, you had better open it.

She was right and he was being ungrateful, but the cost had unsettled him. He looked at it, the knowledge of what it might contain sullied by the method in which he had it returned. He picked it up and sat on the bed, holding it in his lap. Blanche walked to the chair and began to pull it across to him. She stopped as he looked up at her questioningly.

'Should I leave you?'

'No. Stay, please.'

She dragged the chair over, sat opposite Jack and folded her hands neatly in her lap. Her presence was so distracting that Jack almost put the box to one side again. The need to touch her was almost as powerful as the desire to discover his past. He took her hand and squeezed it. Her fingers curled, the long nails grazing his palm.

Jack took a deep breath and opened the box. It had been well crafted as the seal on the lid was tight and fitted into an inner groove with no gaps. He wondered how rich he was to have owned such a possession.

Inside were leather-wrapped packets. Jack picked up the top one. With trembling fingers, he undid the cord and opened it to pull out the contents. They were letters. Thanks to the double protection of their leather wallet and the tight seal on the lid of the box, they had escaped most of the sea's damage. He unfolded the first and read it.

Once he had finished, he refolded the letter and put it to one side.

'My name *is* Jack. Jack Langdon. It appears I am a wine merchant's agent,' Jack said. 'I was in France bidding for contracts on behalf of a company called something ending in *tin* and Rudhale from Bristol.'

'Do you remember the people who the names belong to?' Blanche asked.

Jack shook his head despondently. The names meant nothing to him.

'If you make your way to these people, they will recognise you and your memory is sure to return.'

A wine merchant. Not what he had expected to discover. He was no closer to finding his home, but at least now he had the address of people who would surely help him when he arrived in England. People who would know him and might help him. If he saw the faces they belonged to and walked the streets, then surely his memory would come back to him. More than that, another question had been answered. He laughed with relief.

'There was nothing sinister in my past. I wish I could see the arrogance wiped from Bleiz Mor's face if he could see this.'

'He would say he was still right to take precautions,' Blanche said sharply.

Once again, Jack felt a stab of jealousy that she would defend the pirate's behaviour. He turned his attention to the second packet, which was weightier and rigid. It turned out to be a double wax tablet. Two plain wooden sheets had been bound at one edge to make a book with the wax layers between kept safe. Scratched into the first and half of the second sheet in small, careful script was a series of symbols and letters.

'Is that English?' Blanche asked. She leaned around to look at the sheets. 'What does it say?'

'Not English.' Jack shook his head. It was clearly a code or shorthand of some sort. 'I don't know. I must have been able to once, but no longer.'

His previous relief shrivelled. He had spoken too soon. Why was he writing in code? Who was the recipient? The fact that it was unfinished suggested Jack had been interrupted, or the notes were compiled over a period. His scalp prickled.

'I don't know why I have these.'

'Look at the others,' Blanche said. Her voice was

low. Was she considering what to do if he proved to be a spy or enemy? Surely now she would not betray him to the Sea Wolf?

Blanche ran her fingers over the surface of the wax. 'Some of these are sentences, some are a list. If you work for a wine merchant, could these be a list of purchases?'

Her voice was hopeful and Jack realised she didn't want him to be a spy any more than he did. Could the coded writing be a list of orders or was Blanche grasping at chaff on the breeze? It gladdened his heart to think she cared enough to try explaining it away.

'It's possible, I suppose, that I might have wanted to record transactions without anyone else knowing.' He closed the tablets and fastened them together once more. 'I must have brokered some particularly good agreements if they involve this much secrecy.'

Jack tipped the rest of the contents out. The papers that had not been in the leather wallets had not fared well. They were crinkled from being soaked and dried and were illegible. There was something on finer vellum that might have been a letter of safe passage, but the ink had run beyond reading.

'You have an address and names,' Blanche reminded him. 'So now you can go home.'

His heart sagged at her words. Knowing Ronec was lurking nearby made his spine tingle with anxiety. He couldn't leave her. Not yet. 'Yes.' His voice sounded dull in his ears. 'I can go home.'

He took Blanche's hand. It was a gesture of friendship, but his stomach clenched with desire as she laced her fingers through his and pressed it tightly. He felt a shiver run up and down his arm from wrist to neck, as if she had actually traced her fingers all the way across his bare flesh.

'Thank you for what you did to get the box for me,' Jack said.

'When will you leave?' Blanche asked. She added hastily, 'You're welcome to stay as long as you like. Do you feel strong enough to travel?'

Jack flexed his arm, testing the muscles. Blanche's eyes followed, then she looked quickly away, but couldn't hide the spark of hunger that had ignited in them. Jack tried not to imagine crushing her to his chest with the arms that were feeling more powerful.

'I'll stay for a day or two more at least. I need to decide what plans to make.'

Blanche gave him a warm smile and twisted to face him. 'In that case, I have an idea. Tomorrow is the market day in Benestin, the town not too far from here. Would you like to come with me?'

He looked at her in surprise. She'd been careful to keep him mostly hidden.

'There will be dancing and food. It's usually a pleasant day,' she continued, a blush rising to her cheeks. 'I'd like your company.'

'I'd like that, too.'

She looked at him through her eyelashes in a manner that made his heartbeat pound in his ears. He caught the scent of her perfume again and realised how dangerously close to kissing her he was and, here on his bed in privacy, he would not be content with stopping at a kiss. Perhaps she realised it, too, because she withdrew her hand slowly and glanced at the box.

'I'll leave you alone now. Perhaps something else will come to you.'

Jack escorted her to the door. As he thanked her once again, her eyes scorched him and he was relieved when she slipped out of the room shyly and left him alone, free of the temptations that whispered in his ear.

Chapter Twelve

Blanche met Jack in the courtyard the next morning. She held the reins of two horses and smiled when she saw him. Jack only had two changes of clothes, but he was dressed in his fresh tunic. The deep blue wool jerkin suited his complexion and brought out the blue in his eyes as they wrinkled at the corner when he saw the horses.

'I hope you can ride,' Blanche said anxiously. 'I don't think it is the sort of thing you might have forgotten.'

'I would hope not,' Jack agreed. 'Riding seems the sort of thing a body should remember by instinct.'

He stretched his arms and rolled his shoulders back. Blanche forced her mind from speculating what other physical things his body would instinctively remember how to do. There were six men since Mael and Yann who Blanche had lain with when she had needed money or aid of some sort. Some had been pleasurable, others tolerable, one still had the ability to make her skin crawl. She'd gone into each arrangement willingly, but if asked she would say that she was done with lovemaking and rutting. The bedroom held no interest for her beyond helping her achieve her aims.

So how could contemplating one man's ability reduce her to a quivering wreck of a girl?

She held out the reins of the piebald mare. The mare was twelve and docile, and even if Jack proved to be a complete novice the mare was unlikely to unseat him. She kept the black four-year-old gelding for herself.

'I did hope it would be the other way around.' Jack grinned as he took the reins. He raised one eyebrow suggestively. 'You favour a young stallion when you ride?'

Blanche held his gaze, enjoying the double meaning. 'Young, yes, but he's gelded. Perhaps you can ride him once you have proven your ability. I wouldn't want you to get another injury.'

Jack put his fingers to his head. He'd removed the bandage. The scab over the wound was large, but had begun to show signs of healing. He would always have a scar, but his features were so even it would not mar him. He would always be a remarkably handsome man. He laughed, a warm sound that made Blanche want to do likewise.

'Very well, I shall be happy with my gentle mare,' Jack said. 'Shall we go?'

He held out his linked hands for her to mount. Surprised at the unexpected chivalry, she thanked him and put her foot in his hands. She allowed him to help her into the saddle even though she was more than capable of mounting independently. She settled in the saddle and rearranged her skirts, longing for the freedom of male clothing. She, too, had dressed well for the day in a plain, light wool skirt that she wouldn't mind getting dirty in the market, but with a tightly buttoned sleeveless cote over the top that drew in her waist and gave her a slender silhouette. She smiled to herself. She had dressed for Jack, finding it enjoyable that there might be someone who it was worth dressing for.

They trotted through the gate and towards Benestin. There was a direct route, but the weather was warm and the sea was sparkling so she took the path along the edge of the coast so Jack could see the view.

They passed through Plomarc'h, the fishing village that neighboured Fort Carouel. Fishing nets and crab pots were littered around the jetty. A handful of children raced after a dog, squealing in excitement, while the smell of warm bread wafted from the bakery and mingled with the pervading odour of fish. Jack slowed his mare as they crossed the open space at the top of the slanting slipway. He looked at the low houses huddled together around the edge, then up the winding path that led to the church. His expression darkened.

'What are you doing?' Blanche asked.

'I'm wondering how many people here bear the responsibility for what happened to the ship I was on.'

Blanche frowned. 'Some, certainly.'

She waved her arm round the square. 'Look around you, Jack. This is not a wealthy part of the country. The people struggle to put food on the table at the best of times and the conflict has taken menfolk and left poverty in their place. They do what they can to survive. It isn't honourable or right, but it can be excused, surely?'

'It is easy for you to say that when you have not suffered the consequences,' he muttered. 'Do the authorities know?'

Blanche urged her horse on, anxious to be away and out of the village. 'Monsieur de Larrion doesn't. He's the *Prévôt* of Benestin.'

Jack wrinkled his nose. 'What is that?'

'The—how would you say it in English? The justice? The Man of the Town?'

'The mayor?' Jack supplied. 'The magistrate?'

'Yes, that will do,' Blanche agreed. 'He would not countenance illegal behaviour like that.' She looked at him earnestly. 'I have told the men in my village and farm they are forbidden from taking part in any more wrecking and if I discover they played a part I will inform the *Prévot*.'

'Will they listen to you?' Jack asked, sounding doubtful. Blanche tried to ignore the implied insult. She was strong, but only a woman after all, and Jack didn't know of the authority she exercised.

'I believe they will.' She sighed. 'It will not stop it happening. There are more pressing matters for the authorities. The factions involved in the succession and the war with England concern them more than what a handful of villagers do. If they sink a French ship, that helps. If it is a merchant, that is unfortunate, but surely it is better to use what is salvaged rather than let it sink and spoil.'

'What about piracy?' Jack asked. 'What about Ronec? He hardly seems in need of salvage to survive.'

Blanche sucked her teeth. Jack sounded as if he loathed Ronec even more than he despised the Sea Wolf. He had come to her aid by intervening and when he had learned of how she had retrieved the box he had been furious and protective. It was oddly comforting to have someone caring for her like that. Someone capable of the heady mix of strength and tenderness that melted her heart. She would miss him. Her mind flashed to the cross in her room. How lucky Ronec had taken the box and not that, as he would never have returned it. She felt a flash of guilt at keeping it from Jack. When he left she would give it to him. When it no longer mattered if he was angry she had withheld it.

'Some men fight for glory and riches. Ronec is one of those. He believes de Montfort is the rightful heir, as I do, but *he* sees the disruption as the chance of furthering his own cause. He is a landowner and he makes sure any profits are generously shared with those who matter.' Blanche curled her fists. 'He doesn't care if those who don't matter have nothing. If it wasn't for…for the Sea Wolf, half the villages hereabouts would have starved.'

'He shares his plunder?' Jack sneered. 'How noble.'

Blanche looked at him coldly. 'Bleiz Mor doesn't sail to get rich, but for revenge.'

Jack folded his arms and stared back with a challenge.

'Really. You believe he has such pure motives.'

'I know he does!' Blanche rounded on him.

'He only attacks ships belonging to the House of Blois and their supporters.' Her cheeks felt flushed and the wind caught her hair, causing it to lift and blow around her face.

Jack looked sceptical. 'Really? A man such as he would put his own life at risk with no self-interest?'

'I didn't say there was no self-interest,' Blanche corrected. She tightened her fist on the reins. 'Revenge is a stronger motivator than wealth.'

'But hardly an honourable one,' Jack said.

'It is if the wrong done in the first place was great enough.'

Jack scratched his chin. 'You sound as if you know his feelings well.'

'If you knew him and his past you would not doubt his intentions either,' Blanche retorted.

'And does Monsieur de Larrion know of *his* activities?' Jack asked.

Blanche rearranged the folds of her cloak.

'I believe he turns his face away from the sea so he does not have to see what he doesn't want to. You call the Sea Wolf a pirate. Charles de Blois would say the same. To the House of Montfort and the English, he would be an ally. Someone who works tirelessly to further their cause.'

She pointed a finger at Jack, looking at him levelly. 'You would count him as an ally, I'm sure.'

Jack scowled. 'I would never count someone who treated me with such disdain as an ally.'

'Perhaps not.' Blanche gathered her reins. The day was turning out badly. 'Enough now. We'll be at Benestin soon enough and this sort of talk is not for a public place. Today should be a day for jollity, not anger and judgement.'

She snapped her reins with a sharp cry and rode away. It was doubtful that there would be much jollity if her mood continued to be so black. Rather than ride directly to Benestin, she diverted her path and rode to the Maiden Stones. She dismounted and secured the bridle, then waited for Jack to catch up.

'This isn't Benestin,' he said as he dismounted and left the mare by Blanche's horse.

'No. I come here when I want some solitude. It calms me.'

Jack took a few steps closer to the edge of the cliff and stood gazing out to sea. Blanche let him go. Once she would have feared for his life, but now she had no worries that he might hurl himself off. That seemed to have left him as he discovered more about himself.

'I can see why you like it,' he said. 'It's beautiful. I don't think I've ever seen such dramatic changes in one place.'

Blanche followed his hand as it swept across

the rocks and back over the land. The spring flowers were starting to show. Small buds of yellow and purple were easing their careful way among the gorse and grasses. Soon there would be a riot of colour and the contrast with the deadly black rocks would be even more apparent.

'I wish you could see it in summer.' She sighed. 'The sea turns azure blue and the green stretches for miles behind us.'

She walked back to the circle of stones where she had left her cloak and sat on it. After a moment staring out to sea, Jack followed her. He didn't sit, but walked slowly around the stones, running his hand over the coarse granite and looking curiously at the grooves and indentations. Blanche watched as he ran his hand over the surface as slowly and carefully as if he were caressing the limbs of a lover. She shivered with desire. His hands were broad, fingers spread wide as they stroked the surface. Blanche imagined them moving with equal slowness across her limbs and grew giddy with longing.

'When I saw the stones for the first time, I knew I wanted to be close to them.'

'Who put them here?'

'Nobody knows. They were old before my *grand-mère*'s time.' Blanche stood up and walked between the two lines at the end of the circle and stopped at the stubby, slightly lopsided rock that had always been her favourite as a child. She ran her fingertips of both hands up the length of it, tracing the lines etched by centuries of wind and rain, and looked back at Jack.

'There is a legend that these are women cursed and punished for meeting lovers here rather than attending church. They were transformed to stone for eternity in punishment. Only the women, naturally, not the lovers.'

'Naturally,' Jack said drily.

'Do you think the men took new lovers?' Blanche asked. 'Women who were a little more careful when and where they granted their favours.'

'Some, certainly. Some of them might have grieved so deeply they forswore any other lovers.' Jack's voice was heavy.

'Then that would have been a great shame,' Blanche said. 'We weren't created to be alone, but to live and love.'

'What happened to your second husband?' Jack asked. 'I asked before, but you didn't tell me.'

Blanche stared past him, out towards the sea, and her chin came up. It was more than curiosity or making conversation that made him ask.

'There was a siege in the city of Quimper. The loyal forces of the rightful Duke of Brittany held the city but could not withstand the assault.' She shuddered and felt sick. 'Yann sent me away, but remained. He could have declared allegiance to Charles and been spared, but he refused.'

'If this is too painful—' Jack began saying, but she waved her hand imperiously to cut him off.

'It was painful. It has been, but it is in the past. Refusing to talk about it won't bring him back. Yann refused to submit. He was taken to Paris along with other Bretons and executed as a traitor to France.'

She closed her eyes.

'I'm sorry,' Jack whispered.

Her lips curved into a faint smile of acknowledgement. 'You don't need to be. As far as I know, you were not involved in the matter.'

'I mean I'm sorry for your distress,' Jack said, resting his hand on hers. 'It must have been horrible to hear what happened. I'm glad you did not have to witness it.'

She lifted her head. 'Jack, you don't know me if you think that. I am—was—a loyal wife to Yann. How could I not be there? I rode to Paris and pleaded for his life, but it was in vain. When the time came for his death, I stood beside the block so that the last face he saw before he died would be mine. Then when the night was quiet I stole his head from the spike on the city wall. I fled from Paris and carried it away.'

'So Yann's land and property were forfeit and that is why you must live in the fort?'

'Yes. I was left with barely anything beyond what I had brought to the marriage and a few valuables we managed to hide thanks to Andrey. It is fortunate Mael's brother was generous.' She turned away. 'I even had to sell my horse to afford to make my way back to Brittany.'

'You sold your horse? And bought the fort?'

She shook her head, but smiled. 'Sadly, my horse was not that valuable.'

'You are magnificent,' Jack murmured.

She gave a bitter laugh. 'You would not think me so magnificent if you knew what I did next.'

She had spoken mainly to herself, but loud enough that Jack would hear. Sure enough, he looked at her curiously.

'Please tell me,' he said.

Blanche closed her eyes. She had meant him to hear. Part of her wanted to unburden herself of the secret that she had told no one, not even Andrey. Of the people who she lived close to, only Ronec knew and that was because he had been a part of it. Whatever feelings had grown within her for Jack could not be acknowledged truly until he knew the worst of her, even if it meant he turned from her in disgust.

'Another time,' she said. 'Before you leave.' It wouldn't matter then what he thought of her.

'I've been thinking about when that will be.' He looked into her eyes. 'I would like to stay a while longer.'

She tried to hide her smile. 'Of course you are welcome. Why?'

'I don't like the idea of leaving you.'

She blinked in surprise. 'Why not?'

'The way you had to obtain the box. The fact you live surrounded by wreckers and in the presence of danger. When you speak of solitude coming here, it tears my heart. I worry for you.'

She should tell him the truth and let him leave in confidence that she was safe.

'There's no need. I have advisors. Men I can trust.'

'Men you can confide in?'

'Confide what?' She looked away.

'How lonely you are. Don't deny it. I recognise it in you because I see it in myself.'

Blanche walked back to the cliff edge and looked down at the rocks. The sea in all its fury couldn't rage as fiercely as her heart was now. Jack followed.

'I watch you surrounded by your servants and people like Andrey and Ronec, but you're alone.

Whatever hold the Sea Wolf has over you can be broken. I can help you if you let me?'

She faced him.

'Why would you do that?'

He looked away then met her eyes, his expression intense.

'Because I believe I am starting to care for you.'

Her head spun.

'How can you, when you don't know who you are?'

'I don't need to know my past to know how I feel when I'm with you.'

He reached a hand to her cheek and she let him slide his fingers into her hair, ready to be seduced. The memory of the kiss they'd shared sparked flames in her. She craved another.

'Perhaps if you knew my past you would feel differently.'

'If you think I'd reject you because you've been married, I don't care. I don't insist my partners are young innocents.'

She hoped it was true. Maybe he had in his previous life, but she let her eyes fall down and realised the way his body was behaving now didn't suggest that he was only attracted to innocence and youth. Her cheeks coloured.

'I am neither young nor innocent, Jack. I'm older than you.'

'Maybe you aren't.' He lifted his brow. 'I can't say what my age is. I could be a remarkably well-preserved man of forty.'

'Is that a joke?' Her lips quirked into a grin, feeling lighter in the heart than she had done for an age. Almost dizzy with elation and lust.

'I think it is.' He grinned back. 'You're older by a few years at most. That means nothing.'

'And what of you, Jack?' Blanche asked. 'You are not a virgin, I assume?'

'I assume not,' he agreed.

She wondered what sort of a lover Jack would be and suspected he would be better than most of the men she had known. She was growing hotter, aware of the thrumming in her veins as her heartbeat sped up. Jack edged a little closer to her. She stood her ground, eyes following his movements.

'I don't want to marry any man,' she cautioned. 'I've been married twice and when Yann died I decided that no man would own me. I have my independence and I intend to keep it.'

'Is that all that you need?' Jack asked.

'No. There are other things that I've missed.' She stepped close and put her hand to Jack's chest. 'Things I would like to remember.'

Her heart was beating fast. She'd propositioned men of more importance for greater stakes, but she trembled at the thought that Jack might refuse or scorn her.

'Do I understand what you're suggesting?' Jack said. He spoke in a low, urgent voice.

'Yes.' Blanche took a deep breath and fixed her eyes on his, concentrating on the blue depths. 'We'll say goodbye soon and I want to make love to you before we do. Do you want that, too?'

'Don't you know the answer?' he asked.

'I want you to say it.'

His eyes burned with hunger. 'I want you, Blanche. You have no idea how much. I want you more than any woman I can remember.'

'The thought of being with you has consumed me since I first saw you. But the consequences could be serious.'

'My reputation is my own concern and who is there to witness it here? I've only borne two children over years of lovemaking. Perhaps I don't have that ability any longer.'

'I promise I won't let it get to that stage,' Jack said. 'I know when to draw back.'

Blanche smiled. 'One time, then, in each other's arms with no secrets or recriminations.'

Chapter Thirteen

Slowly, aware that his eyes were on her, Blanche undid the clasp of her surcoat that sat beneath her breasts and gave a shrug. The surcoat slipped over both shoulders and to the ground, the heavy folds pooling at her feet. It was a trick she had perfected that rarely failed to leave lovers breathless with desire and she saw it had the intended effect on Jack. She wiggled out of her skirt and stood clothed only in a light kirtle. The silk caught in the wind and swirled around her, alternately billowing or clinging to the outline of her body. Jack's eyes were fixed on her. The muscles in his neck were tight and she could see the telltale swelling in his breeches that told her he wanted her and was ready to act on his desires. He loosened the laces of his tunic, his eyes never leaving hers, but other than that he did not move.

'Why are you standing there doing nothing?'

she asked. The worry that she had misjudged him reared up. She could not have been so wrong in her appraisal of him, surely?

Jack spread his hands wide and curled his lips into a teasing smile. 'You once told me never to touch you without permission.'

Relief flooded over Blanche, followed immediately by a swell of desire. She gave a gentle laugh, then held her hands out.

'Jack, you most certainly have my permission.'

He was moving towards her even before she had finished speaking and, when the final, crucial word had left her mouth, his was there, falling on hers. His kiss was hot and urgent, lips crushingly firm. She clamped her mouth to his, urging his tongue to seek her own. One of them moaned, but she could not tell whom the primal sound had come from. His lips left hers, travelled along her jaw, down her neck, tasting and lapping at her skin as they settled on her collarbone. Blanche threw her head back as Jack's kisses teased the nerves awake until her skin was on fire. She craned her neck and found his ear, giving it a nip with her front teeth, and heard his choked gasp of pleasure as he ran his tongue around the soft hollow.

His hands moved downwards, pushing the shift from Blanche's shoulders. The soft linen

glided over her nipples, sending pleasure shoot-
ing through her as he eased it further down until
the top of her breasts were exposed. She reached
beneath his tunic, stroking the firm flesh as she
had longed to do for so long. Jack skimmed his
fingers over her neck, then further down, spread-
ing them out wide over the sides of her breasts,
tormenting her with maddening slowness as he
took his time to bring his palms down until he
cupped their fullness. She moaned and he increased the pressure slightly, bringing his thumbs
to her nipples and circling around them gently.

'Is that good?' he asked. His mouth settled
against her neck so his breath was hot against her
ear, then he drew back and looked deep into her
eyes. His gaze was so full of desire that Blanche
almost swooned. He wanted to know, to understand whether what he was doing was making her
happy. It had been so long since a man had cared
whether or not she took pleasure from his touch
that she wanted to fall against him and beg him
to simply hold her in this unaccustomed feeling
of being cared about. But then he brushed his
fingers over the tips of her nipples, already sensitive, and now unbearably so. A throb of heat
between her legs told her she could not—*would
not*—stop at any cost.

'So good,' she gasped, bringing her hands between them to scrape her fingernails up from Jack's abdomen and over the contours of his chest to find his own hard nipples. She pinched gently and felt him shudder.

'Is that good?' she breathed, pinching harder with one hand while sliding the other up behind his head to draw him into a kiss.

Jack's answer was a deep-throated growl of pleasure, then he was lifting her, arms around her waist, and backing her against the largest of the upright stones, pinning her against it with the full length of his body. His length was hard against her. She tore at the tapes at the waistband of his hose to free him. Instead of entering her, he slid his hand down, bunching her shift up and delving between her legs, fingers searching and finding their target, circling around, sliding in and out. Blanche's knees buckled as waves of delight ebbed and flowed, dictated by Jack's strokes that were alternately feather-light or firm. When she sensed herself rising to the top of the highest crest she tore her hands from round his back, reaching down to grasp him and guide him inside her.

'I want you…now…' she said, panting.

He entered her hard, grinding himself against her. Blanche cried out as each thrust brought them closer to the peak of abandonment, her voice mingling with Jack's. She reached the end before he did and would have gone limp with exhaustion but for the weight of him holding her upright, captive against the stone. He was not far behind and as his strokes became faster and deeper, Blanche felt him draw out. She reached her hand downwards, grasping him, hand moving firmly until he, too, shuddered to his climax.

Afterwards they slumped together against the stone, limbs askew, wrapped in what discarded clothing they could be bothered to draw over themselves. Jack yawned. Blanche blinked herself awake. She was growing sleepy. The warmth of Jack's arms was somewhere she could imagine staying for ever.

'Do you think I shall turn to stone for what we've done?' Blanche murmured. She wiggled her hands down into his lap and grinned. 'At one point I suspected you were starting to.'

Jack laughed and pulled her closer. 'Nothing as wonderful as what we did here deserves punishment. I'll treasure these memories as long as I have them.'

Blanche's throat seized. It never ceased to amaze her how each man she had lain with had been so different. Mael had been enthusiastic, full of fun and excitement but, Blanche had to admit, more concerned with his satisfaction than hers and she had never fully been able to articulate what was missing from their lovemaking. Yann had been older, understanding that there was more to a woman's pleasure than the bare bones of the act itself, but preferring the same sequence of events that reached a conclusion swiftly had eventually grown a little dull. Jack was neither and she could already tell that this one time would be remembered more clearly than her two husbands.

'We should go on to Benestin,' she said.

Benestin was not much larger than the village but had a grander square and most of the houses had two storeys. They left the horses in stable down a quiet alley and followed the discordant sound of pipes back towards the bustling square.

They walked arm in arm, not talking of what they had done, but bodies brushing with newly discovered intimacy. The longing to be as close to Blanche as possible even in the public place consumed Jack. He could scarcely believe that less than an hour ago he had been holding her upright as she writhed in ecstasy, pulling him deep inside her until his mind and body emptied of all but the most animalistic sensations. Once only, they had agreed. He should leave as soon as possible before he broke that agreement. But how could he part from her after what they had done?

The scent of oysters roasting in their juices over hot coals competed with steaming pots of vegetables and meat simmering in broth to entice hungry passers-by. Jack's mouth began to water and he inhaled deeply. He was very hungry and the energetic time he'd spent on the clifftop with Blanche had given him an appetite for more than lovemaking.

'Shall we buy some?' Blanche asked. She didn't wait for an answer, but walked to the third oyster seller and returned with a basket of them, cracked open and lying on their shells. They devoured the salty, buttery flesh with their fingers, licking the juices away enthusiastically.

The sight of Blanche's tongue curling round her fingertips sent a frisson up and down Jack's spine. She caught him watching and giggled, sounding like a young maiden.

'You've missed a spot,' she said. She brushed her thumb across the side of Jack's mouth, then held it for inspection, glistening with a smear of butter. Jack turned his head and caught the proffered thumb between his teeth, nipping gently. Blanche gave a small squeak. Jack ran his tongue slowly and suggestively along the inside, down to the soft fold of flesh where it joined her forefinger. Blanche closed her eyes, her face taking on a look of longing that sent Jack's head spinning with lust.

'Monsieur Langdon! You are alive! It is a miracle.'

Jack was tugged from his reverie at the sound of his name. He turned and found himself clutched by the arms and pulled into a hug.

'How good to see you again.'

The man released Jack and looked at him. Clearly, they knew each other, but like all faces, this one belonged to a stranger.

'You know me?'

The man wrinkled his brow. 'You are jesting with me? It is Nevez. Your friend Petrus! You don't remember me?'

He looked confused.

'I'm afraid my friend Jack has lost some of his memories.' Blanche stepped to Jack's side. Her expression was calm and all traces of ecstasy had vanished. He smiled at her. The description of them as friends, and the heat with which she looked at him, made his heart swell.

'Monsieur Langdon, that is a tragedy.' The man who called himself Nevez wrung his hands together.

'But you know him?' Blanche prompted.

'I do. He was a passenger on board my ship when we were grounded on rocks and were wrecked. It was a dreadful accident.'

Blanche and Jack exchanged a furtive look. It had been no accident, but was there any purpose to be served admitting this to Nevez? He recalled the barrels with swords and wasn't sure he could trust the man who had been smuggling them.

'Tell me what you know of me, please,' Jack said. 'I have learned some things.'

'Willingly. But perhaps there is somewhere better suited than the middle of a square? Somewhere to quench my thirst?'

The hint could not have been broader. Blanche led the way to an inn that had opened the front and put tables and stools out into the square where a tumbler entertained the drinkers. They found a secluded corner and squeezed in. The serving girl brought them an earthenware jug of cider and three cups. Jack winced as Blanche paid. Of course Nevez would expect to be entertained while he told his information, but it pained Jack that he had no money of his own.

'I know my name is Jack,' Jack began. 'I have some documents that tell me I am an intermediary for a company.' He didn't mention the coded tablets.

'Yes. You buy wine. You were intending to return to England and were travelling with me to Roscoff. I had hoped to persuade you to commission some of the wine I transport.'

Again, Blanche and Jack exchanged a look. Nevez clearly didn't suspect they knew about the other cargo of swords he had been transporting. Nevez poured another cup of cider and held out the empty jug. Clearly, he expected a replacement. Blanche raised her hand to summon the innkeeper, but Jack shook his head. She ignored him and ordered.

'It is worth the price to discover the truth,' she said.

'My vessel was wrecked,' Nevez sighed. 'But I was fortunate that my boat washed up along the coast and I have my life. I have procured a new ship and will be sailing to Roscoff as soon as I am able.'

'Were you the only survivor?' Blanche asked gently.

'No. All who were in the boat made it safely to shore. Some of us have parted ways. One has gone to join the fight to return Brittany to her rightful heir. One joined the army of Charles de Blois.' He broke off and spat angrily on the ground. '*Pardon*, *madame*, but that traitor's name makes my mouth taste foul.'

Blanche smiled. 'No pardon is necessary. We are also not friends of de Blois in these parts.'

'And what of my allegiances?' Jack said, sitting forward. The salvation of the crew was welcome news, but meant nothing to him emotionally. 'Would I support Charles de Blois?'

'Not from what I know of you,' Nevez said.

The tension in Jack's shoulders eased at this confirmation that he and Blanche were on the same side. It was only a small detail, but it was enough to confirm he was not her enemy. The idea of discovering she had reason to hate him was agonising.

'If only your friend had been here when we found you it would have saved a lot of trouble,' Blanche said. 'You and I are allies after all.'

Her eyes shone and Jack realised the news was as much of a relief to her as to him. Her fingers reached beneath the table and found his hand. She held it tight. They held each other's gaze and warmth spread through Jack. He was growing closer to knowing his past. If he could then begin to look towards a future, was it too much to dare hope it could include Blanche in some way?

'Did I tell you much about myself?' he asked Nevez.

'Not much.' Nevez studied him. 'If you will excuse me, you seem calmer, Monsieur Langdon. When we first encountered each other, you were about to challenge half of Concarneau to a brawl. You were raging and didn't seem to care who you affronted. Whether or not you lived or died did not seem to bother you.'

Jack swallowed. So the craving for destruction was not new. He had suspected as much, but there was still no explanation why he'd been so reckless with his life. Nevez peered at him.

'You are not wearing your cross.'

Jack's hand went instinctively to his neck and a memory flickered to life. He'd sensed on more than one occasion that something felt wrong, hadn't he? There was an absence of something that unsettled him. Was faith an intrinsic part of his life he had lost?

'I don't remember owning one.'

'The cross you wore around your neck constantly. I am so sorry you have lost it.'

Blanche put her cup on the table and sat back.

'Will you excuse me, *messieurs*?'

She slipped from the stool and began walking towards the alley where they had left the horses. A horrible suspicion began to creep over Jack. She had withheld the existence of the box from him. Did she know something about the cross Nevez spoke of? He called her name and she spun around.

'Jack, can you make your own way back home?'

Her expression was tense and her shoulders were rigid. Jack felt his stomach plummet as he recalled what she had done to regain the box from Ronec. He leapt from the stool and ran to her.

'What do you know?'

She walked away, shaking her head. She quickened her pace, but Jack was not going to let that be the end of the matter. She was halfway back to the stable when he caught her by the sleeve. He pulled her to stop with more roughness than he intended and she spun round angrily.

'Don't touch me like that!'

Jack released her immediately, shocked that he had even dared to grab hold of her so brutally in the first place.

'You know what Nevez is talking about, don't you?'

Her mouth twisted and her complexion grew pale. Jack felt sick as he remembered what she had done in order to retrieve the box. He could not bear the thought of her returning to Ronec and having to bargain herself once more. He reached for her, taking her cheeks in his palms, fingers buried deep in her hair.

'I won't let you go to him,' he said, pressing his forehead to hers.

'To whom?' Blanche wrinkled her brows, then as she worked out who he meant, she pulled free and covered her face with her hands.

'I'll go myself and force Ronec to surrender

it,' Jack said. He reached a hand to her shoulder and tried to bring her round into an embrace but she stiffened and pulled away.

'There's no need.' She raised her head and the expression on her face was so full of distress Jack forgot to breathe.

'Jagu doesn't have your cross. I do. I've had it all along.'

Jack dropped his hand. A rushing noise filled his ears. Blanche seized the opportunity and bolted to the stables. When she appeared on her horse and rode away towards the road home, Jack did not even call out to her. He returned to Nevez.

'Your woman is not with you?' Nevez asked.

'She's not my woman,' Jack said, more forcefully than he intended.

Nevez raised an eyebrow.

'She's not mine,' Jack repeated in a softer voice. The rapid throb of his heart reminded him how much he wished she could be.

'You like her, though.'

Jack didn't answer. He filled his cup and sipped the cider slowly to give himself time to consider the question. His feelings for Blanche were too complicated to be easily defined. Yes, he liked her. A lot. He desired her. He wanted her and wanted to be with her. When he had thought even for a moment she was about to return to

Ronec, he had felt such a rush of protectiveness it had startled him. The longer he spent in her presence, knowing her bravery and what she had done to retrieve his box and what she had put herself through after Yann's death filled him with admiration. True, she was hard and imperious, but beneath that there was warmth that he thought he had only just seen the top layer of. When they had made love, he'd witnessed a passionate side that she had concealed so well he still doubted it had really happened.

The way her frosty exterior had gradually thawed to allow him to see her vulnerability spoke to his heart. There were still walls to be broken down and part of him was of a mind to cast off every shackle of the past and stay with her until he had learned every secret, every hope or thought she possessed.

The word that edged around his consciousness was *love*, but he was reluctant to speak it out loud.

But the cross…

That secret made him hot with anger as he thought of it. She had it and had done so all along. If Nevez had not mentioned its existence would she ever have told him? He needed to understand why. He needed to find out what it could reveal— if there was anything significant, he couldn't stay with Blanche.

'When you travelled with me before, you were trying to reach England,' Nevez said. 'I shall be leaving four days from now once my first mate has joined me, and sailing to Roscoff as planned. If you wish to come, I'll be glad of your company.'

'I have no means to pay,' Jack admitted.

'You paid your passage already. I would not charge you twice. You can work as a crewman until Roscoff and I'll pay you. When you reach England, you can persuade your associates to buy my wine on generous terms.'

Jack nodded in agreement. He could find a ship to take him to England from Roscoff.

'Where are you staying?' he asked.

'Here.' Nevez gestured to the inn they were sitting in front of. 'If you wish to join me, I shall be leaving on the morning tide four days hence.'

Jack shook hands. He collected his horse and rode back to the castle at a slow pace. He burned to discover what secret the cross held, but part of him wanted to delay the moment he must face Blanche and confront the betrayal he was sure she had committed.

Blanche was waiting outside Jack's door when he arrived, sitting on the stool the guard had once occupied. She dropped her head when she saw him. He cocked his head, walking past her. She edged into the room behind him nervously. The mannerism was uncharacteristically meek and made Jack more anxious to see the change in her and he wondered what he was about to discover.

'Do you have the cross?' he asked.

Blanche held out her fist. Between her fingers he could see a glint of gold. He was reluctant to take it, fearful of what it might tell him, terrified in case it told him nothing.

'Where did you find it?' he asked.

Blanche's eyes flickered and she dropped her head. 'It was round your neck when I first came across you on the beach. I thought you were already dead.' The implications struck Jack with the force of a hammer to his skull.

'You stole it from me!'

'I was worried the men would take it and it would get broken up and shared as spoils. It was too beautiful to let that happen so I took it to keep it safe. I thought you deserved better than that. I hid it before anyone saw.'

A noble motive, but she hadn't returned it when she knew he was alive. He folded his arms and looked at her coldly.

'You've had it since then? Before you reclaimed the box from Ronec? You could have given this to me at any time, but you kept it secret from me. Why?'

'You were so weak. So ill.' Blanche sounded flustered. 'I didn't know what it would mean to you and thought you needed time to heal. When the box told you nothing of use you were so disappointed. So hurt. I didn't want that to happen again.'

'It wasn't your decision to make,' Jack said. Blanche flinched and he realised he was shouting.

'I know.'

'Give it to me.'

She held her hand out and pressed something into his hand. Jack looked down. It was a delicate cross on a long chain. Not a style he thought a man would choose. He let the chain fall and held the cross between thumb and forefinger, turning it around. The letters *J* and *M* were engraved on the surface of the back. He traced their familiar shape, then rubbed his thumb over the small red stones set into each point of the cross. Once again he was struck with the overwhelming sense that had filled him when he looked at the box. He knew this object. The *J* stood for Jack and the *M* for...

Without him understanding why, his eyes filled with tears.

'What does it tell you?' Blanche asked.

'I'm not sure. I need to think.' Jack clutched

the cross in his fist, swallowing it from view as an immense sense of loss filled him.

Blanche was looking at him sorrowfully. She put her hand to his cheek, but stopped a finger-length away as he glared at her. He yearned to fall into her arms, comfort himself and drive out the pain that filled him, but another voice was whispering in the back of his mind that she was to blame.

With trembling fingers he put the chain around his neck and let the cross drop down beneath his shirt, against his bare skin where it belonged. This was the presence he'd been missing. The nagging feeling that something was wrong righted itself. With it came tumbling a tumult of sensations and memories, and with it a single word.

Margaret.

'What did you say?' Blanche was looking at him with concern on her face.

Jack hadn't realised he had spoken.

'Margaret,' he repeated in a voice crusted with pain.

He drew the cross out from beneath his tunic, clutching it tightly until the garnets pressed into his palms, causing discomfort. He looked at Blanche, but she swam and blurred before his eyes. He was weeping and the grief was swelling up inside him, consuming him with unbearable, agonising memories. His knees buckled and he staggered back against the wall to stop himself from falling.

'My wife. This was hers.'

'You're married?' Blanche's voice was a devastated whisper.

Jack covered his eyes with his hands, feeling tears spilling between his fingers. He knew who Margaret was. Knew where she was now.

'Had.' He looked at her bleakly. 'I had a wife,' he repeated.

He looked again at Blanche whose complexion was ashen. She had a hand out, poised to touch him. To offer comfort to him? To seduce him again?

'What can I do to help you?'

He jerked away. Kindness would end him now. Consolation from Blanche would destroy him more completely than from anyone else.

'Get out.' He flung a hand towards the door.

'You shouldn't be alone,' Blanche protested.

'I want to be.' The grief that was welling up inside him was close to flooding out. He was close to breaking and refused to show his pain in front of the woman who had kept the means from him to discover the truth.

'I could have discovered this a week ago, but

you kept it from me. If I had known, I would never have made love to you.'

He glared at her. 'Is that why you kept it? So I would bed you without realising I was being faithless to her memory?'

'No! I thought both initials were yours. I knew nothing of her until you spoke her name and confirmed it.'

Blanche looked as if she was going to weep and the sight made Jack furious. What reason or right did she have? His stomach twisted. What was it to her if an unknown woman had died?

'Out!' he bellowed. 'I don't want to see or speak to you.'

She didn't protest, but practically ran to the door and fled up the stairs. Jack slammed the door and, feeling his strength begin to ebb, leaned against it, head resting against the wood with his arms limp at his sides. He felt his tears soak into the oak and lost all sense of how long he remained there. It could have been a heartbeat, it could have been a day.

Blanche didn't return. Finally, Jack slumped on to the bed, holding the cross against his heart as memories of his wife rolled over him: a mist of fine golden hair, blue eyes and a sweet, smiling rose of a mouth. Girlish laughter filled the empty room. He gave himself over to mourning afresh. Now he understood why he had the deeply rooted inclination to let his life end if that was his fate. Existence had become so unbearable without Margaret's company. It was too cruel that he had forgotten the memory of her life, but a blessed respite that for a short while he had been released from remembering her death.

Chapter Fourteen

For the rest of the day Jack remained silent, sitting by the window or pacing about the room and grieving. His tears dried, leaving him with a dry hollowness in his chest where the pain had been greatest. He didn't eat, though occasional knocks at the door, followed by the sound of something being placed outside his room suggested someone was bringing food. He ignored both.

He slept fitfully and woke late in the day, but with a greater sense of peace. The shock of the return of such dreadful memories had apparently jarred something in his brain, like a stubborn door finally giving way to a firm kick. They were still insubstantial and half-formed, but with the sadness had come more memories, and now he had an image of a house and a bedchamber as well as his wife. He would recognise the house if he saw it and was convinced now that he would be a whole man again once he returned there.

When there was a lull in activity, he could hear the waves crashing beneath the castle rocks and his soul and heart pulled him towards the sea. England and true understanding beckoned enticingly. Two more nights, then Nevez would be sailing for Roscoff. Jack intended to be on board.

By nightfall, he knew that his seclusion was verging on becoming self-indulgent. He began to notice his hunger and thirst and resolved to deal with those practical matters. He hesitated before leaving his room, remembering how he had thrown harsh words at Blanche. He didn't want to see her. His fury had been reasonable but his conduct insufferable, and dealing with the tangled emotions was a trial he preferred to delay until he had eaten.

Jack waited until the sun had slipped beneath the horizon and the orange glow over the castle walls were consumed by shadows of purple and grey. Once the shadows were black and the building was quiet, he felt safe to slip down. When he opened the door, he tripped over a figure on the stool where the guard had sat on his first days in the tower.

Anger and resentment rose in him. He hadn't been guarded since the first day he had emerged

and he thought enough trust had been built between him and Blanche that she no longer felt
such a precaution necessary, especially now he
had a greater understanding of who he was. His
wrath and the way he had spoken to her must
have caused her to reconsider. He didn't blame
her for that.

All this flashed through his mind before the
figure grunted and looked up from the book in
her lap. It was Blanche herself who was sitting
there.

'What are you doing here?' Jack asked stiffly.

She closed the book and placed it at her feet
before standing and facing him. The flame in her
lantern danced, fingers of shadow caressing her
cheeks. 'Waiting for you to come out.'

She was dressed in a plain brown gown that
looked crumpled as if she had been sleeping or
sitting in it. Her hair was loose, falling in tangled waves halfway down her back. He folded
his arms and glared down at her, still resenting
her betrayal.

'How long have you been here?'

'Since dawn. Andrey insisted I left at midnight
last night and slept a little. He took my place in
case you came out.'

Her eyes were shadowed with deep purple
rings. She didn't look as if she had slept much.

On the floor beside her was a tray with a half-eaten pot of stew and some chicken bones. Jack's stomach growled.

'You must be hungry,' Blanche said. She looked at him warily, clearly uncertain how Jack would behave. 'Shall I bring you something?'

'I'll go myself. That's why I came out,' he admitted.

She picked up the lantern and beckoned him and led him down the stairs, motioning for him to draw back the bolts on the door. They crossed the deserted courtyard to the kitchens in the outbuilding. The evening meal had finished but there was still the scent of the stew Blanche had eaten. In the kitchen she found a clean bowl and ladled him out a large portion.

'I'm afraid it has gone cold and this is all that remains. This was going to be for the dogs.'

Her voice was matter-of-fact and reminiscent of when they had first met and he had been an imposition: an indication that they were no longer friends. Jack's heart squeezed with loss. He took the bowl from her.

'Thank you, this is enough.'

He sat at the table and moved various utensils out of the way to make space. Blanche brought him an earthenware cup of cider. Jack viewed his meal morosely. Now he was faced with food, his appetite had diminished.

'You should eat,' Blanche urged softly. 'Even though the food tastes like wood and sticks in your throat like ash you have to force yourself.'

The description was apt. Jack picked up the spoon and toyed with it.

'The grief feels too big for anything else to fit, doesn't it,' Blanche said.

'I don't want to discuss it,' Jack said curtly.

He glanced at her and met eyes full of gentle empathy that made him melt. She'd lost two husbands and had grieved for them. She understood. He was being unforgivably rude and he loathed himself for it. What kind of mewling lump of self-pity was he?

'Will you join me?' he asked.

She pulled up a stool and sat a little way from him—hesitant in his company, which was hardly surprising given the way he had screamed at her to leave him. He began eating. Blanche nodded encouragement. He felt like a child being praised by a mother, which was a sensation he didn't want to associate with Blanche in the slightest.

'I should have given you the cross sooner,' she said. 'I thought it was for the best but I was wrong. It wasn't my decision to make. I'm so used to being in charge I forget sometimes how to let others make choices.'

It was a simple apology and Jack felt more ready to accept it. His heart opened up a little more at her inadvertent admission of loneliness. 'You should trust others to make decisions. You don't have to rely on yourself all the time. You have friends and if they care for you they won't make bad choices for you.'

Blanche looked doubtful. She poured herself a cup of cider and drank it as Jack ate. They sat in silence but it was a slightly easier atmosphere than it had been at first. He did feel better now his belly wasn't empty. The cider started to make his head a little fuzzy and a warm feeling spread over him. Blanche's quiet presence was comforting too and of course she would understand better than most what he would be feeling. He laid down his spoon and poured them both a second cup of cider. He looked at her in the flickering lamplight.

'My wife was called Margaret,' he began.

'You don't need to tell me,' Blanche said, gripping his hand and shaking her head.

'I'd like to. I want you to understand,' he said.

She withdrew her hand and put it in her lap.

'Her name was Margaret. She died.'

'In the shipwreck? Oh, Jack, no!' Blanche's

face twisted and took on a look of complete horror. 'If I had known, we could have searched.'

'Not then,' Jack answered. Seeing her earnestness confirmed anew that Blanche could have had no part to play in any such brutality. 'She cut her hand while spinning wool and her blood became poisoned. The physician said there was nothing he could have done to save her.'

He took another swig of cider to try fortifying him. He looked at Blanche who gave him a sad smile. 'I wasn't there. I was in France. When I returned, all that was waiting for me was a grave. Her mother told me what had happened. She had been gone three weeks by the time I returned.'

'I left England again. There was nothing for me there. We have no children, thankfully. We'd only been married a year or two I think.'

'You think?'

Jack wrinkled his brow. 'The memories are still hazy. I can remember her face, the sweet smile she had and her hair. It was like sunshine on a spring morning.'

Blanche touched the end of her raven locks. He wondered if she was aware she was doing it. She and Margaret were different in almost every way but he was as drawn to Blanche as deeply as he thought he had ever been to his beloved wife.

'How did you bear the pain when your husbands died?' he asked.

'I had to live. To survive. At first that was all that mattered, but then I found a purpose and gradually I felt myself caring about the world. You will, too.'

'I'm not sure,' Jack said. The impulse to end his life made sense now. A heart filled with grief that had been too heavy to bear. It was a wonder the weight had not dragged him straight down into the depths of the sea. He was past that stage now, at least.

He bowed his head and put his hands to his face. He heard the stool scrape on the floor then felt Blanche's arms come about him from behind. He tensed then relaxed his shoulders, easing himself into her embrace. She gave him strength. This was what he should have done all along rather than hurling anger at Blanche, but taking comfort in the arms of another woman had felt like a desecration of Margaret's memory.

Blanche leaned against his back, resting her cheek against the back of his neck. He felt her draw a deep breath and he shuddered as the softness of her breasts pressed against the broadness of his shoulders. She wrapped her arms tighter around him.

'You'll find the strength once you have the

memories. Once you see where Margaret rests, that will bring you peace,' she assured him.

She knew he was leaving even though he had said nothing of his intentions. He twisted in her arms to face her and didn't deny it.

'What if I don't? I wasn't strong enough the first time, and I don't think I am strong enough now to relive the grief. When I remembered Margaret had gone, I understood why I wanted to die.'

'When Mael died I was devastated,' Blanche said. 'I felt as though my world was going to end, but I was only fifteen when I married him and eighteen when he died. My life had been wrapped in his.'

Jack's heart tightened. She spoke with so much fondness. She must have loved him so greatly to still feel such emotion.

'How soon before you married again?' he asked.

'Three years. Longer than most women wait but I wanted to choose wisely. I didn't love Yann at first but he was a sensible choice. He was ten years older than I was but for our whole marriage we were content. When I learned my pleas had failed and he was to be executed after the seizure of Quimper, I expected the same pain. But the anticipation was worse than the reality.'

She left Jack and began pacing around the

room, then stopped and put her hand on the turn-spit beside the fire.

'Yann did not make a good death. He died begging for mercy and in the end I grieved more over the foolishness that had led him to follow the path he did. He gave me a son and for that I am thankful, but I do not miss my husband now. I mourned him but that has passed and now I merely regret the paths that led us here.'

Jack grimaced. Margaret had not been as young as Mael but that loss seemed most akin to the one he had experienced. Blanche spoke of contentment with her second husband, but not passion or love. It was no wonder she was in no rush to remarry a third time and had grown hard since Yann's death. He stood and took his bowl and spoon to the trough of water and dunked them to clean them.

'I'm glad I saw you tonight,' he said, avoiding her eyes as he told her what she had already guessed. 'I have to leave.'

'You said there is nothing for you in England,' Blanche said.

He looked at her. Could there be something for him here, though? Could the fierce fire of attraction that he couldn't ignore, however hard he tried, become a perpetual flame to sustain them both? He had grown fonder of her than he believed possible, even taking into account the way she had concealed things from him. But he had other matters to deal with first.

'I can't stay. I don't know what else I left behind. There are still gaps in my memory. Huge gulfs. It's as if someone has unpicked a tapestry leaving only shapes and forms and half figures. I need to go back and find out who I am. You understand that, don't you?'

'Of course I do,' Blanche said. She returned to the table and began straightening the wooden spoons Jack had moved aside. 'When will you leave?'

She wasn't going to try to stop him. He remembered how initially she had made no secret that his presence was a trouble to her. Perhaps she would be glad to be rid of him.

'Nevez is leaving the day after tomorrow. I'll take passage on his ship.'

One more day in Blanche's company. One more night under this roof. It was the only choice but telling Blanche made it harder than expected.

Blanche looked at him. 'You already planned this before I gave you the cross.'

'I can't stay here for ever—we both know that. I've been hiding from discovering the truth. When Nevez told me about the cross I was angry that you had kept anything from me. Whatever I had discovered, that was the final push I needed.'

He walked to her as emotions swelled inside him and took her hand, rubbing his fingers over the back of her knuckles. He couldn't look at her in case he saw sorrow in her eyes. Didn't want to in case there was none there. He reached a hand to her cheek, noticing the way the petal softness caused his nerves to heighten in awareness.

'You're a good woman, Blanche. I couldn't have asked for a better place to wash ashore but I've trespassed on your hospitality for too long. You have a life to lead and I must go discover mine.'

She took his other hand, lacing her fingers through his and placed both over his heart. He risked meeting her gaze. Blanche's eyes were wide, her face solemn and her lips pressed together. Jack wanted to soften them with a kiss and feel her melt into his arms as she had done before. Whatever she had done, nothing changed how much he desired her and how his body responded instinctively. If he kissed her once, he wouldn't trust himself not to keep kissing her. And if he did that, how long before he gave in to the needs welling up inside him and made love to her here, on the kitchen table? If he did that, he would be lost and likely to abandon all plans to leave. He could now. He was not married. No one else claimed his heart. Guilt flooded him.

He picked up the lantern and stepped out of temptation's reach.

'It's late and neither of us have slept enough. We should go to our beds.'

Separately. Jack's skin grew hot and his limbs turned to calves' jelly at the thought of taking Blanche into his bed and bidding her farewell in a manner neither of them would forget.

Blanche took the lantern from his hand and led the way back. Jack followed a step behind. She hadn't said she would miss him, but then again, neither had he. It was too raw, too soon after the bitter words to admit such a thing. At his doorway Blanche paused and passed him the lantern.

'I can find my way without this. Sleep well, Jack.'

She left without waiting for a response. He called her name as she reached the bend in the stair and she looked back questioningly.

'You were right about concealing the cross,' he admitted. 'If I had remembered Margaret when I first regained consciousness, I don't know if I would have been strong enough to bear it.'

'Yes, you would.' She gave him a warm smile. 'You've always been strong, even when you were at your weakest. You defied Bleiz Mor and confronted Ronec. You clawed your way back from death on the beach and overcame the fever. You are stronger than any man I've known.'

She left him standing alone, her words sapping his strength more than anything else she had said.

'Our guest will be leaving tomorrow morning.'

Blanche sought Andrey out as soon as she had woken, creeping past Jack's doorway in case he heard her footsteps. She had always known he would go. It had been inevitable from the day he regained consciousness that his presence would be temporary, but saying the words out loud made it too real.

Andrey dipped his bread into the bowl of honeyed milk and bit a chunk before raising his eyebrows. 'What do you want me to do?'

'Do? Nothing. Unless he asks you for help with arrangements, in which case you should assist him. I just thought you should know.'

He continued eating without looking up at her. 'You'll be glad to see him gone, I expect.'

At one time she would have welcomed Jack's departure. Now his forthcoming absence loomed like a storm cloud. She considered herself lucky that she'd had even a short time with him.

Was she lucky, though? To have been given a glimpse of a man she suspected could make her happy and whom she desired so fiercely. It would have been better never to have encountered him and seen the possibility of happiness dangled almost within reach. It was a cruel irony that Jack had withstood temptation while he believed he might be married, but discovering he was free of ties had led to him deciding to leave.

'Of course,' she said briskly. 'It will be a relief not to have to hide what we do.'

'You're lying,' Andrey replied kindly.

Blanche sat on the bench beside him. Her fingers trembled as she picked fitfully at one of the bread rolls, tearing it into small pieces. She gave a bitter laugh.

'I admit I've enjoyed his company. Despite the blunders I've made and the wrong I did him in not giving him the cross, he still thinks I'm a virtuous widow living quietly in seclusion.'

At least her final secrets had remained hidden. Jack would leave without ever knowing she was the pirate he despised. She sighed wistfully and crumbled the bread between her fingers. 'His faith almost makes me wish I was the woman he believes me to be.'

Could she stop and let Bleiz Mor die? Or let Andrey take over the guise. After the revulsion she had felt seeing the bloated bodies of the drowned crew, she was losing her taste for death.

She'd spared the crew on the recent attack and if she were not careful she would hesitate to strike and find herself on the end of a sword. She'd avenged Yann's death fivefold by now and her luck would not last for ever. Didn't she deserve to rest after so long fighting? Brittany would continue without her.

It was something to consider, but the idea of such a momentous decision made her head ache.

'Tomorrow we'll sail up the coast,' she said, standing and brushing the crumbs away. 'Today I shall do nothing. I'm tired.'

The sun was bright and there was no wind. She craved solitude and a favourite spot called to her. She could think and plan in peace for the day.

'I'm going to spend the day thinking alone. I'm going to the Maiden Stones,' she told Andrey. She lowered her voice even though no one else in the hall could hear them. 'If you speak to Jack, will you ask him to join me there later in the afternoon?'

Andrey grunted and a gleam entered his eye. Blanche ignored it. Let him suspect what she hoped might happen. She wouldn't confirm it and couldn't deny it.

Blanche watched Jack climb the last corner and make his way across the steep incline to join her at the steps. He was breathing heavily from the effort. At some point he had unlaced the ties of his tunic and the linen hung open, fluttering in the breeze. Perspiration trickled down his neck, tracing a path that disappeared between the firm muscles of his chest.

Blanche shuddered as the hunger she had been keeping under control rose up again. She stood, placing herself between the two guard stones and held herself erect.

As he reached the top of the path, Jack bent and caught his breath then looked around and spotted Blanche. His eyes filled with suspicion and he looked at her, face carefully expressionless. A twinge of anxiety caused Blanche a moment of uncertainty. This was the wrong thing to have done after all.

'Andrey said you wanted to speak with me.'

Blanche nodded. She didn't trust herself to speak because the lump in her throat threatened to make her voice waver. She would rather face a dozen Frenchmen than Jack bearing the look of hurt and grief when she had given him the cross. She didn't want him to see how greatly his presence affected her. She walked to where he was standing, close to the path where the gorse was thinnest. He didn't seem to mind her joining him and for moments they stared out at the sea.

'I thought if we were going to say goodbye it should be somewhere beautiful that hasn't been tainted by any of the deception or arguments.'

There was longing in her voice and she knew Jack could hear it too because his lip quirked and he lowered his eyes. She hadn't intended to dwell on their parting but regret welled inside her that they were parting less than warmly.

'I'll be sorry to see you go,' she admitted quietly.

'So we are saying goodbye now?' Jack grimaced. 'Do you not plan to see me tomorrow?'

It gave Blanche a little hope that he regretted it, too. She shook her head. 'No. I dislike partings and I've said goodbye to...'

She stopped before admitting she'd said farewell to too many people she had cared about. It seemed a foolish thing to admit that he had come closer than any man to breaking through the shell around her heart. She had no right to lay that burden on him after the deceptions she had been guilty of. Nevertheless, he looked at her with understanding in his eyes, and she knew he was finishing the sentence in his mind. She felt a weight of sorrow that someone who seemed to understand her so perfectly without words was leaving.

'I don't remember my goodbye to Margaret,' Jack said quietly. 'I wish I did. It would mean more to know it was a kind one.'

The pain and remorse in his voice twisted Blanche's heart. Of course he had to leave. With such grief in his past, how could he not return to his true life and the people who understood and loved him.

She held her hand out and he took it.

'Live a good life, Jack. I hope you find what you need to find when you return home.'

Jack nodded. He kissed the ridge of her knuckles, lips pressing firmly, then his eyes darted away. He dropped her hand and walked back towards the path. Two paces later he spun around.

'Know that you are in my head and my heart. I'll always regret the things we never did or said.'

A keening hunger began to wake inside Blanche to touch Jack and have him return her touch. To feel his hands on her body in the most intimate ways possible.

'It isn't too late,' Blanche said.

Jack walked past her to the stone where they had made love. He laid his hand on it and looked round, his expression bleak.

'I think I fell in love with you without knowing I shouldn't have. I betrayed Margaret's memory without even realising I was doing it.'

Jack's face twisted, grief enveloping him. He dug his fingers against the rock as if he hoped it might crumble between his hands. He cut such a lonely figure that Blanche couldn't resist walking to him and resting her hands on his arms. She expected him to shrug her off but he didn't.

'Would Margaret have wanted you to grieve this long? She loved you, yes?'

'Of course she did!' Jack sounded indignant. Blanche put her hand to his cheek to appease him.

'Then she would have wanted you to live, not to become as chaste as a monk.'

'How do you know that?'

'I don't know, but I suspect it. If you had been the one to die, would you have wanted her to spend her life pining from sorrow or would you have wanted her to find another? Not to take your place, but to be her companion when you no longer could?'

Jack looked at his hands. 'The idea of Margaret in the arms—let alone the bed of another man—rips my heart to shreds,' he admitted. 'She had the sweetest smile that had lit her face, and a laugh that caused anyone nearby to join in. That she might never have used those again would have been unbearable.'

Jealousy flared in Blanche but subsided as quickly as it had reared up. Of course his wife would have been young and sweet. Jack, with his deep well of kindness and urge to comfort and protect, would choose no other sort of girl.

'I would have wanted her to be happy,' Jack said eventually. 'How could I not?'

Blanche gave a gentle smile. 'Then you know she would have said the same about you.'

Jack bent his head and touched his forehead to Blanche's. Warmth flowed through her as he tightened his arms around her back, and there it was again: the unmistakable, undeniable *something* that burned between them. Something deeper than physical attraction. Her lips sought his but as soon as she began to relax into the kiss she came up against a solid wall. She put a hand to his chest and looked at him seriously.

'I promised to tell you what I did after Yann died,' she said. 'I need to tell you now.'

He looked puzzled. 'Can't it wait?'

'No. Not this. You need to know what I am.' She took a deep breath. 'I sold everything I possessed and when that had gone I sold what remained.'

He looked at her, brow furrowed. She wanted to slap her hands against his chest in frustration that he didn't understand what she meant without having to say it.

'I sold myself, Jack.'

Chapter Fifteen

Blanche watched as understanding filled Jack's eyes and changed into revulsion. She turned her back, unable to bear it any longer and not wanting to see his condemnation. When he spoke behind her, his voice was level and low.

'Why?'

'Because it was all I had,' she said.

He gave a sharp exhalation. Blanche looked back at him. The disgust had vanished and his face was as neutral as his voice. She lifted her chin and met his gaze with a challenge.

'I'm not proud of what I did, but I'm not ashamed either and I won't be condemned for it either. A woman does not have as many resources to draw on as a man. She must use what talents and skills she has.'

'When was the first time?' Jack murmured. He held a hand up and looked away. 'No. Don't answer. I shouldn't ask that. It isn't any of my business.'

Blanche felt her legs begin to buckle. She sat down on the grass, curling her legs beneath her.

'I don't mind,' she said. In truth, now she had begun to share her secret, it felt like a weight had been lifted from her heart.

'Sixteen miles out of Paris I was at an inn. I had run out of money. I had enough to pay for some bread and a meagre bowl of soup, but not enough for my board. The innkeeper suggested I had a choice of sleeping in the stables with the other poor travellers or spending the night in his bed. I'd walked so far and was so weary by that point that it wasn't a hard decision.'

She laughed, seeing his expression growing solemn. How could men imagine the anxiety that women faced on a daily basis when they lived without protection.

'The innkeeper wasn't an ill-looking man and seemed kind. His wife had died not three months earlier and he was lonely. If I had slept in the stables I'd have most likely spent the night awake trying to fend off men in any case. Better to have only one and a soft mattress afterwards.'

Jack gave a grunt that sounded angry, but Blanche knew enough of him to know she was not the one he was cross with.

'The next morning, the innkeeper sent me on my way with a basket of food and a kind word.' She smiled at the memory. 'I sometimes wonder what would have happened if he had asked me to stay longer. Whether I would now be living as an innkeeper's mistress or wife.'

'How many men?' Jack asked quietly.

Blanche felt her lips start to quiver as she counted the times she had allowed men to take their pleasure with her. It was not the memory of the men that made her quake, but knowing what Jack must be thinking of her.

'Less than ten. When I kissed the innkeeper it felt like I was dreaming—not me doing it but someone using my body, and after the first time it became easier. I didn't mind giving myself to men when I had no other possibility. My heart was dead so it didn't matter what I did with my body.'

It *had* been worth it to achieve what she had, and there had even been men who took care to ensure she found the experience enjoyable, but in Jack's company she found herself wishing she were as innocent and whole as she had been on her wedding night with Mael.

'I didn't plan it at first, but I discovered men wanted what I could provide and often I needed what they could offer, be that a bed for the night or money to dress my children. It was a transaction I found easier to make each time, and each time a little more of my heart hardened.'

She folded her arms and waited for Jack to turn his back on her in disgust. He was silent for too long to bear.

'You want me to condemn you for what you did,' he said finally.

Blanche dropped her head but Jack placed his palm beneath her chin, raising it again so she looked into his face.

'Well, I won't. I can't. I only have pity that you were left in such circumstances.'

His voice was gentle. His words themselves choked her. How many in a thousand would be as understanding? She reached for his hand and nestled her fingers deep in his palm. Jack curled his hand round them, keeping her hand within his. He looked out to sea.

'Who can say what I might have done if I had found myself destitute and friendless in a less welcoming home than yours,' he muttered.

'You said you would do honest work. I could have scrubbed floors or carried trays, though it would not have made me as much money. You're better than me, Jack.'

Blanche bit her lip. Now was the time to stop what she intended to do. Ignore the urge she fought so hard to control. If Jack surrendered to

the same urge as she felt, there would be no turning back. She walked slowly back to the stones
and looked at him. He looked puzzled but his
body was tensed, a hunting hound, alert and
ready to spring after a quarry. It excited her to
see the vitality exuding from him.

'Why did you tell me now?'

'Because I wanted you to understand how it
was different with you. I haven't seduced a man
for a long time. When we made love before, I did
it with all of me. I wanted you, Jack. With my
body, but also with my heart. I still do. We both
have so many bitter, painful memories. Let's create a beautiful one together.'

There was a moment then where she thought
she had ruined everything, that Jack had invoked
the memory of Margaret and it was too much for
him to contemplate. He blinked away his thought
and looked back at Blanche. He opened his arms
and she walked into them. They cleaved to each
other, arms tight, bodies crushed together. Jack's
lips found Blanche's and he kissed her with a
slow, measured thoroughness that made her head
spin. They sank to their knees, still clutching at
each other as their kisses became more frenzied
and they could hold back their passion no longer.
As they began to make love Blanche felt whole for
the first time in longer than she could remember.

* * *

Afterwards they lay together, simply holding each other. Blanche discovered that as much as her body yearned for Jack's touch, it was this embrace, this companionship and warmth that her heart had been craving. She felt like a cracked pot, mended so skilfully that the original damage couldn't even be seen.

Clouds began to gather on the horizon. Grey and greyer, they rolled inland, obliterating the sun from view and chilling the air. Even the heat from Jack's body couldn't prevent Blanche from shivering now and it gave her the impetus she had been lacking to move.

She shifted against Jack, reluctant to break the contact between them. He inclined his head to kiss her, and though Blanche responded with enthusiasm, there was sadness looming the edge of her mind now. This was goodbye. She had known all along that Jack was not hers to keep, that this stolen moment of lovemaking—and it was clear to her that there was a deeper emotion than pure physical satisfaction—was the only time they could spend together. The grief welled up as harshly as if he was already in her past. Jack seemed equally disinclined to move and gathered his discarded clothing lethargically. They dressed quickly, with the slightly awkward air of people who had been more intimate than they should have been. When fully clothed once more, they stood facing each other and it seemed to Blanche there was an insubstantial barrier between them created by more than layers of clothes.

'You go first,' she said. 'The path isn't wide, and in any case it will be more discreet.'

'We've just made love in the open on a cliff-top,' Jack said, his mouth twisting into a crooked grin and his brows lifting. 'I think we've left discretion long behind us.'

Blanche smiled, 'Perhaps you're right. But I think I'll stay here a little longer. I know you must be eager to prepare for leaving.'

'I don't have much to pack,' Jack said ruefully.

'Tell Andrey it is my instruction that you can take anything you need—clothes, a weapon, food. Whatever you require.'

'You're too generous. I haven't the means to repay you,' Jack said.

'You aren't in my debt. You've more than paid your way.'

Blanche leaned over and gave him a hug but felt him stiffen in her arms and looked up. Jack was staring down at her with an odd expression.

'I didn't realise I had been paying in advance,' he muttered.

'I don't understand,' Blanche said. But she did, and his next words confirmed her suspicion.

'Was I settling my debts ahead of time just now?' Jack asked. 'Doing what you did to earn your bread?'

He thought she was treating him as she had been treated by so many men.

'Of course you weren't.' She pushed him away and stepped out of reach. 'I meant how you'd defended me from Ronec and worked in my house. Chopping wood and mending nets, not bedding me.'

'I want to believe that,' he said.

'Then believe it!'

She was shaking with anger, unable to believe he was actually saying such things after the closeness they had shared. That he doubted why she had seduced him. The fact that the notion of suggesting payment in kind had crossed her mind when they first met made things worse.

'I would have given you anything you needed in any case,' she snapped, 'but like all the men I've been with, you think I'm doing it for a reason,' Blanche said scornfully. 'Well, I was, and the reason was that I desired you as much as you desired me and I didn't want you to leave without making love to you one more time.'

She threw her arm out in the direction of the

pathway. 'Just go. Take what you need, *without* any obligation. The only payment I shall exact is a memory for myself. I shall dine in my room tonight so we shan't see each other again.'

Jack took a step towards her but halted as she stepped back, hands up before her.

'You do not have my permission to touch me!'

His eyes blazed but he bowed his head and strode away without a word. Blanche watched him go through a film of tears. She slumped back against the stone and sat in the same place she had so recently been in Jack's arms. The argument had flared so quickly and now they would part on hostile terms. She wiped a hand furiously across her eyes.

It was definitely for the best, she told herself, as she made her way down the path. Because if she was not furious with Jack, she did not know how she would be able to endure him leaving. She didn't follow him down to the castle but instead took the concealed turning to the harbour. Even her joy and pride at sitting on board *White Wolf* felt muted and diminished after the argument. Her ships and her identity as Bleiz Mor had been her only comfort during dark times, but as she leaned against the railing and watched until the sun set, that comfort was nothing compared to what she had found in Jack's arms.

* * *

Remorse hit Jack like a fist to the kidneys half-way down the path, as the last traces of resentment slunk away like a dog with a tail between its legs. He leaned against a tree and wiped a hand across his eyes, then stared bleakly back the way he had come.

Had he ever really believed that making love to Blanche had been in return for the clothing and food? Of course not, and he couldn't if his life depended on it work out why he had said such cruel things to her after they had shared such ecstasy. His skin fluttered and tightened, making his frame feel too small for itself at the thought of Blanche's hands skimming over his body, teasing him and summoning him to greater and greater heights of pleasure. At the crucial moment he had pulled away in his determination not to risk pregnancy, she had taken him in her hand and led him to completion.

Perhaps it had been that—the skill and assuredness with which she had drawn the climax from him that made him think of her doing it for the men she had given herself to. He'd been overwhelmed with the richness of the feelings that had enveloped him and had lashed out in jealousy.

How could he have ever said such things aloud? It was far from his finest hour and he ground his teeth in contrition. He'd told Blanche that her past did not matter then proved otherwise in the worst way at the worst possible time. He'd insulted her, and remembering the wounded expression in her eyes was a penance he would perform for the rest of his nights.

He started to walk back up the path, but as it wound around on itself he had second thoughts and turned back. She'd made it clear she wanted to be alone and he would not force his presence on her when she had made her wishes so clear. He would seek her out and speak to her later to beg the forgiveness he had no right to deserve. He'd go down on his knees and swear endless devotion if she would only pardon him for such base accusations.

He returned to the castle and saw Andrey who was sitting with Marie in the courtyard, catching the sun in a corner. The couple were resting with their heads together, hands linked and speaking quietly, laughing over some private matter. The simple sight of such contentment was almost too much for Jack, but he watched from the gateway until Marie kissed her husband's cheek and left him. She passed Jack as they crossed the courtyard and she gave him a nervous curtsy.

'Marie,' he said. 'I want to thank you for the care you gave me. I wish you well.'

She smiled nervously and continued on her way. Jack joined Andrey.

'Did you find Blanche?' Andrey gestured for Jack to join him in Marie's vacated place.

Jack confirmed he had, hoping to convey that nothing had taken place which could not have done in full view of the entire household. There was a knowing look in Andrey's eyes that made Jack wonder if the older man had known what fate he was sending Jack to meet with when he had passed on Blanche's message. He fervently hoped not. He did not want this man, who was protective over Blanche and who Jack had started to regard warmly, to think any less of him for what he had done. He passed on Blanche's instructions with a guilty conscience. It would be better to leave with nothing but the clothes he stood in, rather than let her think he still believed what he had said, but he was not so foolish as to begin his journey with nothing.

'When I'm gone, will you take care of Blanche?' he said.

'Do you think she needs taking care of?' Andrey's brows met in a grey thatch.

'Yes, I do,' Jack said earnestly. 'From men like Ronec, or whoever would seek to use her or do her harm.'

Men like me, he thought grimly. He'd done just as much harm if not more than Ronec ever could.

'I know she's strong but she shouldn't have to be all the time.'

'She's shouldered too many burdens for too long. If only the fighting was over she might cease, but until then she'll carry on doing what she does, even if it destroys her.'

'Running the fort and estate would be taxing even on a man,' Jack agreed. 'I admire her more than she knows.'

Andrey gave him another inscrutable look and Jack got a sense there was more that he knew. Did Andrey know how she had supported herself? Had she lied when she told him she had stopped?

'I care for her but I can't stay,' he said gruffly.

'You have to go. Doesn't mean you can't return,' Andrey said with a shrug.

The thought had crossed Jack's mind before but now it solidified, growing larger. What did England have for him other than sadness and a grave? Here could be a new beginning at the side of a woman he knew now he loved. A woman he suspected loved him back. He needed to speak to Blanche and see if there was any possibility of her wanting the same thing.

Blanche didn't appear at dinner and Jack barely touched his food. He lingered after the rest of the household had left but Blanche seemed to be keeping her intention of dining alone. Jack returned to his room but instead of entering he paused at the turn of the stair. Blanche's room was above his. She forbade anyone from entering but the thought of not seeing her left him trembling. He climbed the stairs and knocked on the door. There was no answer, even when he knocked more firmly. She wouldn't know who was knocking and he worried she had decided to refuse all visitors. He should go, but his need to see her and make amends was too great. Cautiously, he lifted the latch and pushed the door open a crack.

'Blanche?'

There was no answer and he sensed the room was empty. Knowing he was trespassing but drawn irresistibly to discover Blanche's home, he entered.

The room was light and airy but not what he had expected. Unlike the richly decorated hall on the ground floor, with the tapestries and expensive furniture, Blanche's suite was almost bare. Tapestry frames stood before the windows but there was almost as little furniture as there was in Jack's own room. All her wealth was displayed in the public rooms.

The bed that stood in the centre of the floor was hung with mismatched curtains. Jack ran his fingers over the threadbare blue drapes at the end and found tears that had been repaired with neat, almost invisible stitches. The scarlet curtains that hung at each side were in better condition but faded to dull pink where the sunlight had bleached the colour from them. In winter they must provide little protection from the bitter winds. The bed itself was covered in an intricately embroidered counterpane, repaired carefully and partially hidden beneath a pile of furs similar to the one on Jack's bed. He suspected his had once belonged here. He stroked the nearest fur, his imagination wreaking havoc on his senses as he pictured Blanche lying there. His conscience pricked, regretting that he had ever intruded, and he turned to leave.

Blanche was standing in the doorway, hands rigid at her side, her eyes blazing with fury.

'I told you never to come up here,' she said, each word a shard of ice. 'You are the first person ever to disobey my orders. First you insult me, now you violate my hospitality in the basest way possible. Tell me why I shouldn't throw you out right now?'

Chapter Sixteen

Blanche flung a hand out, pointing to the door.

'Well? Why shouldn't I summon my servants and throw you out of the fort?'

'I can't. You'd be right to.' Jack's guts twisted. 'I have no defence. I should have left when I realised you weren't here but I was surprised by what I found. Your room is so bare.'

She nodded, face like thunder.

'Shall I tell you why I live like this?' Blanche snapped. She continued without waiting for his answer, though he would not have dreamed of interrupting her. 'It is because I have so little and every week is a battle to survive. I spend all my money on the rooms that visitors might see. I could spend some on this room but I choose not to, and what does it matter. I am—usually—the only one who sees it.'

She walked to a small table before the window. On it was a casket not much bigger than her hand, with a plain clasp. She opened it and Jack saw the glint of silver before she closed the lid again with a snap.

'As long as I keep up the appearance of a wealthy widow, I stand a chance of keeping my liberty.'

'Liberty?'

'From marriage,' she said, turning her eyes on him. 'Ronec would not miss the opportunity to take me as a wife if he could claim I could not support myself. Others would have the same idea. They would take what little I have left and my independence along with it.'

She gave him an arch smile. 'Sleeping on a lumpy mattress in threadbare hangings is a small price to pay. Don't you agree?'

She was right, but such fierce pride made him sad. Was this what Andrey meant about her living as she did? If she were so determined to keep her independence, why would she ever agree to what he had come to ask?

She stood up, facing Jack, and her face became marble.

'Now you know. Is there anything else you need to see? You're leaving soon so I trust you'll keep my secret. I have no fear you'll share your knowledge with Ronec.'

'You don't have to ask that,' Jack said fervently. 'I would die before I told him anything.'

He stepped closer to Blanche. She did not move away.

'What did you want?' Blanche asked. Her voice was still cold.

'I was looking for you. To say farewell.'

'We already said goodbye,' Blanche said. 'It didn't end particularly well if you can recall it.'

Her expression was as cold as her voice, with disdain in her eyes, though her cheeks were beginning to blaze red.

'That's why I came. It wasn't the farewell we should have had. I wanted to see you again,' Jack said. 'I can never say goodbye to you too many times. I have so few memories you can surely forgive me for wanting to create more, however sad they make me feel.'

Blanche frowned. 'Being with me made you sad?'

'Leaving you makes me sad. Being with you gives me more joy than I thought possible.'

'You've got a tongue of silver,' Blanche said. Her cheeks flushed, but a little of the ire in her eyes faded.

'Will you pardon me?' Jack asked.

Her eyes flickered. She bit her lip. Jack held his breath.

'You've forgiven me so many times,' she said. 'It would be churlish of me not to extend you the same courtesy on this occasion.'

'Thank you,' Jack said.

'Perhaps I would like a better farewell, too.'

A small smile played about Blanche's lips. Instinct told him she wanted him as much as he wanted her, physically at least, even if the emotion that filled his heart wasn't reciprocated as deeply. She had said often enough she didn't want a husband, but a man to satisfy her needs was a different matter, and he was more than willing to be that man.

'I wanted to ask you something,' Jack said. The mention of his departure reminded him of why he had come searching for her. 'I'm still leaving tomorrow but that doesn't mean I can't return. If you'd like me to, that is.'

He looked at Blanche expectantly.

'What for?'

'To see you again.' He stroked her arm, feeling her skin flutter in answer to the beating of his heart, which leapt to life as he touched her. 'To be with you.'

She watched him with uncertainty in her eyes.

'Blanche, I care for you deeply. Don't you realise that? This afternoon wasn't just about making love. It was about more than just gratifying our physical desires. For me, at least. Is it wrong to hope that you care for me, too?'

Blanche put her palm on his chest, causing fires to ignite within him. 'Jack I do…care for you. But your life is in England.'

'What if it isn't?' he said. Her hesitation plagued him. Had she been about to say more, or less than *care*? 'What if I get there and find there were good reasons for me leaving beyond Margaret's death?'

'What if you don't?' She eyed him seriously. 'Don't make any promises until you know.'

He slid his hand down her arm and watched her shiver. She looked away and he thought he had pushed her too hard. Or maybe he had misjudged her feelings.

'If I were to offer you my heart, would you accept it?' he asked.

She looked back at him. 'Would you expect me to marry you? I've told you I don't want another husband.'

She was like a bird that would die if caged. Jack did want to marry her now she had spoken the word, but like a bird, if he clutched too tightly she would fly from him.

'Would you want a lover?' he said. 'For as long as we both choose to be with each other. Whatever I did in my former life brought me to France. Could I be a part of your life when I'm here?'

'You think you know me but we've spent so little time together. You may decide you don't like me after all.'

'Life is a risk,' Jack said. 'You told me it took you time to remember how to live after you were widowed. We can learn together.'

Blanche put her arms around herself. Jack couldn't remember seeing her looking so vulnerable. He wanted to lift the cares from her shoulders.

'What's wrong?'

Blanche looked at the floor. 'I hear your offer and I feel like it is pulling me towards a cliff edge. I worry that to accept it would be leaping out over the whirlpool and plunging to the rocks below.'

So she wanted to. Jack put a hand to her face, lifting it so he could see her eyes. They were brimming with uncertainty.

'My love is not the whirlpool,' he whispered. 'It is the light on the shore that guides you to safety.'

He ran his hands up her arms from wrist to shoulder then slipped them round her back and down to settle in the curve at the space of her spine.

'A silver tongue,' she repeated with a sigh.

'Let me stay with you tonight,' he breathed. 'Decide in the morning.'

She wound her arms around his waist, edging closer until their hips brushed, causing Jack to shiver with suppressed lust. He growled softly in the back of his throat and Blanche's smile grew more sensual as she lifted her mouth to his and kissed him slowly. She dragged her fingers down his back and up again, her nails scraping as they reached his neck and he grew hard. A groan escaped his throat, muffled against her soft neck. Blanche opened her eyes and smiled at him with the same wanton look that had driven him wild on the clifftop. The raw longing and wildness in her eyes sent blood rushing through him.

Her fingers were already pulling determinedly at the tapes at his waist to free him and though he strained against the constricting cloth, he covered her hand, staying the motion. When they'd coupled on the clifftop it had been a frantic, purely carnal act. They hadn't even had the self-control to undress before hurling themselves at each other. Now he intended to savour the experience. Blanche was used to being in charge and there had been enough times Jack had been under her control. Now he intended to redress the balance a little.

'Slowly,' he commanded. 'We have all night.

We're not going to touch each other like that until we're both naked and lying atop those furs.'

Blanche's black eyes gleamed and she nodded meekly. She put her lips close to his ear. 'Then you had better help me. I'm wearing a lot of clothes.'

She held her arms out wide to the sides and her eyes flickered to her girdle, held in place by a semicircular buckle.

'Undress me, please, Jack.'

Jack grinned. As he had suspected, this was a new experience for her and he intended to take his time. He unbuckled the girdle slowly and let it fall to the floor, easing the heavy velvet mantle over her shoulders. Her sleeves were narrow at the wrist, four buttons on each. One arm at a time, Jack undid them with hands that trembled. He regarded the veins in her wrists as though they were the most sensual sight in the world. He lifted her hand and blew a long, measured breath over the delicate flesh and heard her sigh. He moved around behind her, hands travelling slowly across her form until he was able to loosen the laces and slip her gown down until it fell to the floor. She stood clad only in her cream shift. His final act was to draw the combs one by one from her hair until it fell tumbling free. He couldn't resist running his fingertip down the nape of her neck and she dropped her head back, moaning.

'I want you now.'

Jack burned to touch her but instead he stepped back and gave her a stern look.

'No,' he said. 'My turn.'

She looked back at him over her shoulder then turned around and circled him, slipping her arms around him from behind and easing the jerkin from his shoulders then lifting the tunic over his head. The exhilaration consuming him deepened. Undressing Blanche had been erotic, but to stand submissively while she returned the favour was even more arousing.

He only had to help when it came to removing his boots, balancing on one foot in turn while Blanche tugged them off and threw it behind her with a cry of victory. They smiled at each other, eyes laughing. When Jack was clad only in his hose, Blanche dropped to one knee before him and resumed untying the tapes at his waist, her eyes never leaving his. He was panting like a virgin on his wedding night, hot and agitated, by the time she slid the hose down his legs and he stood naked before her.

He wanted her to stay down there, to take him in her hands, in her mouth. He wanted to lift her and fill her, to claim her as his own.

She solved the dilemma by standing and slipping her arms around his neck and drawing him into a kiss. He put his hands on her buttocks and lifted her bodily, backing her towards the bed with her legs around his waist. By the time he had laid her down, he was so hard and desperate for her that obeying his own dictate to be unhurried would be a challenge. They kissed slowly, arms about each other, hands stroking and exploring, teasingly light and hungrily firm.

Jack ran his hands over the length of Blanche's body, feeling the contours through the thin cloth. She was not yet naked and the hidden secrets were a torment.

'Take this off,' he said, sliding his hand beneath the neck and running his hand over her shoulder.

He saw a warning in Blanche's eyes that made him hesitate and lift his hands away.

'I'm not a young woman, Jack,' she said. 'I've borne children and had pregnancies. I might not be what you hope for.'

How could she even think for a moment that was a concern? The frankness was what he had come to expect but the self-consciousness was startling and at odds with the Blanche he had grown to treasure. A rush of protectiveness filled him. Whatever she pretended, she was more vulnerable than she liked to show.

'I want to see you,' he said. 'All of you. I want to feel you, taste you…'

He knelt between her legs and put his hands beneath her shift, sliding them up the length of her legs and teasing the garment higher and higher. The scent of her filled his nostrils, spinning his head and waking the remaining senses that still lay dormant. He forgot about being slow and dragged the shift up and off her, then gazed at her naked form.

Her waist was slender but her belly was soft and slightly plump. It bore the trace of fine lines where the skin had stretched as she had carried her babies. There were similar lines beneath her breasts and across her thighs. They were lighter in colour, silvery in the moonlight against her creamy skin. To Jack they were beautiful—nothing like the red lesions that crisscrossed Jack's chest from the rocks. He traced the outline of her belly with his fingertip, causing Blanche to shiver.

'You are beautiful,' he said. He kissed her. First on the lips. Then between her breasts. Then on the round mound of her belly. She sighed and spread her limbs out. Jack's lips continued downwards slowly and methodically, kissing the lines beneath her belly, then down between her legs.

Only when Blanche was whimpering and her fingernails threatened to tear the skin from his back as she pulled him towards her did Jack permit himself to satisfy the desires that consumed him, too.

When he woke, Jack was disoriented. When he looked towards the window the light was brighter than he was used to in his room. He couldn't locate himself at first and the panic that had first descended on him when he awoke after the shipwreck threatened to return.

Blanche lay beside him, face down, her black hair spread across her naked back and one arm crooked up around her face. Jack's eyes followed the length of her spine down to the covers that lay jumbled around her hips. The shape of her buttocks and thighs rising beneath the sheet was enough to bring him out in a sweat.

He should get out of bed and dress. It was daybreak and Nevez's ship would be leaving on the morning tide. Jack would need to hurry to make his way to Benestin in time to meet him. The longer he stayed here, the harder it would be to leave Blanche.

He had been wrong to come here last night. Wrong to make love to her again, but he'd been unable to resist the pull towards her. Deep warmth spread through Jack, stirring more than his cock. It spread throughout his limbs and plucked at his heart. This was where he should be. With Blanche. In her bed and arms.

Blanche stirred and half rolled over. Her eyes focused on Jack and she stiffened as she realised she had a bedfellow, then her body relaxed and she gave him a sultry smile. She rolled fully on to her back and pulled the coverlet up, concealing herself.

Jack plucked at a stray thread.

'I have to go.'

'Yes, you do. You don't want to miss your tide.'

Blanche craned her head and Jack bent to kiss her. Only briefly, because if he allowed himself to indulge to the extent he wanted to, he would never be able to leave the room. She was stronger than he and pushed him away gently, ending the kiss.

'Please come back when you can,' she said. 'I would be glad to see you.'

Jack squeezed her hand, heart swelling. He climbed out of bed and walked to the window. He was naked but no one could see him from the courtyard. He didn't remember his marriage to Margaret being so free of inhibitions but she'd been younger and modest. There was nothing that would come between him and Blanche. Nothing they could do that would cause shame or censure. Freedom stretched before him thrillingly and he knew his decision was made.

He looked at the jewel case and wondered if that was where she had kept his cross and pushed the thought away. He had left it in his room rather than wear it to come up to Blanche's room. Had he been intent on seduction from the start? He was honest enough to admit it to himself that he had nurtured those hopes. Beside the jewel case stood an open pot of some waxy substance. He sniffed it and caught a trace of the scent Blanche wore. He breathed it in, storing the smell in his memory. He'd be able to see her as soon as he brought it to mind.

His clothes lay strewn across the floor, mingled with Blanche's where they had undressed each other. He stooped to pick them up and as he bent he spotted the heel of a boot peeping from behind the folding screen. He walked towards it, wondering how it had been thrown so far. Blanche cried a warning to stop but by then he had found himself behind the panel and bent to retrieve the boot.

It wasn't his. It was too small to fit his foot, but was a man's boot, none the less. He looked at it in confusion, not understanding who it could belong to. Blanche was standing before him with the bed sheet wrapped around herself. Her face was white and her eyes were wild.

'I told you to stop!'

Jack looked around and his eye fell on a folded bundle with a hat on top and his heart seemed to stop with an almost audible thud.

He recognised the hat and cloak. They belonged to Bleiz Mor. His heart gave a painful thump, lurching back into life. The man's clothes were folded alongside Blanche's, clearly belonging there. He unfolded the cloak and saw the mummer's mask.

'You lied to me,' he said. He picked up the mask. The wolf's face grinned up at him. 'You told me there was nothing between you and Bleiz Mor, yet I find his clothes in your room.'

Blanche strode forward and snatched the mask from his hands.

'Is this why no one is allowed here?' Jack asked. 'Is the Sea Wolf your lover?'

To his astonishment, Blanche began to laugh, holding the mask to her breast, her eyes shut tight. Her shoulders heaved and Jack realised to his horror that the gulps were turning into sobs. A nagging sense that he had misunderstood the situation grew inside him. She had always been at such pains to point out she had no lovers. Was she an unwilling participant in whatever took place?

Cautiously, he reached out and took her by the shoulders. She did not protest as he drew her closer, wrapping his arms around her until she was pressed tightly against him. The scent of her perfume and the feel of her against him sent a rush of desire coursing through him.

'Does he force you? Say the word and I will kill him.'

'Kill him? Oh, Jack.' Blanche raised her head and looked into Jack's eyes. She bit her lip. 'You still don't understand, do you?'

'Then tell me,' he urged. He ran his thumb along the ridge of her cheekbone, capturing a stray tear and erasing the tracks.

A haunted look crossed her face.

'The Sea Wolf is not my lover.'

He looked at the mask that Blanche was twisting around in her hands and he understood what he had been missing. Another stitch in the tapestry. He raised his head slowly and met her eyes. She knew what he had guessed.

'It's you, isn't it.' He had to force the words from his throat. 'You are Bleiz Mor.'

Chapter Seventeen

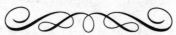

Jack's complexion had become as grey as when he was close to death. His eyes brimmed with hurt and anger.

'You have lied to me about everything!'

'Everything I told you before was the truth,' Blanche protested. 'I walked to Paris and claimed Yann's body. I worked my way back. You know how I supported myself on the journey and how I raised the money I needed to buy my home.' She raised her chin and put her hands on her hips, looking deep into his eyes. 'I told you then I am not ashamed of what I did, and I refuse to be judged by anyone for that.'

'But you didn't tell me the whole truth, did you.' Jack's voice was a snarl that tore into Blanche's chest, ripping it open and exposing her heart to the cold air.

'No. I didn't.'

'Why did you do it? Once you were home?'

'I've told you that, too. Bleiz Mor sails for revenge. I bought the house, and I fitted out the ships. I cannot bring my husband back but I will send every man to join him that I can. We fought for the same cause and I have not stopped fighting because he is dead.'

At the word she felt the iron returning to her blood, strengthening her. 'The French have ravaged Brittany, destroying lives and families. I will do everything in my power to stop them.'

She gripped the mask, grinding it in her fists. 'The country is divided, Jack. How can it heal when the two factions believe such opposing things? We know who our rightful Duke is, but rich and powerful men insist on twisting events until they get what they want. Now I have the means to redress some of the wrongs, I use them.'

'By fighting and killing?' Jack asked. Now his voice had more scorn than she had heard when she described her whoring.

'Would you ask that of a man? Would you judge a man for fighting for his home and defending his country? Of course you would not! Don't judge me more harshly because of my sex!'

Fury rose in her. She didn't care if he was outraged and hurting. 'If that is what it takes, then, yes, I will fight and I will kill if necessary. Just as you would to defend your home.'

He grunted a grudging agreement and looked at his hands.

'Did you manage to kit out two ships with what you made with your body?'

'Like the horse I sold, I'm not so valuable.' She looked at him drily. 'No. I bought jewels and clothes. When I presented a wealthy appearance it allowed me access to the commander of the English navy who were in support of de Montfort. I threw myself on his mercy.'

'Just his mercy?' Jack asked in a low voice.

'Yes! I told them of the sacrifice Yann had made to ensure the safety of the English forces and that I wanted to avenge his death. I spoke convincingly and thanks to the grace of King Edward the English gave me *White Wolf* and paid for it to be fitted out. The condition was that I provided the stake to equip *White Hawk* and used them to further our mutual cause. Then I asked the men who had fought with Yann and the fishermen in the villages here to be my crew.'

She walked to the window that faced the way Jack's didn't and leaned her hands on the sill. She could tell him that her ties to his country went deeper, that the household Fransez now lived in was in England, but he had forfeited the right to learn anything else about her.

Jack picked up the hat, turning it round in his hands. 'All this time you let me think someone else was Bleiz Mor. I thought you were helpless. I knew Ronec held something over you but I had no idea what.'

He tightened his fists against his sides and looked back at Blanche. The anger in his voice was terrible to hear but the look of betrayal in his eyes was worse than a sword through her guts.

'I had to do it,' Blanche said. Tears made her eyes blur. She wiped them away angrily.

'No, you didn't,' Jack snapped. He spun away and walked swiftly to the window, leaning his hands on the sill and bowing his head. 'You've lied constantly.'

'That's unfair!' Blanche exclaimed. 'I told you my biggest secret—my worst shame.'

'You didn't tell me this one.' His face was bleak.

'I didn't think it mattered. I thought I could hide it until you left. Until you asked me this morning, I never dreamed that was possible you might stay. I delayed giving you the box at first because I thought it was for the best. I didn't know if we could trust you and Ronec would have demanded your death or arrest if it had held something incriminating. I couldn't let that happen.'

'Why not?' Jack asked. He looked over his shoulder but past Blanche and would not meet her eyes.

'I wanted to keep you here a little longer. Because I was growing to care about you.'

He met her gaze but there was none of the tenderness she had seen when they made love. Only disbelief and pain filled his eyes.

'How can I believe that after all your other lies?' he said bitterly. 'You've dripped out the truth when you had no choice and this is the same. What other secrets have you kept from me?'

'None!' Blanche cried. 'There is nothing else. I thought it didn't matter, because you would be gone soon. Then you told me you would stay and I realised I couldn't tell you.'

She held her hands out, wanting to hold him but he shook his head.

'Don't touch me now. Not ever.'

His words broke her.

'Were you ever going to tell me?' His voice cracked. It tore Blanche's heart to shreds.

'I knew you would despise me.'

Her voice was small. She hated the sound of it, knowing how openly she was showing her despair. Where was the woman who bedded men without a care? Who laughed at their pleas and hardened her heart? How had Jack managed to crush the walls she had so carefully built around herself?

He laughed bitterly.

'Do you know I suspected Ronec might be Bleiz Mor, even though I had seen the two of you together? What hold does he have over you? Don't even think of lying to me now.'

Blanche felt nausea rising. 'I had to raise the money to equip the ships and pay the men myself but I couldn't do it without help. He had been a friend of Mael's family. I thought I could trust him.'

'You went to bed with him, didn't you?'

Blanche writhed at the contempt in Jack's voice but she reminded herself that she had sworn to regret nothing. She lifted her chin and looked him in the eye. 'Yes, I did.'

'How many times?'

She couldn't bear the disgust that filled Jack's voice. She didn't want him to see her own loathing for herself and the man she had given herself to.

'Does that matter?' she whispered.

'I don't know.' His jaw tightened and he glared at her. 'How many times did you make love to him?'

'I've never made love to him!'

She faced Jack, cheeks growing hot, and folded her arms around herself as if that could offer protection from the searing gaze that burned her.

'I had to beg Ronec for more money than he had originally pledged. The cost was a week in his bed. But I've been paying the price for his silence ever since.'

'Why does he want to marry you?' Jack asked. 'If he can claim you when he likes, what more does he need?'

'A husband controls his wife's possessions. He wants control of the ships. He thinks that limiting ourselves to attacking the French is a waste when the sea is full of cargo vessels. That's why he encourages the wrecking.

'You know I refused to take part in the wrecking. I've banned all my men from doing it again. I saved you because it was the right thing to do and I'm glad you lived.'

'But if I had been on a ship you attacked, you would not have hesitated before ending my life,' Jack pointed out.

'No. Not through choice, but because it is what I have to do.'

Jack covered his face with his hands.

'I believed you to be virtuous and innocent. I came to your aid! I offered to protect you.'

'I didn't ask you to!' Blanche said. 'I told you time and again that I needed no one to defend me and that I am no frail woman who must cling to a man. If you chose to ignore what I said, that is your doing. The mistake is yours.'

But she had tried to give that impression, hadn't she? She'd wanted him to think her virtuous and chaste—a poor widow living in solitude. She dropped her head so he didn't see the pain she felt.

'A mistake I shall put behind me as soon as possible,' Jack said. He looked suddenly tired. As weak as the day he had woken from his fevered sleep.

'It is your countrymen who aided me, Jack. You and I are on the same side. Why can't you see that?'

He looked at her wearily. 'We're not on the same side, Blanche. The only side you are on is your own.'

She spun around, glaring at him. 'And I have to be! Ultimately, who else is on my side? No one! Ronec isn't. I was on my husbands' sides as a loyal wife to both of them for many years. Now I stand alone.'

She dropped her head. 'I was foolish to ever think it might be different.'

Her legs began to tremble. She locked her knees, refusing to show her weakness.

'You said you cared for me,' she whispered.

He stepped close and reached out a hand, holding it close to her cheek. She felt the warmth emanating from his palm and for a brief moment thought he was going to caress her but he withdrew it.

'I do care for you, but how can I stay knowing what you did?'

'I will not insult you by asking.'

Jack nodded, his jaw tightening. He pulled on his shirt and shrugged himself into his jerkin. He bent down and picked up the hat then held it out to Blanche. When she did not take it he tossed it on to the bed.

'Thank you for your hospitality and care, Blanche. I shall try remember those rather than this.'

He walked away and she made no attempt to follow.

Blanche waited until she knew Jack had left the castle. She had plenty of thoughts to keep her occupied. Recriminations and self-loathing. She waited longer still, until she could be sure he would be at Benestin and probably on board Nevez's ship. She wondered which port in England he would land in. Now there were two reasons her heart clenched when she thought of that island. She dressed in the costume of the

Sea Wolf, which now seemed hateful to her. She pinned her hair and curled it tightly and jammed it under the hat. A lump in her throat threatened to choke her and she craved a cup of wine to force the lump away. She marched downstairs and found Andrey. He raised his eyebrows at the sight of her.

'Jack left,' he said.

'I know.' She forced her eyes to stay clear and dry.

'Word came from men at St Petroc. The French are sailing from Brest tonight.'

He looked at her keenly. How could she tell him she wanted to hide away and curl into a ball rather than attack? He would never understand. Tonight she would sail. Tomorrow she would explain.

'Make ready the crew. We sail to meet them.'

She mounted her horse and made her way to Ronec's house. She found him alone and strode up to him with a purposeful manner. She told him of Andrey's message. 'We sail on the evening tide,' she said. '*White Hawk* needs her Captain.'

Ronec lifted his chin. 'It's been a while since I saw you wearing that. I had wondered if you had surrendered it for ever.'

Blanche ground her teeth. 'No. My guest has left. Now we can continue as I promised.'

Ronec gave her a lecherous grin. 'Then does *White Wolf*'s Captain need me, too?'

Blanche turned her back. She'd lost Jack and the possibility of happiness. What did it matter if she gave herself to Ronec? The thought was abhorrent but she barely cared. No. She could not do that. No man would have her now. Jack would be her final lover.

'I'll see you by the dock,' she told Ronec, and walked away.

Blanche stood on the deck of *White Wolf.* There was no need for her to give orders. Andrey was a more than capable First Mate and gave commands efficiently. She watched as the oarsmen rowed beyond the inlet into the open sea. The dusk sun had sunk low and the waves were a palette of gold and purples. Foam crested them and salt spray misted her face, damping the mask over her face. The cog surged forward. Blanche breathed deeply, drawing the clean air into her body. She loved the tilt of the deck beneath her and the wind gusting around her but tonight the elation was shadowed with sadness.

Tonight would be her final voyage. The notion had been creeping up on her like a sea fret since her abhorrence at the wreck and with Jack's condemnation it had solidified. Bleiz Mor would retire. She would miss this feeling of freedom more than anything once she gave it up.

Not quite everything. She would miss Jack more than anything else.

You find a way to live, she had told him. The words seemed hollow now. Blanche would try to live the life that she had led Jack into believing she led. He would never know but it would satisfy her to do it.

She gazed out at the ocean to hide her emotions from the crew and watched the gulls flying overhead.

A shout from Andrey brought her attention back to the present. She looked where he was pointing. A sail came into view in the distance and another one far beyond that. Both cogs. These must be the French ships that she was searching for. She bellowed to the men.

'For Brittany. For our freedom and honour.'

As they cheered and set to work turning the ship and relaying the message to *White Hawk* through a series of whistles, Blanche climbed up to the front tower to get a better view, drawing her sword. Her ships were sleek and light and cut through the water with ease. *White Hawk* came alongside, ready to trap the ship if the Captain tried to break free. They gained on the closest cog that was tacking lazily around the coast. As they drew near enough to see the figures on deck, Blanche drew her sword and threw her arm into the air. Her crew screamed and hollered their intent.

The crew of the cog began hurrying around, passing boxes below deck. Blanche narrowed her eyes, puzzled. She would not expect the crew of a warship to behave in such an odd way. They should be arming themselves and ready to repel the attack.

This was not the French warship, but a private vessel carrying cargo. The cog was similar to Blanche's ships but without the fore tower that marked it out as a military vessel.

No one on this ship deserved to die. Blanche sheathed her sword and began giving the order to call off the attack.

'Enough,' she screamed. 'Stand down. We are not taking this ship.'

A susurrus of anger and surprise enveloped her.

'I was mistaken. This is not the ship we're looking for,' she said forcefully. 'This is not our enemy.'

She repeated her orders and slowly *White Wolf* began to wheel about. Blanche turned back to look at the cog and a figure moving towards the front of the boat caught her eye. The man walked to the prow and climbed on to the rail. He raised himself up, standing straight backed and staring directly at *White Wolf.*

Jack.

Blanche couldn't hold the cry in, though the wind tore his name from her and she knew he wouldn't hear it. He saw her though, and for one moment that chilled her blood, she stared into the eyes of the man she loved. This was Nevez's ship but it should have sailed on the morning tide. Something must have caused a delay and now they were in Blanche's path.

The intention to retreat had been relayed to *White Hawk*, but Ronec gave no indication of preparing to follow the order. Blanche leapt on to the rail, standing in the same spot Jack was standing. She drew her sword and pointed it at Ronec.

'You give the order to turn now,' she bellowed, 'or the ship I sink will be yours!'

'Have you lost your mind?' Andrey cried, coming to her side.

'Jack is on that ship.'

She would rather sink her own ship than see Jack's life snatched away. The sea had surren-

dered him once but he could not be so lucky a
second time. Andrey repeated Blanche's order.

Ronec finally believed she was in earnest
and she heard him giving the order to his crew.
Both ships came about, heading back to the cove.
Blanche ran to the back of the ship and climbed
on to the rear tower. Jack was still standing
watching. As Nevez's ship began to move away
he walked down the length of it, keeping Blanche
in view. She couldn't see his face clearly any longer but raised her hand in farewell. Slowly, Jack
raised his and they stood watching until the other
became too small to see.

Too small for him to see the tears that streamed
down her cheeks and too far away for him to hear
her whispered words.

'I'm sorry.'

As soon as *White Wolf* had moored, Blanche
walked towards *White Hawk*, intending to explain
to the crew her reasons for withdrawing. Ronec
stepped in front of her.

'What were you playing at?' His face was
florid with fury. 'We had a perfect opportunity.
We could have crushed that ship like swatting
a fly.'

'It wasn't a French ship,' Blanche explained,
aware of both crews gathering round to listen. 'It
was a cargo vessel.'

'Cargo be damned!' Ronec spat. 'What do I care for that?'

Blanche lowered her voice. 'Jack was on board.'

Ronec spat at her feet. 'Now I know why you retreated. He's gone now, and I've tolerated your waywardness long enough.'

He took her by the wrist, fingers tightening.

'What are you doing!' Blanche exclaimed, trying to pull away.

'What I should have done a long time ago. I'm relieving you of your command.'

'Mutiny?' Blanche sneered.

Ronec laughed. 'Call it that if you wish. I call it sense. I knew a woman was too weak to lead and now I've seen the proof. Twice in a row you stayed your hand when you shouldn't have.'

'You have no right to do this!'

'And how do you intend to stop me?'

Ronec looked around at the men watching. Blanche realised that although Andrey was reaching for his sword and a handful of others were shifting and looking disapproving, most of the crew were standing passively and watching. Ronec had said once that the men looked to him as a leader and he was right. She would get no support from them.

'I'm taking control of the ships, and you are coming with me now.'

He pulled on her arm to lead her away. Fury blinded Blanche. It didn't matter now that she had intended to give up anyway. She would die before relinquishing control to Ronec and fight to the end before letting him take her. She reached awkwardly behind her back with her free hand and pulled out the slender dagger from her belt. She swung it wildly upwards, hoping to strike deep in his throat, but she was not using her usual hand and the blow caught him across the centre of the chest, slicing the flesh rather than stabbing as the tip raked upwards. Ronec cried out as blood seeped from the cut. It was not deep enough to do any damage. Blanche twisted round and drove the blade into his shoulder, feeling the hardness of bone.

Ronec let go of her wrist with a roar of pain and pushed her away. He pulled the knife free then delivered a backhanded blow to the face that felled Blanche. Everything went quiet then started to buzz. She barely had time to recover before he aimed a kick at her face and she had to roll, shielding her face with her arms before he struck. His second blow caught her in the stomach, knocking the breath from her and making her feel sick with pain.

'Bitch! Whore!'

Andrey drew his sword and rushed forward.

'No. Don't,' she wheezed. Someone had to look after the castle and her people. If Andrey was taken too, or worse, Blanche would be completely friendless. 'I'll go with him.'

Blanche pushed herself to her knees, hands spread before her, breathing heavily. Her vision cleared and she saw the dagger had fallen within her reach. Ronec was clutching his shoulder and ashen and hadn't noticed. As he came to haul Blanche to her feet she threw herself at the dagger, grasped it and stabbed out wildly. It embedded in his thigh and he screamed.

'Three strikes to me,' she whispered, smiling up at him triumphantly.

'You'll die for this, whore.'

'I won't die alone,' she crowed, looking him up and down. Ronec looked at the blood welling on the front of his trouser leg and frowned. His cream-coloured tunic was already crimson at the shoulder. He was growing paler and paler. Blanche had seen men die before. She'd been the cause enough times. Some deaths had caused her to mourn, others had left her impassive. If Ronec died she would sing with joy. But if he didn't, she was damned.

'Get her out of my sight,' he wheezed.

Hands seized Blanche from behind, pinning her arms, clutching her waist and that had to be her only satisfaction as his men pulled her upright and dragged her up the cliff path. She looked back and saw Ronec being carried up by four of his men. His shoulder had been dressed in makeshift bandages and a rope tourniquet was around his thigh. He drew near and despite his obvious pain and the sheen of sweat on his brow, he gave Blanche an evil smile as he was lifted into his saddle.

'The *Prévôt* will hear that you attacked me at first light. Your fate will be in his hands. A woman with no man to support her, who attacked an influential member of the community? You have no friends. You are alone.'

Her legs gave way. Alone. No more than she deserved.

She was bundled on to her horse and her hands bound behind her back so she could not seize the reins and make a bid for freedom. With a man at either side holding the bridle, she was taken to Ronec's home and pushed into a storeroom, not unlike the one Jack had been kept in when he first arrived. She screamed and bellowed, but no one came. Finally, she sank on to the floor in despair. Her face and belly ached and her throat was parched. Unlike Jack's room, there was no straw pallet to lie on.

Jack was alive. That was the only victory she

could claim from the day. At least he would return to England in safety. Despite her taunts, Ronec was unlikely to die from the blood loss as the wounds weren't severe enough to be fatal. Infection might taint his blood. It struck her as ironic that her life would depend on his.

She'd ruined everything. She'd been so close to true happiness but now Jack knew what she was and he had gone. He'd forgiven her for so many lies and secrets but seeing what she truly was had been too much, even for a man so understanding and compassionate.

And he was right to condemn her. She had been the gentle, innocent woman he wanted her to be but life had hardened her. Vengeance had allowed her to become a killer and thief. She was no better than the wreckers. The weight crushed her like the boulders that lined the shoreline around her home.

Her only consolation was that he had recognised her and knew she had called off the attack. The hand he raised in answer to her own had to be a simple acknowledgement of that. If he bothered to think of her at all, she hoped that in time he would remember the times they had been fond of each other instead of the lies and deception. The memories of the happiness she had felt in Jack's company and the ecstasy she had known in his arms were her only solace now. Whatever fate she was due, she was alone and friendless and could do nothing but wait to see what the morning would bring.

Chapter Eighteen

It was mid-morning when Jack stood on Winch Street in front of Fortin and Rudhale's Bristol offices. He was travel stained and weary from the week-long journey first to Roscoff then to England, but old Gilbert Rudhale greeted him warmly. Jack felt embarrassed he couldn't quite return the embrace with genuine affection that the reunion obviously merited. It was clear the wine merchant was obviously pleased to see him back.

'We received your last report,' Rudhale explained. 'When you didn't follow as expected we feared you had been lost at sea.'

Jack explained his predicament over bread and cheese, accompanied by a bottle of extremely good wine, omitting certain facts that he had decided would be his secret until the day he died. He finished by asking if Rudhale knew where Jack had lived. Rudhale named a village where a house could be found and, in a sorrowful voice, where Margaret's resting place was.

It was within half a day's easy ride and Jack decided to leave straight away. As he thanked Gilbert again, another man entered. This was Henry Fortin and the entire process was repeated, but as Jack finally exited, Henry exclaimed, 'Your chest! Did you take your chest?'

Jack raised his brows.

'You leave a chest here when you travel. I believe it is important documents you want to keep safe.'

As Gilbert bustled off to find the item, Jack commended himself on his foresight. Not everything he owned was at the bottom of the sea. He was presented with a substantial-sized box with two locks but only one key. He tried it in both locks but it refused to turn in the second. Presumably, Jack had hidden the other for safekeeping and he suppressed his irritation at himself for being so conscientious.

'A man came asking after your whereabouts not three days past and if you had left anything,' Henry said. 'I didn't like the look of him, pasty-faced whelp who couldn't recognise a good Burgundy from a slice gut! I told him to be off.'

Hiding his regret at the missing key, Jack thanked them once again, strapped the box to the horse's pannier. He rode away, pondering who might have been looking for him.

Rain was threatening for the entire of Jack's ride to the village of Rooksridge. By the time he had found the burial ground there was a steady shower of fine rain that penetrated every layer Jack wore. He ignored the discomfort and knelt before Margaret's grave, clutching her cross in his fist. His eyes were dry and he thought it odd that he couldn't weep now. Maybe it was exhaustion that led him to feel so numb, but the grief was not as raw as it had been when Blanche had given him the cross and the memory had returned.

He pushed Blanche from his mind. His wife's grave was not the place he wanted to think about the woman who had briefly been his lover but his mind kept returning to the final time he had seen her. She had called off the attack and he suspected she had done so before she had seen him because the sail had already turned before he had run on to the deck and they had seen each other. It tortured him not to know why she had done it and he had to suppress the urge to return to discover the mystery.

He waited at the grave until the shower turned into a torrent then walked the short distance to the house that was apparently his. Neighbours nodded to him as a friend. He couldn't face admitting he didn't recognise any of them so murmured polite greetings and passed on.

The house came as a surprise. He was wealthy. He hadn't expected that and Master Fortin hadn't mentioned it. Why an agent for a wine merchant would hold property as substantial as he appeared to was something Jack didn't fully understand. The house was three storeys high, with the timber-framed gable end facing on to the street. A shop selling wooden cups and bowls took up the front space downstairs but once he had taken the second door down a passageway, Jack found himself in an airy room away from the noise of the street. The light was familiar, a warm glow through the small-paned front window where sheets of horn had been nailed. There was a pervading smell of mustiness and neglect, but beneath that was a layer of familiar sandalwood, beeswax and straw. This was the kitchen and he remembered sitting with Margaret while a large grey and white cat slunk around their feet. He smiled at the memory and wondered what had become of the cat. The hearth was clean and free of ash and no lingering scent of cooking remained. Clearly, Jack hadn't bothered to find a tenant for the property once he left.

The furniture that remained—a heavy table, a sturdy chest and four low-backed chairs—were covered with a layer of dust. If there had been hangings on the walls they had been removed for storage. Jack examined the furniture, feeling the association with his belongings but not particularly caring for them. The chest was unlocked but contained only the wall hangings and some plain candlesticks. A stub of candle remained in one so he sparked a flint and lit it, then shut the lid and made his way upstairs, his recollections strengthening with each footstep.

There were two rooms on the upper floor. The larger was the bedchamber he had shared with Margaret. He couldn't face crossing that threshold yet so went instead into the smaller room at the front that he recalled had been his private chamber. As in the kitchen, the furniture was dusty but a small chest pushed beneath the table in the corner caught his attention. To a casual observer it might have been missed, but Jack was looking for anything significant and the beam of sunlight caught the clasp. He picked it up and discovered that behind the chest was a small hole, big enough to put his arm inside but not more. He laughed, remembering this hiding place in a flash. He rooted inside and produced a large key. Holding it in his hand he knew without question it was the missing key that fitted into the lock of the chest.

The box contained more papers. Jack's scalp prickled as he recognised the writing that matched what he had found in the box Blanche had taken from Ronec. He sat on the table, lifting the sheets to the light and reading his past and discovering himself.

When he finished he sat deep in thought, clutching the papers tightly. He *was* wealthy. Considerably so. More than that, he knew why.

He was an envoy for the Crown. His work with Fortin and Rudhale had been a subterfuge to explain his business abroad. That explained the coded account in the tablet. He looked at the other object he had found. A heavy ring engraved with the initials *JS*. John Sutton. His initials. His name.

Jack would have laughed if he had not been so weary. A spy after all! There was still no cipher but the chest had also produced a single letter bearing a name and a wax seal. Richard Marten, resident outside Portsmouth. Jack needed to retrace his steps back to the port to discover what that man could tell him.

It was growing late. Jack finally steeled himself to enter the bedchamber. It was cowardly to delay any longer. He had seen the place where Margaret now rested. He owed it to her to see where they had lain together. The room was empty as he expected, save for a settle and a bed-frame with no mattress, only the strings running back and forth. Spiders had begun to make webs between them. He perched on the edge of the frame and rested his hand against the headboard. The memories were clearer now he had a place to associate with the woman. He sat and remembered Margaret and the time they had shared, not with the all-encompassing grief, but with a blend of sadness and fondness.

'Forgive me, my love,' he murmured. 'I didn't know. I would have come if I had known.'

He listened for an answer but knew her shade had passed beyond hearing. They had loved each other but she was gone. She had been a loving and warm-hearted woman and Jack suspected Blanche had been right, that she would not have wanted him to live alone dwelling in the dark place he had exiled himself to. Blanche's face passed before his eyes and he felt a twinge of pain. He loved Margaret, even if his mind refused to stitch together the whole tapestry, but he knew also that a substantial part of his heart was filled with Blanche. He rested his head against the wall and closed his eyes.

Whatever she had done, he couldn't stop the swell of love that rose at the thought of Blanche. Beneath the resentment was an affection as true and deep as anything he had felt for his wife. He pictured her asleep in her tower. The moonlight would be streaming through the threadbare hangings and bathing her as she slept. He hoped her dreams were peaceful.

Jack spent the night sleeping on the settle rather than in the empty bed. The next morning he closed up the house and began preparations for his trip back to Portsmouth, hoping that a meeting with Richard Marten would complete the missing pieces of his life.

Richard Marten was a severe-faced man of fifty. He lived in a sprawling manor house along the river from Portsmouth. He welcomed Jack and listened to his tale of memory loss. He gave brisk orders for a room to be prepared. Jack presented Marten with the tablets he had discovered in the case, apologising for his inability to translate them. He bathed and changed into fresh clothes before joining Marten to dine.

'You seem different, John,' Marten commented as they sat beside the fire. 'More peaceful. Less set on a course to destroy yourself.'

Jack considered Marten's words. Even being called by his true name was odd. He still thought of himself as Jack, though in time he would doubtless grow used to John again. He did feel calmer. The man who had courted death was a stranger to him now.

'Can a blow to the head do that?' he wondered aloud.

'I don't know. It might. Nothing else has influenced you, has it?'

Jack paused before answering. 'Nothing significant. I remember some emotions but not everything. I feel like I'm watching a tapestry of my life as if it belonged to someone else. I know I should recognise things but they seem strange to me.'

'Will you work for us again?' Marten asked.

Jack shrugged. 'I might as well. There is very little to keep me here.'

Marten raised an eyebrow. 'You said the same before. There are always places a man of your skills can go and work that needs to be done. The succession in Brittany is still not settled and you would doubtless be useful there.'

Jack frowned. Brittany was the one place where he had felt a bond strong enough to hold him. And was the one place he had vowed never to return to. Blanche had turned her ships away. Why? It nagged him like a sore tooth. Could he let the resentment go? Blanche had accepted his offer right before he had thrown it in her face. Could he live with her while knowing what she was? His heart, his body screamed that he could. Only the stubborn part of his conscience refused to yield.

He realised Marten was waiting for an answer.

'I don't know. Let me spend a few days here trying to remember what I can. I'll answer as soon as I am able.'

'Try not to wait too long,' Marten cautioned.

Jack slept long into the following morning. It had been too long since he had slept in a proper bed. The last time had been when Blanche had lain in his arms but remembering that only twisted his stomach into knots.

Marten was waiting when Jack entered the long central hall in search of breakfast.

'While you are staying here I have a task for you.'

He delved into the deep folds of his gown and produced Jack's wax tablets. 'I haven't looked over these. The task can be yours.'

He led Jack into a smaller chamber and placed the wax tablets on a sloped scribe's desk beside a scroll.

'This is the cipher. Perhaps if you translate it yourself you will remember it.'

Marten took another scroll to the chair by the fire and Jack began his task, carefully transcribing the symbols and words on to a fresh tablet.

The report was dull, a series of thoughts and statements about the situation in Brittany. Place names where support was wavering or strengthening.

Jack translated without much interest, but halfway down the second tablet something caused his heart to stop.

Sea Wolf. Blaze Mor. Pirate. Rumoured ally? Investigate and remove?

He exhaled loudly in a jagged breath and covered the tablet with a trembling hand. Here before him was the evidence in his own hand that he was a danger to Blanche. She should have let Ronec slit his throat on the beach that first night. He didn't want to contemplate what might have happened if he had recalled how to read the code while he was living in her house.

'What have you found?' Jack hadn't realised Marten was standing behind him. He could not erase the words, so unwillingly moved his hand.

Marten read it and shrugged. 'An ally, as you suggest.' He sighed. 'Removal will not be necessary, though I commend you for the discovery.'

Jack sagged with relief. Blanche was safe. It was at that moment, when his heart lurched and soared, that he realised how deep his love for her was. The thought that he might have been the instrument of her downfall was appalling.

'Come, I have something that might interest you,' Marten said.

Together they walked to the gardens where a number of the children of the household were enjoying a brief respite from work in the company of a grey terrier. They ran after a ball, laughing and squabbling while others munched on pastries from a trestle table.

'See that boy there,' Marten said, gesturing to a black-haired child.

The boy's profile was familiar, but it was only when he turned that Jack realised why. The angular jaw was hidden beneath boyish chubbiness and the nose was wider, but the black hawklike eyes were the ones he had last seen staring at him from the deck of *White Wolf.*

While he was in France, Jack had grown used to not recognising anyone, and the gradual fitting of faces to names after his return to England had been disconcerting. To see a face he knew intimately on a person and in a place it should not be was a great shock. He feared his brain was still addled and he was putting faces where they did not belong.

'Who is he?'

'A French lad. A ward of our King.'

Blanche had said her son by Yann was living in another household but she had never said where.

'What is his name?'

'Fransez Tanet,' Marten said. He pulled at his greying beard and his gentle eyes filled with sorrow. 'That poor boy has already lost one parent to the French. He will likely become an orphan before the summer is out.'

Was there another, deadly, secret Blanche had withheld from him? She had not seemed ill. She was strong and full of life. Thoughts of Margaret filled Jack's mind. Arriving too late to be by her side at the end. Finding only the grave to mourn at. All his fury and resentment at Blanche's deceptions were swept away on a tide of unbearable grief.

'Why?'

Marten looked taken aback at Jack's urgency. 'Unbelievably, his mother is the pirate known as Bleiz Mor. She came begging to us after her husband died and asked us to help her fight against the French in her husband's name. Personally, I would have told the unwomanly upstart to marry again and support her husband as a good woman would, but apparently she was very persuasive. Can you believe that a woman could command a ship and crew?'

Jack grimaced, which Marten took to be agreement at how unlikely such a thing could be. If Marten had met Blanche he would never doubt her ability, courage or determination.

'I believe the right woman could do anything she sets her mind to,' he said.

His conscience shamed him. By scorning Blanche, Jack had belittled everything she had worked for. Now, defending her actions to Marten, he realised what a great thing she had managed to accomplish. Her face flashed through Jack's mind, image overtaking image of her laughing, then furious, then her head thrown back in ecstasy, before finally settling on the awful twist of her lips as Jack had walked away from her for the final time.

'But that doesn't explain what you said,' Jack prompted.

'The woman proved to be unexpectedly competent,' Marten said. 'Unfortunately, we received news only yesterday that the local *Prévôt* grew tired of her activities and she has been relieved of her authority.'

Jack bunched his fists at his sides. Erwan de Larrion would not have acted unprompted and he had a suspicion as to who the real culprit was. 'She is now under house arrest awaiting trial and may well be executed.'

Jack's cup slipped from his hand. He righted it

to give himself time to rein in the stab of dread that caused his heart to miss a beat. 'Trial? For acting on orders?'

'For attempted murder.' Marten sucked his teeth. He refilled his cup and carried on blithely speaking, unaware of how his words were in the process of destroying Jack.

'Bloodthirsty woman attacked her own Captain, it seems. He lives, but it will be a while before he can sail. It is a blow to our cause, especially at a time when we need all the ships we can muster.'

Jack could barely concentrate on the words for the feeling of utter horror that was enfolding him. Blanche in custody awaiting death. He didn't blame her for attacking Ronec; he'd have done the same, and if the man walked through the door he'd have felt Jack's boot across his windpipe, slowly crushing the life from his worthless carcass, but he despaired at how rash she had been.

Marten sighed and looked at Fransez as he threw the ball for the dog and chased after it out of the yard. Jack felt sick seeing the boy's carefree manner. He ground his teeth to stop himself crying out in despair, wishing he could step across the miles that divided him from Blanche and be at her side.

'The boy will stay here and learn to be English. When he returns to his own country he'll be loyal to us. He's too young yet to take his mother's place, unfortunately.'

'Does the boy know of the events?'

Marten frowned. 'We aren't cruel. We've taken pains to ensure he doesn't hear of it. In any case, her sentence might not be death. If she can plead well and soften the heart of those damned French she might escape with her life and end her days under guard in a convent.'

This was not a comfort to Jack. Blanche would loathe being caged and confined. She might even prefer a swift death. It was unthinkable to him, however.

'Will you send men to defend her?'

Marten pursed his lips. 'Unfortunately, we have no one to spare.'

'I'll go.'

The words left Jack's lips almost before Marten had finished speaking. As he said them he knew the decision had been inevitable as soon as he had heard the news. He could not leave Blanche to face her ordeal alone.

'I know the area.' He pressed his hands to his eyes and swallowed, trying to keep his voice steady. 'I know the woman. She took me in when I was lost recently and I know she is honourable. She does not deserve this fate.

'I think I can get you the ships, but I want something in return.'

'What?' Marten asked.

He was rich. He owned a house he didn't want. Wealthy enough to buy a ship.

'If I secure the ships I will only want reimbursing for the cost of one,' Jack said.

Marten looked at him with narrowed eyes. Jack considered spilling out the whole story but Marten gave a brief nod.

'It is unconventional, but our king will be happy to share the expense. Very well. What do you need me to do?'

Chapter Nineteen

Jack arrived at Fort Carouel just before sunset and hammered on the door. It was opened by Marie, who gasped when she beheld Jack. She shrieked Andrey's name over her shoulder followed by a rapid torrent of words Jack only caught half of. He'd never heard her speak so much. Andrey appeared and his face broke into a weary smile.

'I knew you would come back. I told her so but she didn't believe me.'

It pierced Jack's heart. Why would Blanche believe Andrey when Jack had made it so clear he wanted nothing to do with her?

'I heard she was awaiting trial. Is she…?'

He couldn't bring himself to utter the dreaded word.

'She's in Benestin,' Andrey said. 'She's being held in the *Prévôt*'s house.'

Jack sagged with relief. Still alive. 'Not Ronec's home.'

'No, though he tried his hardest to convince *Prévôt* de Larrion that he would be the best jailor for her. Luckily for Blanche, the *Prévôt* said Ronec was too ill after his injury.'

The injury Blanche had caused. The *Prévôt* was a wise man to keep them separate. It would make his mission easier.

'I need to see her,' Jack said.

Andrey frowned. 'That is unlikely.'

'Don't you think she'd want to see me?' Jack asked. They'd parted so badly maybe she wouldn't welcome his presence.

Andrey smiled. 'If you have to ask that question you'll never know the answer in your heart. No, the difficulty is she hasn't been permitted any visitors. I haven't seen her myself, though I've gone twice weekly.'

Anger boiled in Jack's belly at the thought of Blanche as a prisoner with no recourse to a defence or friends. He should have been here for her. He tugged his cloak into place and glanced at the sky. His instinct was to mount his horse and ride to Benestin now but the sun would have set long before he got there.

'May I beg leave to claim my old room for the night? I have a case to present that might help

Blanche. If I am going to demand entry to the *Prévôt*'s house I'll stand a better chance in the morning.'

Andrey brightened. 'You think you can help her?'

Jack agreed with more confidence than he felt. He dined with Andrey and Marie that night. It felt like visiting an old friend. Everything was familiar, save the absence of Blanche, which he hoped would soon be rectified. Andrey clearly felt the same. He finished his tale of what had happened to Blanche by pressing Jack's hand.

'I'm glad you are here, Jack. Ronec is demanding that Blanche face the consequences. The sooner she is safe, the easier I will rest.'

Jack muttered an answer, the description of Ronec's mutiny and treatment of Blanche rending a hole in his heart. He made his way to his old room, feeling a curious chill as he passed through the door into the place he thought he had left for ever. He visited Blanche's lonely, threadbare room. She'd taken no benefit from her piracy. All Bleiz Mor's spoils had helped others as she had once told him.

He lay awake long into the night, going over his plan and speech, not daring to contemplate what would happen if he did not succeed.

The following morning he dressed in fresh clothes and presented himself downstairs.

'This is unexpected,' Andrey commented, taking in the heavy pine-green robe trimmed with dark brown beaver fur, the black velvet hat and the rings adorning Jack's fingers.

'I want to look my best. I intend to ensure Ronec does not get what he wants.'

'You have my best wishes,' Andrey said. 'If it comes to it, you have my sword, too.'

Jack smiled. 'I hope that won't be needed, but it is good to know.'

He rode to Benestin and found the *Prévôt*'s house, where he requested entry. If the servant who opened the door was surprised to see a well-dressed Englishman standing there, he hid it well. 'Tell the *Prévôt* it concerns Madame Tanet and that I am here to settle matters. I have a message from my masters to yours that cannot delay.'

The servant did look surprised at hearing the stranger speak of the *Prévôt*'s prisoner. He closed the door and reappeared shortly afterwards to admit Jack into the inner hallway and from there into a small chamber. Erwan de Larrion arrived shortly afterwards. He listened to what Jack had to say, then nodded.

'I'll send for Ronec.'

* * *

Another weary day staring at the same four walls. Blanche paced the room. Seven steps in one direction, nine in the other. She had been in this room for nine days. It was an improvement on the cellar which had been perpetually gloomy and cold. The window was small and faced over the back of Erwan de Larrion's residence. If she stood on tiptoe all she could see was the rubbish heap and pigpen, but she could feel the sun on her face as it rose. She scratched another mark into the plaster behind the door to mark the passing of time and tried not to cry.

The door opened and Erwan de Larrion's servant, Gui, appeared carrying a tray of bread and cheese. He nodded at Blanche. At least here she was being well treated, which was some consolation.

'Someone is asking to see you.'

Blanche glanced over her shoulder. 'If it is Ronec tell him to go hang himself from *White Hawk*'s mast.'

Gui grinned. Ronec had not made himself popular. The last time he had visited Blanche to gloat at her situation it had required three servants to pull her off him. Blanche turned her attention back to the basket of wool and the carding brush. She would have preferred to sew but since driving her

needle deep into Ronec's thigh when he had tried
to lay his hands on her, she had not been allowed
the implement in case she used it as a weapon.
It was worth the sacrifice to remember Ronec's
howl of pain that had brought half the household
running.

'It isn't him. It is an Englishman.'

The spindle slipped from Blanche's hand.
She loathed the way her heart leapt to her throat.
'What is his name?'

'He is called Captain Sutton,' Gui said. 'He's
here on a matter with the *Prévôt*.'

Blanche's heart became lead, plummeting to
the bottom of her belly. For one glorious, foolish moment she had believed Jack had returned
to her.

'I don't want to speak to him.' She tore the
hank of wool into smaller tufts roughly. 'Whatever business he has with Erwan doesn't concern me.'

Gui stood his ground. 'But he said…'

Blanche rounded on him fiercely. 'Didn't you
hear what I said? I'll see no one. Now get out.'

She brandished the carding brush and Gui retreated, muttering beneath his breath. She heard
him turn the key loudly in the lock and immediately regretted her harshness. Gui had always
treated her kindly but she seemed incapable of

being kind herself. She put her head in her hands and wept. Jack was not coming. Jack would have been glad to forget her, and even if he had forgiven her deceit, how would a wine buyer from Bristol ever learn of her predicament? She hadn't even been allowed to see Andrey. She was completely friendless and it was no more than she deserved.

By mid-afternoon she was regretting turning away the visitor. Anyone would be worth seeing rather than the silence she was faced with. Erwan was a fair jailor and did not keep her completely in seclusion. She had been invited to join him to dine on three evenings and he behaved towards her almost as if she was a guest.

When the key scratched in the lock again, she looked up eagerly. It was not Gui this time but two of Erwan's guards.

'You're to come with us,' one of them said.

'Where?'

'Your case is being heard. *Prévôt* de Larrion is waiting.'

Blanche tensed. The Englishman's visit could not be unconnected. News of her plight must have reached King Edward's lieutenant. Now she wished she had taken the opportunity to throw herself on to his envoy's mercy. Her legs began to shake as she stood.

The second guard produced a pair of manacles from behind his back. 'You have to wear these,' he said, looking shamefaced.

Blanche rolled her eyes scornfully. 'Am I such a dangerous prisoner that I must be fettered?'

'Jagu Ronec insists,' the guard replied. 'And yes, you are.'

Blanche grinned despite her unease. The guard was young and breathtakingly handsome. She'd considered trying to seduce him when she arrived but was firm in her determination that Jack would be her final lover. She would not break that vow over someone with as little influence as the guard, however his eyes flashed when he looked at her. She sighed and obediently held her hands out, managing not to shudder as the cold iron enclosed her wrists.

The guards were courteous enough not to manhandle her to Erwan's chamber but allowed her to walk between them untouched. She was taken into the small room and motioned to sit at one of two tables that faced de Larrion's larger lectern. It had the air of a courtroom and Blanche steeled her nerve. After captivity, any result would be better than being forced to imagine various fates. The two guards stood behind her chair.

Ronec entered and shot her a look of loathing followed by a leer of triumph as his eyes fell on the manacles. He was limping slightly, to Blanche's satisfaction and she smirked back. The door opened again and she heard voices before de Larrion entered in the company of the Englishman. Blanche barely glanced up, but when she did her heart leapt. She had no idea why he was travelling under an assumed name, but the man at Erwan's side was none other than Jack.

He looked different. His bearing was tall and he was dressed in formal robes, fingers laden with rings. His hair was clipped and lay around his ears in soft waves, save for the section that fell forwards, covering the worst of the scar. He surveyed the room as though he was master of it, not the *Prévôt*.

Blanche's whole body gave a tremor, reacting instinctively to the sight of him. Lust and confusion vied for supremacy in a whirlpool of emotions. She wanted to shout in joy. Fall at his knees and beg forgiveness. Throw herself across the table and wrap her limbs around his body, smothering him with kisses. Scream at him for leaving. Weep that he was returned. His eyes met hers and he gave a subtle shake of the head, warning her to say nothing. She searched for any kind of affection in his face or bearing but saw none. Only coldness. Distraught, she sat back in the chair and drew her hands into her lap. The links between each manacle clinked.

'Is it necessary for the woman to be chained?' Jack asked. Only Blanche knew him well enough to spot the suppressed fury beneath his cold tone. *The woman*, though. Such distaste in his voice.

'She is temperamental and given to sudden rages. A frailty of her sex,' Ronec said. He looked at Jack and pursed his lips, frowning. Blanche suspected he did not quite recognise the well-dressed Englishman as the feeble and dishevelled shipwreck survivor. If it came to that, Blanche was hardly certain her mind wasn't tricking her.

'Not so frail I couldn't strangle you with these chains,' she snarled, eager to draw Ronec's attention from Jack.

'Enough!' Erwan de Larrion rarely raised his voice but when he did, his voice was a whip. 'Madame Tanet stays restrained, for the time being. Now, please explain your purpose here.'

Jack walked slowly to the centre of the room and faced de Larrion. He barely glanced in Blanche's direction. Blanche held her breath.

'I have been sent here as envoy on behalf of Richard Marten, who in turn acts as proxy for the Lord Lieutenant of Edward, King of England. It is my duty to inform you that the vessels known as *White Wolf* and *White Hawk* once belonged to the English crown.'

'I am aware of who they used to belong to,' de

Larrion said, taking his seat. 'What I don't understand is why you are here now. This meeting is to decide the fate of Madame Tanet.'

'My master is aware there is currently some question over the conduct and position of the ships' current owner. I have been entrusted with a communication from His Lordship to yourself concerning her sentence. However, the matter of the ships is his first concern,' Jack said. He gave Blanche a sharp look. 'As it is mine.'

Her throat tightened. Duty had brought him here, not affection.

From his case Jack produced a scroll bearing a plum-coloured wax seal.

'King Edward is preparing to sail to France in a month's time. The army is intending to raid Normandy and weaken the forces of the French. He needs every ship that is prepared to ally with him and carry troops and supplies. This bears the seal of Richard Marten and states both ships shall be placed under the command of John Sutton, previously—and once more—Captain in the service of the King's Lieutenant in France. Any and all debts will be paid off to those who have a financial interest remaining.'

Ronec jumped to his feet. 'This is an outrage. I've never heard of this John Sutton. Who is he?'

For the first time since cautioning her to sit quietly, Jack shared a look with Blanche.

'I am,' he said.

He paused to let the muttering, which had naturally sprung up, die away before he continued. Erwan de Larrion was watching with a carefully blank face. Ronec, however, was clearly furious. Blanche held back the protest that sprang to her lips, though she was outraged that Jack was commandeering her ships.

Jack passed the scroll to Erwan de Larrion who snapped it open and read it. He met Jack's eyes then glanced at Blanche.

'This also stated that Blanche Tanet, the former Captain known as Bleiz Mor or the Sea Wolf, is to be taken into English custody, by order of the King's Lieutenant.'

'What!' Now it was Blanche's turn to leap to her feet. 'My ships are one matter. My person is another entirely.'

De Larrion looked up from his reading and glared at her. 'I see this declaration also notes Madame Tanet's efforts to aid the House of Monfort and thanks her for her work. It suggests that Madame Tanet should retire from her part and be taken into Captain Sutton's custody, to spend her days living under his supervision.'

Jack's custody. A life with the man who had

turned her world upside down and made her remember the woman she had been. It was too
much to take in. Blanche began to shake. No,
not Jack. Captain Sutton. She tried to meet his
eyes but he kept them averted. He didn't want
her. Erwan walked round the table and passed
the document to Ronec, ignoring Blanche who
reached for it. She exhaled angrily, slamming her
hands on to the table and causing the manacles
to clatter, furious with the men deciding her fate
while she was ignored. Erwan fixed her with another hard stare.

'We have not heard whether Madame Tanet
consents to accept this sentence,' Jack said.

'Madame Tanet has no say!'

Ronec practically burst from his seat, one hand
grasping Blanche by the arm as if he expected
her to try fleeing to Jack. 'She is a woman and
has no legal authority. She needs a man to speak
for her and make these decisions. If she is to be
placed in anyone's custody, it should be mine,'
Ronec insisted. 'I am the man she wronged and
I deserve compensation.'

'Blanche is not compensation. She doesn't
want you. She doesn't need a man to speak for
her, but she has me to stand beside her,' Jack said.

He'd called her Blanche. For a brief moment
she heard a hint of the passion they had shared

in the sound of her name on his lips. But Jack, or John, or whoever he called himself, was preparing to dispose of her as coldly as Ronec. To treat her as a chattel for whatever purpose served him best.

'I will speak for myself and as *Prévôt* de Larrion says, I have not agreed to anything.' Blanche set her jaw. His face remained as emotionless as an effigy.

'Captain Sutton rightly said I can speak for myself. In fact, I would like to speak to him now. In private.' Blanche rose again and faced Jack. '*Prévôt* de Larrion, will you permit this?'

Erwan nodded. 'Be quick.'

The guards escorted Blanche and Jack to a small chamber that served as a cell. They left at Jack's command but Blanche had no doubt they were waiting within earshot.

She faced Jack. He was standing arms folded forbiddingly across his chest with the same aloof expression he had worn since his return. A day ago, if she had been offered the chance to speak to him again, she would have planned words of apology or entreaty. Or love. Now her mind was empty.

'Is your name really John Sutton?' she asked. She folded her arms across her chest and tried to look stern.

'Yes. I really am an agent for the crown.' Jack laughed bitterly and raised an eyebrow. 'So you were right to suspect me of being a spy after all.'

Blanche put her hands to her face. Ronec had been right. She felt sick to her stomach wondering what would have been the outcome if his identity had been discovered while Jack was under her roof. Would she have killed him before she had grown to know and care for him? The Blanche she used to be would have without question.

'So I am not the only one guilty of subterfuge,' she said.

'You're the only one guilty of it intentionally,' Jack countered.

Blanche scowled again. The indignation that had risen at being forced to sit quietly while her fate was decided welled up once more.

'You said you were leaving for ever, yet here you are to steal my ships!' she snapped. 'What motivated you to come here, *John Sutton*? Spite or revenge?'

Chapter Twenty

Jack blinked. Of all the accusations he expected Blanche to level at him, theft was the most unexpected. Her cheeks were flushed and they stood out in stark contrast to the paleness of her skin and the shadows ringing her eyes. What had her time been like, a prisoner not knowing if she was to live or die? He wanted to hold her tight and offer belated comfort but she stepped close to him, jabbing her finger out angrily.

'I thought I would never see you again. When you walked into the room my heart missed a beat, but you came here to use and control me. I'd expect that of Ronec, but not you.'

She sounded…tired. Not even angry. It was as if the fight had gone out of her after her initial accusation.

'I'm not here to *steal* your ships,' Jack said. 'They've already been taken. I'm here to reclaim them for a better purpose than Ronec would use them for and to help the cause you've been fighting for. The cause we're both fighting for as I know now.'

She rallied, glowering briefly, but dipped her head in acknowledgement.

'More to the point, how am I trying to control you?' Jack asked.

'Blanche Tanet retires and lives under the supervision of John Sutton?' she said in a sing-song voice. 'Why, when you despise me? Did you decide that, or did your master? What do you want in return?'

'I want nothing from you,' Jack said stiffly. 'If you wish, I can decree that my supervision extends no further than putting you back in your tower to live alone.' She gave a little cry, her face twisting. Jack forced himself to calm down. This was getting nowhere and time was short.

'Why didn't you tell me about Fransez?' he asked.

Blanche's eyes widened. 'What do you know of him?'

'I saw him in England. He's living in Richard Marten's residence. He's so like you he could only be your son.'

Blanche shot forward, grasping Jack's hands.

'You saw him? Did you speak to him? Is he well? Has he grown?'

Jack gripped her hands tightly. His body grew warm at the touch, heat racing through his limbs and blood. His heart sped too fast. How could he ever have thought he could live without her?

'He is well. He's a tall lad. He has your features. He looked happy.'

Blanche dropped his hands, her shoulders sagging with relief.

'Did they take him by force?' Jack asked.

'No. I told you, I asked them to take him.' Blanche walked slowly around the cell. She gathered the chain that linked the shackles and bunched them in her fist, raising her head proudly. 'No one made me do anything I didn't want to do. I stand by my actions. I'm happy that Fransez has a secure future, even though I miss him. Don't imagine me now as a victim needing your pity.'

'I don't see you as a victim,' Jack said. 'I think I understand a little more now than I did when I first realised it was you. I'm not angry, only sad I didn't know and couldn't help you.'

'Don't be sad. I'm not.' Blanche smiled and a little of the woman who had captivated Jack shone through. 'For Fransez it is a good position, better than if he had stayed with me. He might even train to become a chevalier if he proves to be a good learner. I had hoped to see him again but that is just a mother's weakness.'

She tailed off and rubbed her eyes.

'You still will. I'm here to save you if I can,' Jack said firmly.

'I don't need saving!' Blanche said, against all evidence to the contrary. Jack tried to keep his eyes from the chains binding her wrists. He hadn't expected a warm greeting after the bitterness of their parting, but to hear her swearing she could manage by herself was infuriating. He lifted his chin.

'Really? Shall I leave now with the ships? Would you prefer the sentence likely to be given if you don't agree to my suggestion?'

Misery coursed through him that death was preferable to a life with him.

'You don't have to die,' he snapped. 'You wounded Ronec but he lived. There has been no crime to be punished by a sentence as severe as death.'

Blanche's mouth fell open in astonishment. 'Did you think I was destined to die? Is that what brought you back here?'

Jack's heart lurched at the endearment. Blanche stepped towards him and for a moment Jack thought she might embrace him but she lowered her hands and stayed out of reach.

'It is what I heard in England. Isn't it true?'

'As you say, there is no reason to execute me. I'm not a murderess and no one could accuse me of being a traitor to Brittany. My worst crime is setting myself against Ronec and for behaving as a man would.'

Now it was Jack's turn to flush. It was true he would not have recoiled from her activities so hard if she had been male. She nodded, eyes narrowed.

'The *Prévôt* suggested I retire to a convent and take holy orders, but I suspect Ronec has other plans for me. There is a more conventional way to dispose of a difficult woman.'

'Marriage.' Jack spoke the word for her.

'Erwan told me that Ronec proposed that solution almost immediately after he had recovered. Naturally, he put himself forward, suggesting he was best likely to succeed in "taming" me. He even suggested I be kept at his house until the matter could be decided.' Her mouth twisted in revulsion and she wrapped her arms around herself.

'I think I would rather have died swiftly than submit to him for years.'

'Yet you have to think before agreeing to spend your life in my charge?' Jack muttered, allowing resentment and hurt to seep into his voice. 'Is the thought of life with me even more abhorrent?'

'I didn't say that,' Blanche snapped. She looked

at her hands, twisting them in the folds of her skirts. 'It must be abhorrent to you, though. Why are you trying to help me after the way I deceived you? You have the ships. You don't want anything else from me, as you made clear.'

She looked utterly dejected. A shiver went down Jack's back.

'You're wrong, Blanche,' he whispered. 'That's not all I want from you.'

He watched her closely, spotting the slight twitch of her lips and tightening of the fine lines around her eyes. His words mattered to her and it occurred to him it would have saved a lot of time to say this first.

Jack lowered his head.

'There was once a ship's captain who fought in France. His wife died before he could return to say goodbye and for a long time all he wanted was to join her. He thought he was a brave man, but he discovered his bravery was only in battle, not in life. When he lost everything including his name, it took a woman much braver than him to show him how to be strong again. A woman who rose instead of falling when she had lost everything. It took her strength to give him a reason for wanting to live. It took her compassion to give him a reason to love again.'

His hand shook as he lifted Blanche's chin and

looked deep into her eyes. The black orbs surrounded him, swallowing him and claiming him. He could hold his feelings back no longer.

'I want everything from you, Blanche. I want your laughter and your sighs, your kisses and your touch. I want to fall asleep in your arms and wake at your side. I want your love,' he breathed.

Blanche's eyes were glistening. Jack's throat tightened as a lump of emotion filled it.

'I thought you didn't care,' Blanche whispered. 'In the *Prévôt*'s chamber you were so cold and distant. You looked as if you hated me.'

'I had to be. I don't want Ronec or the *Prévôt* to think I have anything personal to gain from the result otherwise they will never agree to it.'

'Do you forgive me for not telling you who I was?'

'Yes and no. I'm still angry and hurt, but when I thought you were in danger that stopped mattering. I'd lost one woman I had loved. I couldn't do it again if it was within my power to prevent it. My journey here was a living nightmare in case I came too late.'

He reached for her hand. 'I thought of you all the time I was in England. I couldn't help it. Even when I was hating you for what you had kept from me, you were always in my mind. Life is too short to bear resentments and harbour regrets.'

He stroked her cheek. She closed her eyes and he saw the same yearning on her face that had tugged at his heart for so long.

'I'd vowed never to love again after Margaret died,' he said. 'I fell in love with you when I didn't know I shouldn't. I tried to resist you. I tried to deny my feelings but I can't and won't any longer. I love you, Blanche, as deeply and truly as I've ever loved anyone. I want to be with you for whatever time either of us has left on Earth. We've both been damaged but together we could build a life worth living. If that is what you want? Be with me. On whatever terms you wish. Be my lover or my wife, just say you'll be in my life.'

'I will.' Blanche put her hand to Jack's cheek. Jack cursed the chains that prevented her from putting her arms around him.

'I'll never forgive that cur for demanding you are chained,' he growled. 'Blanche, I wouldn't do you the disrespect of suggesting you need rescuing but I would consider it an honour if you would allow me to assist in thwarting that bastard Ronec to the satisfaction of both of us. You once asked me if I would be prepared to sail under the flag of the Sea Wolf and I refused.' He held his hand out. 'Will you ask me again now?'

Blanche clasped his hand and shook firmly. 'Nothing would give me greater pleasure.'

'Nothing?' he purred. He lifted her hand to his lips, turning it palm upwards and kissing the delicate skin of her wrist. She shuddered in pleasure.

'Lots of things, now I think of it,' she said, 'but I'd rather not do them in chains and in this place. Free me and I'll gladly pay any price.'

'No.' Jack dropped her hand and put his hands on her shoulders. 'No price, Blanche, my love. No trade or bargains.' He touched her cheek then dropped a kiss in place of his fingers.

'What we do, we will do for love and nothing else.'

She gazed into his eyes.

'There is one more lie you should know about. I said I don't need rescuing, but I do. I need rescuing from myself. I've been friendless for so long that I'm too stubborn to admit I need help. Even today I thought the worst of you rather than trusting you. I want you to teach me how to love again and how to live again.'

Jack slipped his arms around her, holding her to his chest. 'I can do that. So, are we agreed? You will accept your sentence?'

'I will.'

Jack kissed her. Not as thoroughly as he wanted to, but there would be time for that later.

He hammered on the door. 'We've made a decision. Open up.'

They followed the guard back to the chamber where de Larrion and Ronec waited. Blanche sat back at her table.

'I agree to the terms of the proposal.'

De Larrion nodded his head. 'Then the matter is settled. All parties agree.'

'I don't,' Ronec snarled.

Jack spun on his heel and faced Ronec. He almost welcomed the protest.

'I've seen you before,' Ronec said, finally looking Jack in the eye.

Jack walked to where Ronec sat and lowered his voice.

'Yes, you have. On the beach and in the entrance hall to Blanche's home. Shall we tell *Prévôt* de Larrion where, and how I came to be here originally? What would he think of the circumstances in which I was washed ashore? I believe he takes a stern view of such activities as lighting unlawful beacons and luring ships on to rocks. Shall we test my theory?'

Ronec glared at Jack, then at Blanche. He would not risk being put on trial and with his fortune and liberty in jeopardy.

'No,' Ronec muttered.

Jack smiled grimly. 'In return for our silence

you withdraw your accusation against Blanche, discontinue all claims for damages and do not challenge this decree. You relinquish your captaincy of the ships.'

Ronec scowled. 'This is blackmail.'

'Yes, it is,' Jack said agreeably.

'She still owes me three nights in my bed,' Ronec said, glancing at Blanche.

Jack slammed his hand on to the table, palm down. 'She owes you nothing. You'll be paid in coin and you'll accept it. But if you prefer, I can meet you outside and beat an agreement from you. I'd welcome the chance and I'm no longer as weak as I was.'

Fear flickered in Ronec's eyes. He was too cowardly to confront Jack at full strength, and Jack was clearly strong now.

'Silence now and for ever,' he said through clenched teeth.

'Very well.' Ronec pushed his chair back and stood, facing de Larrion. 'If Madame Tanet chooses to place herself in this man's custody I do not object.'

'Then everyone is in agreement,' Erwan said. 'Madame Tanet, I release you into the custody of Captain Sutton.'

Blanche stood and walked around the table to Jack. They stood opposite each other.

'Will you consent to live under my roof and in my keeping?' Jack asked.

It was not the usual way to offer marriage and he could not throw his arms around Blanche and smother her with kisses as he wanted. The promises they would make to each other would be done in private and intimacy. Blanche bowed her head and tried to look meek and submissive. It did not come naturally but Jack would not demand that of her anyway. She gave up the pretence and gave him her widest smile. Jack stopped caring what the onlookers thought and beamed back.

'I consent,' she said.

'And what of the ships?' de Larrion asked as the manacles were struck from Blanche's wrists. 'You will have to begin a hunt for captains, I presume?'

'I shall captain one myself.' Jack gave the *Prévôt* a warm smile, purposefully not looking at Blanche. 'As for the other, I believe I know where I can start my search.'

They left before Ronec decided this was too much and objected after all.

The sun was beginning to set as Jack and Blanche walked along the clifftop to the Maiden Stones. They would have come earlier in the day but once they reached Fort Carouel, and Blanche had greeted Andrey and Marie with tearful embraces, she'd wanted to bathe. With a wicked smile she had invited Jack to join her in the wooden tub, which he readily agreed to. Which had, inevitably, led to a very wet floor, a lot of laughter and the afternoon disappearing without either of them noticing the passing of time.

Now, they strolled arm in arm through the wildflowers and bushes Blanche had described before. It was as breathtaking as she had promised it would be. In the distance, a ship followed the line of the coast, ploughing through the azure waves. Three days hence, *White Wolf* and *White Hawk* would begin their journeys to join the number of King Edward's fleet.

Jack laid his cloak on the grass and they sat side by side, Blanche leaning close while Jack put his arm around her. Every opportunity to be touching was seized upon.

'Did you find your memory?' Blanche asked.

'Not completely.' Jack sighed and stretched out his legs. 'I know more about myself but a lot of it feels like remembering a dream I once had. The only place that feels real is by your side.'

'Should I call you Jack or John?' Blanche asked, snuggling down beside him and laying her head on his shoulder.

He considered it. Jack felt more comfortable.

John belonged in the past, a dimly remembered acquaintance. He wondered if his memory would ever return completely but discovered he didn't care one way or the other. A new future lay before him.

'Call me either. Or better still, call me "my love".'

'I can do that,' Blanche answered.

They kissed, and when they drew apart Jack looked into her eyes.

'I saw you that day when you called off the attack,' he said.

'I know. I called it off even before I knew you were on board. Will you believe that?'

'I already did,' Jack replied. 'But why?'

'Because yours wasn't the ship I needed and to take those lives would be wrong.' She sat up. 'Perhaps to take any would be wrong.'

She leaned her head on his shoulder and gazed out to sea. 'We'll sail to Calais as ordered, but after that I don't know what I'll do. If Bleiz Mor sails again it won't be me beneath the mask. I think Andrey would make a fine captain. He's trustworthy and honourable. Don't you agree?'

Jack smiled. 'I do. And what of you, Blanche? What do you intend to do?'

'Make a life and a future.' She took his hand and smiled into his eyes. 'Perhaps in time, even a marriage.'

'A marriage?' Jack grinned. 'I suppose I'm a rich man now. I command two ships. Are you marrying me for my ships, Blanche?' he asked wickedly.

'I must be,' Blanche murmured, draping her hand in his lap. 'Unless you can think of another reason?'

Jack slipped his hands to the back of her neck and drew her closer, intent on showing her what compelling reasons there were. Together they fell back on to the blanket. The sun was still warm and they had the evening to themselves. Looking into Blanche's eyes, Jack knew she had the same thought as he did. Love and excitement, desire and happiness coursed through him.

'Life,' he murmured as he leaned in to kiss her. 'I like that idea. Let's do it together.'

* * * * *

MILLS & BOON

Coming next month

STOLEN BY THE VIKING
Michelle Willingham

'I am Breanne Ó Callahan,' she answered. 'My foster father is King Feann MacPherson of Killcobar.'

'I know who he is.' He turned at that moment, and his gaze fixed upon her. 'I recognised you the moment I saw you. And you are worth more than a slave.'

'How could you possibly know me?' she demanded. 'I would have remembered you.' Heat flared in her cheeks when she realised what she'd said. But it was too late to take back the words. Breanne tightened her grip upon the drying cloth, and in that heated moment, she grew aware of his interest. He studied her face, his gaze drifting downward to linger upon her body. There was no denying that he wanted her.

But worse was her own response. She was caught up in his blue eyes and the dark hair that framed a strong, lean face. There was a slight scar on his chin, but it did nothing to diminish his looks. The *Lochlannach* warrior was tall and imposing, his physical strength evident. Only the slight limp revealed any weakness.

'What do you want from me? A ransom?'

He reached out and cupped the back of her neck. It was an act of possession, but instead of feeling furious, his sudden dominance made her flesh warm to the touch. His blue eyes stared into hers as if he desired her, and